TAINTED GLASS

KODA POINDEXTER

Tainted Glass

Copyright © 2025 Takoda Poindexter

2nd Edition

e-book ISBN-13: 979-8-9930812-3-6

Paperback ISBN-13: 979-8-9930812-4-3

Hardback ISBN 13: 979-8-9930812-5-0

Cover design by: Susan Roddey

Edited by: Lynn Picknett & Jason Roach

Layout by: Jason Roach

Publisher's Note

This book contains elements of suicide, SA/sex, and the complex, real-life aspects of teenagers coming of age.

Dedication

To my friends and family, who never stopped listening, and to my Nana, Martha, who never gave up on me. This book is for those who have felt broken yet still found the strength to keep walking. This is for you.

Prologue

The brightness from the full moon illuminated two side-swiping vehicles. The metal screeched through the dense forest, causing the airbags to deploy, hitting both James and George from all sides. George's breathing was shallow, letting the reality of what'd happened set in. He unbuckled his seatbelt, trembling as he hopped out of the truck, examined himself, then broke out in a nervous sweat at the emptiness of the highway.

George used the light from the clear night sky to investigate the damage. The rear passenger's side was scraped and dented, the front grille bent inward, and an outline of an unrecognizable creature was wedged between James' truck and the guard rail.

Fumbling through his pocket, George pulled out his phone and turned on the flashlight. A giant pool of blood inched toward George's sneakers. A splash broke the silence as a doe's head landed at his feet. Splotches of blood decorated his gray Skechers.

"Look! Look on the fucking ground, James!" George yelled, pointing the white light from his phone directly at the head.

Panic set in. George's knees began to buckle, and he quickly braced himself against the truck bed before shouting, "Where's the other car?

Where's the other fucking car, James?"

"Calm down, George. Take deep breaths, man," James said, struggling to get the driver's door open.

"Blood! There's fucking blood everywhere! And where is the other vehicle we slid into?" George yelled. "We are so dead!"

James stumbled over to the edge of the mountain, where the skid marks on the pavement seemed to vanish off the side of the cliff, leading to an immediate decline into the woods below. Yellow caution tape— now split into two— fluttered on both sides of where a completed guardrail should have been. The void was wide enough for a truck to slide down.

James walked over to George, then answered arrogantly, "No one is around. We're the only witnesses. If we keep our mouths shut, no one will know we were here.

George pointed towards the embankment, "Those people, whoever they are, may need our help! We can't just leave them down there! What if they're hurt!" He expressed, wiping beads of sweat from his forehead. "Why? Why did I even allow you to convince me to go to Becca's party? I'm not a drinker. I'm a goddamn saint compared to you."

James climbed back into the truck. He glared over at George saying, "You have five seconds to get back in or ..."

George's eyes filled with terror, "I'm not getting back in the car with you. I...

"Get in the fucking truck before I leave you here for cop food! Fuck!!!" James yelled, starting the engine. The blood-covered glass blocked his view. The wipers did prove to be much use. They tossed it off the side of the truck, smearing it into the cracks like the tainted grout of a mosaic.

George dodged red crimson drops by jumping back into the truck.

His past experiences with James told him any type of reasoning would trigger the onset of an alcoholic rage. He mumbled to himself, "I told you to let me drive." As James pulled back onto the highway, George noticed something feasibly impossible. The doe— the decapitated carcass he'd been standing so close to— had mysteriously vanished from the scene. "Ummm, James?"

Ignoring the sound of his name, James sped off. He had one hand on the steering wheel and the other rubbed his temple. "Pipe down! Fuck, you're giving me a migraine with your bitching! I need to think! My dad will murder me if he finds out about the grille, the dented hood, not to mention the fucking airbags, and the blood-soaked, shattered windshield.

"How the fuck can you even drive with this tainted glass? Can you even see?" George asked. "Oh, and to give you the answer to all your problems, I suggest you tell your dad the truth about driving drunk, hitting a deer, and running someone off the road. But I know you, you'll never do that," George said, staring out of the window at the trees passing by.

Out of nowhere, James slapped the steering wheel. "I've got it!"

"Stop! There's a stop sign," George screamed. "You're going to run a fucking stop sign! Urggh …"

James slammed on the screeching brakes. "Sorry. Hear me out! I'll convince my dad I went to your house to hang out and catch up. However, you also needed to help me study for my college Anatomy test. Havoc broke loose when several deer jumped out while I was driving home. How does that sound?"

"Well, it's believable... but... I... I don't know if I can go through with being your alibi. Besides, I feel shitty for not going to the hospital with Becca and Meagan. I feel even shittier leaving people behind who may be hurt!" George confessed, staring at the floorboard— tears starting to form in the corners of his eyes.

"Did you forget the woods are off limits! They broke the law the moment their truck went over the embankment and landed in the woods! Just be glad it wasn't us flying down the mountain! If you won't be my alibi, your head will be the newest addition to my shrunken head collection!" James threatened as he dug his fingernails into the leather steering wheel.

"I swear, James, this will be the last time I help you!"

Chapter 1
(Two Months Earlier)

"Timothy, do you think I'll get the job? This is nerve-racking, and I can hardly stand it! I mean, my collar is lopsided, and my cowlick won't stay down. Besides, what if I mess up in my interview!?" George fumbled nervously with his collar, making it even more disproportionate.

Timothy turned George around to face him. "Relax, you'll do just fine," he said, adjusting his collar. "There, better?"

George turned to examine himself in the mirror one last time and sighed briefly. "Yes... better... You'll be waiting for me outside, right?" Timothy responded with a nod, and George felt him ushering them both out of the men's restroom.

Everything will be fine... no more than thirty minutes! Why am I so nervous interviewing for a bagger position!?

George breathed in deeply, exhaling hot air while doing his best to stay composed.

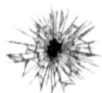

An hour later, George grinned as he walked out of the store, scanning the parking lot for Timothy's '98 Camry. His face became puzzled with confusion. The Camry was missing. George's queasy stomach, which had settled from the interview, now filled the back of his esophagus with bile.

Panicking, George shoved his sweaty hand into his pants pocket to retrieve his phone, then dialed his boyfriend. But after numerous rings, it went to voicemail.

"I thought you were going to wait for me, babe? I know I was a little longer than expected, but I hope you're okay. I guess I'll walk home..." he tapped the end button.

On a brighter note, he was relieved he didn't butcher the job interview, even if it was only for a bagger and cart position in the town's only local grocery store. Despite being stranded, he was eager to share the news with his significant other and his parents. For him, it was one more step to becoming independent.

Other than an actual emergency, what could be more important than stranding your boyfriend at a job interview? He's been acting strange lately. No texts, no phone calls, no hanging out, nothing! We just graduated, so what else could be keeping him occupied?

Lost in thought, George raised his head and fixated on the sun settling below the horizon, casting a red-orange haze across freshly cut lawns.

Beautiful!

Abruptly, George heard rhythmic clicking in the humid summer air. "Huh?" hissing like venomous vipers, a dozen water sprinklers in unison sprang out from the ground striking George.

"AHHH!!!" Freezing water sprayed from the ground, causing him to throw his hands in reflex, shielding his glasses. In a desperate need to escape, he sprinted towards the end of the block. George leaned his back against the stop sign, using the pole for support, his fingers clutched to his knees.

I'm fucked! My dad is going to kill me! These are his fucking Gucci three-piece suit and loafers. Just another thing I can't do right— walking home without getting soaked.

He found himself disheartened from his boyfriend ditching him and now soaking wet, anxiously awaiting the scolding he was going to receive from his father. Suddenly, his neck hairs started to prick up. Something was wrong. George had an odd sense he was being watched. His eyes searched the houses with soft yellow beams, highlighting the shrubs and water sprinklers. The leaves on the trees began to rustle from a gust of wind blowing east toward the woods.

Twilight had turned into night. George noticed a pair of shimmering white eyes from within the forbidden woods lock onto him. Discomforted by the unblinking stare, George slowly slipped off the soaked loafers, then bolted across the road, down the next block, and finally onto his porch, adrenaline pumping through his veins.

George waited outside— catching his breath— before proceeding into the house, dropping his dad's loafers at the door. Hearing dishes clank together in frustration, George entered the kitchen, seeing his mom cleaning up the dinner table.

"Hey, Mom! I got the job! I can start tomorrow!" George leaned against the counter, now in control of his breathing, and fluffed up his damp hair.

"Supper is in the fridge, we've already eaten. I have a lot on my mind right now. Your younger siblings now need a babysitter." His mom seemed disappointed, as if she was laying on a guilt trip for him getting a job.

"You know why I needed to start working— college and starting my own life. I need money for textbooks and tuition! Scholarships only get you so far. I could babysit on the days I'm off."

"Don't you get it, George? I still need a damn babysitter for the rest of the week!" his mom snapped.

"Aren't you happy for me? It's my first job!" George exclaimed, hoping his mom would at least understand the milestone achievement in his life. George waited for a response, but his mom continued cleaning like he wasn't standing right across from her.

"You don't have to clean up after me. I'm not that hungry anyway." George climbed the stairs, taking refuge in his room.

He threw his dad's wet clothes into the corner, deciding it would be tomorrow's problem, and dove underneath the covers.

Now in his briefs, George stared absently at the ceiling.

Those eyes wanted me. They were stalking me. But why and what were they attached to?

His eyelids grew heavy, falling asleep. He dreamt only of the pair of white eyes fixated on him in darkness.

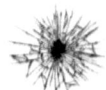

"RISE AND SHINE! IT'S YOUR FIRST DAY OF WORK! IT'S ALREADY NOON!" George's mom jerked the covers off him, then rattled him until his eyes were open.

"I'm up, I'm up!" He wiped his eyes dreamily, snatching his phone from the nightstand. A new message flashed across his phone. Seeing it was from Timothy, he promptly opened it.

George, forgive me for running off and not answering last night. My mom called me raising hell to do chores; and as soon I was done, I fell asleep. I know you did fine in your interview. You're smart, you know how to handle yourself under pressure, and above all, talented. I love you more!

George tapped the home button, noticing his mom hovering over him. "Who texted you? Meagan? You text so much these days, I'd be surprised if you hadn't slept with her yet." She giggled at her conjecture, leaving her son in utter silence.

If you only knew I was bisexual, but you wouldn't understand me if I told you. You would disown me as your child and abandon me if you knew who I truly was: I have a boyfriend. As if you cared enough to know what's going on in my life. You didn't even care that I got a job... She's in a good mood, though. Should I risk messing it up? Last night...she was in one of her bad moods.

The vision of his parents knowing frightened him. He briskly shook the feeling away as he freshened up for his first day of work. "God, I hope I don't make a fool of myself."

The automatic doors slid ajar, and the fluorescent lights shone down on him in a spotlight. Baggers and cashiers stared at him with tired, distasteful eyes, except for Timothy, who was waving slowly, smirking. George gave a nervous smile and waved back, then headed upstairs to clock in.

It seems Timothy is the only one I'd want to talk to. But after last night? Ugh, the rest appear to be in no mood to talk, or maybe they were suffering from lack of sleep? Not a friendly environment this afternoon. I should find out where to start—

"George? I didn't know you started working here! Cool beans!" A high-pitched, enthusiastic, familiar voice startled him as he clutched his heart from the shock. George turned around to face Meagan, one of his only friends from high school.

"Jeez! Don't walk up on me like that! It's my first day," he said. "You never told me you worked here."

Meagan punched his arm.

"Sorry, I saw you were in deep thought, but I couldn't resist it! You should stay with me today, and I'll show you the ropes! I want you to meet Becca and Hannah!" Meagan jabbed the bewildered George with her fist again.

"Are you alright...? I mean... normally you're not this ecstatic."

"Oh, tonight we don't get off until late, so I ate three candy bars before coming in. Not exactly lunch, is it? I still have five more in my locker! This will be fun tonight; it will be like when we first met. You know, back in physics class last semester!" Meagan grabbed his wrist, then dragged him downstairs.

"Meagan, slow down! Wait!" He yanked his arm from her grasp. They stopped near the health and beauty aisle.

"What is it?" she laughed nervously. George put his hands on her shoulders. He noticed her pull away, but continued on: "Take a deep breath and calm down. You might bring some unnecessary attention if you can't control yourself."

Meagan slowly let out a deep breath. "Sorry, George. Getting hyper like this helps me engage with the customers on days I don't want to be here." She pushed up her glasses and tied her long brunette hair in a ponytail. "Thanks. I'm fine now. Let me introduce you to Becca and Hannah. It'll be a great way to start off by making friends. You already know Timothy, right? I saw you two hanging out with each other around school."

George's cheeks flushed, nodding. "Actually, can I meet them some other time? I want to dive into work, if you know what I mean. With my anxiety high... could I just bag for you?"

"Oh, yeah. No problem." They passed the long line of registers until they came to register fourteen. "I'll start off slow; but remember to put cold with cold, produce with produce and non-foods with non-foods, got it? Hey, once you're fast at bagging, maybe we can have a competition. Who knew grading each other's test papers would spark a friendship! It was fun, we became study partners, and we aced the finals like it was nothing!"

George smiled as Meagan turned on the aisle light.

I didn't have many friends in general. One semester, I had a couple of friends, and then the next, none of us had the same classes. Meagan was different. We walked together at graduation. It didn't feel like a one-and-done friendship anymore, whereas my other 'friends' moved on. She stayed, and now we text on a regular basis. Being the friend that she is, she doesn't pry into my personal life. I'm not sure how she would react with me being—

"Meagan, he doesn't need to be reminded what his job is. Let George handle it." Timothy appeared beside George, bagging on thirteen and pulling him out of his thoughts. "I'm sorry I missed out on you getting hired yesterday. Don't worry, I'll protect you from her, you're welcome," he said, giving him a sly wink.

"I don't need protecting. I had to walk by myself, nearly in the dark. My clothes were ruined, and now my dad is going to hang me. I'd like to be left alone."

After a few orders, George was a tornado, bagging faster than any other baggers. However, Timothy kept staring at him with the intention he wanted to say something.

Once the five o'clock rush let up, Timothy turned toward him. "Hey, I wanted to ask you something. Do you trust me?"

11

You've trusted before in past relationships and been hurt. I love him though...

"Yes, I trust you. Why?" George asked suspiciously.

"I get off at eight, but since you're not getting off until later, do you mind if a friend spends the night?" Timothy asked. "I think... You know... Just so mom doesn't get suspicious of anything, *someone* else should spend the night for a change."

George bit his lip. He knew one key to successful relationships was to trust each other. "Only for one night?" he asked.

"Yes, only one night."

George cracked a warm smile. "Alright, then. I trust you!"

The rest of the day grew more vacant as co-workers were relieved of their duties and fewer customers came in. George went to lunch around eight; however, he didn't have much of an appetite and instead went into the restroom. George studied his reflection with uncertainty. His emerald eyes glimmered in the light, his long coffee-colored hair gently fell into his eyes, and his smile faded.

We spent so much time together while we were in school. I helped him with Chemistry class, so he could skip junior year. He was able to graduate early with me. I know he was held back a year, but now it's summer, and we've already walked the stage... why am I doubting—

George was deep in thought before arms embraced him in a hug.

"What are you thinking about? The sleepover? You have nothing to worry about," Timothy smiled as he kissed George's cheek.

"No, not that. I was thinking how we have to keep this relationship hidden from everyone... and how my parents would kick me out of the house if they knew I was bisexual."

Timothy turned him around and caressed his chin. "It'll all work out, you just have to be patient. I'm heading out... so I'll text you in the morning, okay?"

George nodded silently as Timothy left the bathroom.

The next morning, George woke up to rays of sunlight beaming down onto his face. He flung aside his comforter to check his phone. He had one new text; his heart nearly stopped:

George, my mom tried to wake my friend and me up this morning, but realized the door was jammed. I didn't hear her at first, but she nearly kicked the door off the hinges. She was furious, and told me I couldn't have anyone else over. Guess this means I'm grounded. Don't worry, though, I'll win her back after work today. I'm going to buy her flowers and chocolates. I'll text you tonight. I love you!

George's heart jumped into his throat, and it felt as though a fist had knocked the breath out of him.

Today is your only day off. Enjoy it— his mind reassured him.

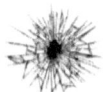

As much as he tried, he couldn't enjoy himself for one moment; either he would ponder what Timothy had texted him or he would doubt himself – the constant struggle he faced daily. After constantly glancing at his phone for an update, no texts were sent.

George eventually fell into a deep sleep; dreaming, he found himself standing in the middle of a hallway surrounded by cobras. He could feel the presence of someone behind him, but couldn't turn around to see who it was. There was a ladder at the far end of the hall. He ran as fast as he could to it; the cobras and the unknown presence followed. He could feel tears rolling down his face as he climbed up the ladder.

Reaching the top of the ladder, he found himself in another hallway – repeating the same scenario. "Stop following me! Leave me alone!" George cried, kicking the cobras away. They regrouped and hissed angrily, arching their heads. Icy fingers reached around, grabbing George from behind. There was a high-pitched scream, and he felt the cobras biting into his flesh.

"Get off me!" George kicked and screamed, realizing he was waking up from his dream. He broke out in a cold sweat as he sat up.

"Ugh! What is wrong with me?" he wailed, checking his phone to notice he'd received a new friend request. He gently clicked on the name, and a picture of a guy popped up on his screen.

Michael Banes? Who the fuck is Michael Banes?

George dropped his phone, all trust drained from him, and his world turned splotchy black as he fell to the floor.

Chapter 2

Meagan's thoughts focused on George.

He was extremely dismissive yesterday. What is up with him? Should I text him?

Meagan searched for George's name in her contact list and began typing, her thumbs tapping away:

George, I know we haven't texted in a couple of days, but I wanted to make sure you're fine. I wanted us to catch up after the late shift, but you seemed... distant.

After George had come back from his lunch, he'd barely spoken a word to her. She tried to make him laugh, tried to introduce him to Becca and Hannah before they'd left, but he just shook his head and didn't respond.

Meagan watched the neon yellow stars on her ceiling, studying each one, and noticed one flickered when her phone buzzed. She viewed the message, but it wasn't from George. Her heart melted into her stomach, and her sea blue eyes sparkled with excitement. Since she'd started working at Arcae's Whole Foods a few months earlier, she'd met the sweetest guy who helped her stock and bag and would listen to her explaining Physics. Dom.

He had to be at least two years older than her.

Meagan, I was wondering if you wanted to go get Froyo tomorrow after work? Only if you're okay with it. I know it would look bad if we were seen together because of work policy, but I can't resist! You're easy to talk to!

The hottest guy in my department wants to go on a date with me. She thought to herself in disbelief. Hoping she read the context correctly, she reread it. *Yep, that's what it said.*

Dom, is this your way of getting a date? I'm flattered, but I will only go with you as friends. You understand, right?

Meagan sent the message, satisfied with her reply, though the thought of getting into the dating pool scared her immensely. The thought of someone even giving her a hug freaked her out. She *wanted* to go on a date with him, but feared her haphephobia would keep it from being anything other than just a date – a friend's date. Not to mention if anyone found out they were dating, she'd never hear the end of it – especially from George – and they'd both get fired on the spot. Besides, it wasn't like she was in love with him, it was only a simple crush. Although she'd rather date Dom, she knew she'd have to fly under the radar by "hanging out" occasionally to lower suspicions. Her cheeks felt hot in the faint glow from the fluorescent stars. She heard the buzz of her phone:

Of course, as friends! Wait for me after work. Goodnight. Sweet dreams.

She plugged in her earphones and began listening to *Red*, a hard rock band, falling asleep to the rhythm of the drum and the thumping of her heart.

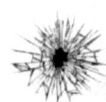

BZZZ, BZZZ! Meagan's phone awoke her with a fiercer vibration than usual, as if her phone sensed danger. She yawned and rubbed her eyes, then reached for it from underneath the covers. A reply from George awaited. Smiling, she viewed it:

I'm fine, don't worry about me. I'll see you today at work. I want you to introduce me to Becca and Hannah…

Meagan was relieved her friend was fine, and with her worry extinguished, she knew she would have a bright day.

George hid himself underneath his covers and refused to believe what he'd discovered. A picture of Timothy and Michael together in Timothy's room was posted several hours ago on this so-called Michael's profile. George pressed his head into his pillow tightly, bawling with despair to the point he could barely breathe. The pain his heart felt spread all over his body and washed him with numbness. After shedding all the tears he could manage in a decade, he rallied, then balled his fists in anger.

"I won't let my parents know I've cried. I have to act normal in front of them. God knows I don't have time to play fifty questions. In fact, I can't let anyone know…" George picked himself up, mustering enough strength to drag himself into the bathroom to take a shower. The steaming water ate away the numbness, making him feel a bit more optimistic, and a new George stepped into existence.

When George arrived at work, he could feel Timothy staring at the back of his head while he clocked in. He made no effort to acknowledge him. His supervisor directed him to bag for Meagan once again.

"So, Meagan, where's Becca and Hannah?" George asked, and her eyes lit up in delight.

"Becca. She's over there," she quickly pointed to a tall girl with dyed red hair and glasses at the express lane. "She is the sweetest person you'll meet here. She knows where everything is and almost all of the produce numbers. All you have to do is say hi and be respectful, and she's your friend!" Meagan began scanning items while the customer unloaded their buggy.

"Hannah is two lanes down from us, bagging. We call her Ginger because she's the only ginger here, but if you need sassy comebacks or memes, she's your gal! She's hilarious, so try to talk to her sometime!" George nodded and began to bag as fast as he could, deep in thought.

Making new friends right now won't be bad... I need to be more social, but... my damn timidness always gets in the way.

Meagan handed the receipt to the customer. "Have a wonderful day, ma'am!" She kneeled and pulled out the cleaning spray and napkins. "Do you mind helping me clean the conveyor belt?" She handed him napkins, spraying the belt.

"Um... Meagan... can I ask your thoughts on Timothy?" George stared down, wiping in circular motions.

"He's nice to me sometimes, but other times I feel like he has an attitude, I don't know. He seems shady at times. Why?"

"Oh, I was only wondering— wait, shady?"

Meagan set the spray bottle underneath her register. "Well, he seems to get along with everyone, but recently I've noticed he's on his phone more than usual. Every time someone walks near, he jams his phone back into his apron pocket."

"Hmm, I don't know why I asked," he sighed heavily, keeping his

18

head down, not letting her see his eyes.

"Are you two not talking?"

George threw the wad of paper towels in his hand away, shaking his head in regret. "Forget it, it's nothing."

"Alright, well... I have awesome news! I'm going out with Dom tonight. We're going to Froyo Fantasy across the street." Meagan replied ecstatically, changing the subject.

"Well, you'll have to text me how that goes later tonight!" George smiled. A finger tapped his shoulder. It was Timothy. "What...?" he asked without emotion.

"Why are you ignoring me? Did you read my texts? I made up with my mom. All I had to do was butter her up. You can't be mad at me." He stared at him with an innocent puppy face.

"I didn't read your texts and I am mad at you. Go do your job and don't bother me. I'll talk to you after work, *friend*," he spat out harshly, making him walk away dumbfounded and speechless.

Meagan kept silent in front of the register, waiting for the next customer. George had the urge to tell her what was going on, but hesitated on impulse in fear of losing a friend.

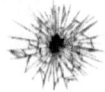

After his shift was over, George found Timothy waiting at his car.

"What?" he said, approaching the driver's side door.

"Can we talk?" Timothy asked.

"Get in..." George swung open the door, crawled in, and slammed it shut behind him.

Timothy reached over, gently caressing George's hand, but he pulled away in reflex. "What's wrong, baby?" he asked in a soothing voice.

George stared out the window as he spoke: "Michael sent me a friend request this morning. When I looked at his profile picture, I saw the two of you in *your* room, and it said he's in a relationship. What is going on!?"

George's jaw clenched, and his hands clutched the hem of his shirt, his eyebrows squinching.

"George, look at me." Timothy grabbed George's jaw, slowly turning his attention to him. "Nothing is going on between us. I'm honestly dealing with a lot of drama with my friends; and since we aren't out yet, I wanted to tell them, including Michael, that I'm talking to someone. Michael and I aren't dating. He has a boyfriend. You trust me, don't you?"

George wanted to believe him, but his mind whirled in a thousand directions, and his stomach churned like a washing machine. "I'm slowly coming out to my parents. I'm trying to find the right time. Why can't you tell your parents that you're talking to me, and not him? You're already out of the closet. I told you, my family doesn't approve of being gay or bisexual. This new profile picture makes it harder to trust you!"

Tears began streaming down George's flushed cheeks, Timothy wiped them away with his thumbs. "I know it looks bad right now, but you have to trust me! I love you, not him. If you don't trust me, then we don't have a strong relationship, which means you truly don't love me. And I trust you."

"But you're putting words in my mouth... I love you and I'm trying to trust you! I'm scared all the time you'll leave me out of the blue for no reason. I feel as though I'm never good enough for anyone for what I've been through." His mind took him back to that horrific night. The night he felt his stomach lurch into his throat when Kat, his ex-girlfriend, had gently ran her fingers through his palm.

"You've got it all wrong, George. We are second cousins; he lives in the town over. We hadn't seen each other since the start of summer before senior year. I'm being honest." Kat had stared into George's eyes and told him what he thought was the truth. He trusted so easily.

If he hadn't been so excited to give Kat the Christmas present, he probably would have never realized she was cheating on him. The empty feeling he felt turned into resentment. The guy even looked like him, maybe a little taller and much stronger. George resented her to this day for the lies she told.

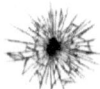

George snapped back into reality just as quickly as he'd left it.

"I'm so stressed with everything, and I'm paranoid!" he said, jerking away from Timothy once more, then cupped his hands in his face, and laid his head on the steering wheel.

No one understands what I'm going through. I hate keeping everything a secret. I have to in order to maintain the love of my friends and family.

"George, I'm going to leave this with you: I promise to never hurt you, I promise to never leave you, and I never break my promises. Hopefully, you will understand and be a little more relaxed. Be safe, I love you." And with that, Timothy got out of the car, slamming the door behind him, sealing the three promises he'd made to George.

Chapter 3

Meagan's breath grew sharp, patiently waiting outside for Dom. She watched Timothy get out of George's car.

What is with those two? One minute there's tension, then the next they are smiling at each other. Are they... dating? No, George told me he was straight; yet I haven't seen him with a girlfriend before or after Physics class. I shouldn't jump to conclusions: he told me about Kat. What she'd done to him was awful... she humiliated him on Christmas break. He'd bought her a necklace with a golden hourglass pendant that had the letter 'G' on the top and 'K' on the bottom. When he went over to her house to give it to her, and discovered another guy was there, locking lips with her on the couch.

If we had been friends then... I think I would have locked her in a freezer to die. George deserves to be happy, but he—

"Thanks for waiting on me. Are you ready to go?" Dom appeared beside her, and she lost her thought.

"Oh, of course!" She replied, following him to his car.

He surprised her by opening the door for her like a gentleman, with a fresh pine scent wafting out. It reminded her of the exciting, refreshing scents of a forest.

If that's even what a pine tree smells like, considering it was forbidden to enter.

She sat awkwardly, dusting off her dress pants, realizing she could feel the tension in her feet rise.

Say something, Meagan, don't let it get awkward.

"Thank you for opening the door, it seems chivalry isn't dead yet!"

Smooth as a cucumber.

Dom chuckled, cranking the car when a blast of country music startled Meagan, making her curse. He lowered the volume. "What kind of music do you listen to?"

"I usually listen to Killswitch, Red, and Skillet," Meagan answered.

"Oh, so you're more hardcore. I have a few Skillet songs, but I'm more of a country guy, even though I clearly don't dress that way." Dom pressed track two and turned the volume up, driving across the street to Froyo Fantasy.

"No one's ever asked me to hang out anywhere with them before. I honestly don't get out much," she blurted out truthfully, hearing the squeaks of Dom's brakes as he pulled into the parking space.

Dom smiled sweetly. "Well, it's my pleasure to take you out tonight!" As if on cue, he killed the engine, then swiftly moved around to her side and opened the door again as if they were on an actual date.

Entering the frozen yogurt shop, they saw machines frothing different flavors, a splash of reds, blues, yellows, greens, and pinks decorated the walls. Picking out two large cups, they began filling yogurt to the brim. Meagan finished with a swirl of whipped cream and sprinkles on top.

"Oh, I'll pay for yours! It's no problem," Dom placed both cups on the scale, paying the cashier.

This feels wrong because I'm used to paying my own, but also lovely because a friend has never bought me anything before... not even George.

Her face burned bright, murmuring, "Thank you."

Dom picked out a table in the corner, and Meagan realized they were the only two in the shop.

"So, Meagan," Dom sat down opposite her, "which college were you thinking about going to?" He stared into her brown eyes before scooping a spoonful of yogurt into his mouth.

"There are only two here; it's not much of a choice. I want to be a computer engineer, but neither college has that many classes to take in that field. What about you?" Meagan said, pushing the focus towards him instead of on herself.

Dom stared down at his melting yogurt as he spoke: "I haven't decided yet. I wanted to be a doctor, but I can't handle blood well. I was hoping the money I saved up from this boring cashier job would somehow make the decision for me; and yet here I am still contemplating. I know... stupid me for thinking we could venture outside of this town or any neighboring towns for that matter." He raised his eyes up to her, smiling.

Meagan took a deep breath, finally mustering up enough courage to ask, "Why do you have your eyes set on me? I don't consider myself the 'pretty' type."

Dom chuckled, "You're funny, smart, and easy to talk to. I know you're probably thinking I'm just a player, but I really just want to see what you have on the inside."

Meagan was completely shocked. Cupid's arrow was piercing her heart and this honestly scared her.

He is evaluating me from a spiritual level, not appearance. This is making it harder to resist only having a friendship, because I doubt he knows I'm crushing on him...

"I do think you are very attractive, but from what I've observed with some of the other girls at work, you tend to flirt with them, and they are prettier than I am. That's why I'm confused." Meagan challenged him, taking another bite of her froyo.

"I get it. But you're not like the other girls. Are you on your phone right now? Are you trying to get into my pants?" Dom explained.

"Now see... that's just plain rude and shallow in my opinion. I'm more of a romantic type. Well… I would like to think I am, but I haven't been on a date before."

Meagan could feel Dom's eyes trying to search into her soul.

"I have a confession." Meagan continued. "I have had a crush on you since I laid eyes on you a few months ago, but I must admit I have a hard time expressing my emotions to people I care about, but for some reason, with you, it comes naturally. I'm not sure what I'm talking about anymore! Listen at me rambling." Meagan's eyes dropped slowly. She couldn't look into his eyes. She hoped he didn't think she was too absorbed in him.

"So... if you have a crush on me, and I have a crush on you, what does this mean? I could take you out sometime and buy you dinner. Or you could come back to my place and stay awhile, only if you felt comfortable doing so. I only ask we get to know each other more beforehand. You're easy to talk to."

Meagan raised her eyes to see him ruffle his dirty blonde hair.

"Well, I do agree we should get to know each other more, but going out on a date? What if it doesn't work out? Wouldn't that affect the friendship we have now? Then again... part of me wants to try it. Oh my gosh, what am I saying? We'd get fired if work found out!"

Dom's demeanor shifted. "How else would we know if we were compatible? I wouldn't worry about work. Tonight, if we can get to know each other more, maybe we can see where it leads. What's your favorite movie?

He's smirking... that grin... a sly reassurance. He secretly wants to be in a relationship with me.

Meagan grinned, *"Star Trek: The Voyage Home."*

Stinging pain flooded into George as blood dripped down the back side of his wrists and painted the white sink red.

It doesn't hurt, it doesn't hurt. I trust Timothy. I want to...

He washed his razor and arm quickly, then wrapped it tightly with a gauze.

I'm going to have to wear long sleeves for a while, but I'm fine, I'm okay.

George slipped on a long-sleeved black shirt before his door creaked open.

"It's late. I'm not going to scream or wake anyone up," his dad said, stepping into the room.

George set his phone on the table, hoping his dad hadn't noticed the bandage.

"I let you borrow my loafers one time. You can't even take care of something without it getting ruined. Your mom found my dirty, wet clothes in the corner of your room. You need to get your shit together. You're going to start learning your actions have consequences. You're paying me for a new suit and loafers since you're working now. And with that job of yours, don't even think about asking to borrow anything of mine again. Got it?"

With an unbothered face, George nodded. His dad grumbled and closed the door.

George locked the door behind him and glared at his phone.

Should I?

Before George realized it, he held the phone and viewed his newsfeed. Nothing. He typed in Michael's name and viewed his profile again, his paranoia eating him slowly. A new post from him flashed into his eyes.

Going to the movies with him and his mom tonight!

It was him and Timothy in the car with Timothy's mom. George's heart began to crack. Dropping his phone, he fell numbly onto his bed.

We're the ones supposed to go to the movies. We're supposed to be together, and yet... Fuck it... Why do I even try? I just want to...

George unwrapped the gauze wrap, stared at the cuts apathetically, then dug his nails into them, reminding him how it felt to not feel good enough.

This feeling. I've felt it before. Resentment? No, that feeling was from Kat. Worthless. I didn't know what it felt like until it happened with Kai. I thought I might've been the only one in this town who wanted to experiment with guys. Then, you came along and promised me the world. It was odd because Kai claimed to be a senior and lived in a neighboring town when we met. Kai lied about his age. He was always infuriated when I didn't feel comfortable doing anything with him. He beat the shit out of me, and I had to fight for my life, ending up with several bruises to avoid being raped. I felt useless and worthless. My parents didn't even care why my wrists were purple or my eye blackened.

George winced before forcing himself to fall asleep, blood dripping onto his shirt from the reopened wounds.

I'm never good enough...

George mentally counted the cuts.

28

One... I'm ugly... two I'm overweight... three... I'm gullible... four... I'm passive...
five... I'm stupid...

Meagan's stomach churned as Dom's face came closer to hers. *Surely, he wasn't*
trying to kiss her while she was getting back into her car. She quickly opened the car
door to block his advance.

"We'll have to do this again sometime. I enjoyed every minute of it."
Dom forced himself around the door, enclosing Meagan with a hug.

I... I... This warm, fuzzy feeling... I don't like it!

Meagan refrained from hugging him back; instead, she pushed him
away. Her haphephobia had kicked in.

"I'm sorry, I'm not the juxtapose kind of girl… this is what I meant
from earlier. I don't know how to explain it, but I hate having physical touch.
I yearn for it, but I can't have it. My body... well... mind won't let me. I
immediately panic." She rubbed her right arm, trying to wipe the *touch* off.
"When you have haphephobia, you're just a can of bug spray, constantly
repelling guys. Now you know why I haven't been actively dating. It's a deal
breaker."

"You have nothing to apologize for. You went out of your comfort
zone tonight. I'll make a deal with you. If you come over to my house next
time, I'll cook us dinner, and in return, I'll help you with your phobia. You
just have to get used to me first, but you will soon enough. Text me when
you get home safely." He winked and got into his car, driving off, leaving
Meagan with yet another cold, icky feeling in her stomach.

She took her phone out and immediately texted George:

For the first time, I think I could be in love! I'll tell you about it tomorrow!

George felt himself falling into an abyss, swimming in an endless black ocean, trying to see if he was actually falling, floating, or rising. All he saw was darkness, and darkness is what he accepted.

Am I dead? Is this the end?

"No, you're not dead." A soft, but deep voice echoed all around his murky surroundings.

Who are you?

George could not speak, feel, or see any of his body.

"I am not you, but I could be you. It depends on how you interpret the predicament."

Are you God?

"If that's who you want me to be."

I don't know who I want you to be... I just want to be fine.

"What is your definition of fine, George?"

To be happy, instead of miserable.

"There's only one way you can be happy."

Which is?

"Look inside yourself as you're doing right now. You can't see anything right now, because you're standing in the way of finding yourself."

How am I...

"You will understand soon."

George was left in silence. He felt nothing. He saw nothing. He heard nothing.

Chapter 4

The next morning, George skipped breakfast and headed to work without speaking to his family. He didn't care to interact with them and take the chance of them noticing the five cuts on his arm. He parked his car, then he glanced at his phone. Nothing. George sighed heavily and texted Timothy:

Good morning, how was your sleep? What time do you come into work today?

He waited for a moment to send, then went inside, acknowledging no one. All he wanted was to hide his pain from everyone.

"Can I go get carts today?" George asked his supervisor numbly.

The manager tilted her head in confusion. "Normally, no one asks to go get carts when their shift starts, but if it's what you want to do, then yes."

George slipped on the orange vest, grabbed the double-ended hook used to retrieve carts, and ran outside. He needed time to himself, time to process the feelings that were all screaming at him.

The dream... who was that? How can I be the one in the way of my happiness? I haven't done anything wrong. I just want Timothy and me to be together and happy...

BEEEEEPP! George nearly pushed the carts into a backing vehicle, the driver screaming at him to pay attention. Pulling the carts back, George heard a soft chuckle from behind him. He turned around to find Hannah laughing and covering her mouth.

"What's funny? Almost ramming carts into a car?"

"No. I mean yes... and no. I hate the customers here, so... I'll give you props for nearly damaging their vehicle, but I hate some of our co-workers even more, which is why I'm out here." She sighed heavily and rolled her eyes.

This is your chance to get your mind off things, he thought.

"Oh? Why do you hate our co-workers? What happened, if you don't mind me asking?" George began pushing the carts again as Hannah strode along beside him.

"Linette... she doesn't like me, and I have no idea why! She throws shit down the conveyor belt at me! I didn't do anything to her. I became so mad I was about to tackle her like a quarterback and pound her face to the ground." Hannah's voice rose and grew more heated, "I decided to come out here to destress."

"That doesn't make any sense to me. She can't be mad at you for no reason..." George replied, pushing the load into the lobby, then turned around to go get another.

"I don't know... I try so hard to be nice to people, but they keep teasing me." Hannah said, following him back outside.

"I understand how you feel. I try so hard for everyone, but it seems as though it's never good enough. You know... we should have fun. Fourth of July is coming up in a few weeks. Meagan, Becca, Timothy, you, and I could pitch in and buy some fireworks to let off!" George grinned at her as her face lit up.

"Yeah, I'll ask my parents! You've just made my day! Thanks!" Hannah snickered, then stopped as she saw George's arm. "What happened to your arm?" she asked with concern.

"I... uh was fixing dinner last night and burnt my wrist on the stove." He scowled to himself for not making up a better excuse.

"Did you burn the food?" Hannah teased, latching the hook onto several carts and pulling the strap tight.

"No, I'm a great cook. I wasn't paying attention. Anyways, how long have you been working here?" he said, diverting the conversation.

"Two months back, at the end of April. I'm also a cashier, maybe they'll let you on register. Either Meagan or I could teach you!" she said.

"Yeah, maybe," George took a deep breath, not thinking he could learn in his state of increasing depression.

"How old are you, Hannah?" George stopped in his tracks.

"I'm eighteen. I graduated with you and Meagan. I've seen you around the halls. I'm guessing you never noticed me." Hannah replied, studying him.

"I had my head down most days, almost always invisible and avoiding conflict and drama. I never realized..." George tried to explain when a smooth voice interrupted.

"Hey, Hannah!" Dom shouted as he walked past them and into the store.

"H-Hi, Dom." Hannah's personality shifted, forgetting George was there for a minute.

"Ahh, I can see someone is crushing with dreamy eyes and a slobbery mouth," George pestered.

Hannah opened her mouth when a voice echoed from the lobby.

"Hannah, you're needed up front on the register. It's getting busy," Timothy informed them from behind.

"Oh my God, I don't want to go back in there with them! I swear that old bat will get what's coming to her." She ripped the orange vest off her shoulders, then handed it to Timothy as she stomped back inside the store.

"Hi," Timothy said to George, but he completely ignored him.

"Are you angry? George, listen, I've been getting your texts. I've been hella busy. I just got a second job yesterday to help out my parents financially. I do hope you understand." Timothy laid his hand on George's shoulder.

"I see, but you could have sent me a text explaining the situation. I would've understood," George said, pulling his next load of carts out of the corral. He started to struggle as he realized he hadn't pulled the rope tightly enough. George growled at himself, but his frustrations were stopped by Timothy.

"Here, let me do it," Timothy tightened the carts more. "My mom was watching me like a hawk yesterday. I couldn't text you back because she monitors my phone. Trust me."

And again with the trust card. He went to the movies last night... why should I trust him?

George nodded silently.

Maybe I'm just too paranoid I'll get hurt again... what is this heavy feeling in the pit of my stomach?

George clutched his stomach, confused on what to believe.

"Hun, what's wrong? Are you sick? And what the hell happened to your wrist!?" Timothy forcefully grabbed his wrist.

"I'm fine! I burnt myself last night making dinner!" George lay, wincing in pain from Timothy's grip, and pulled his arm away.

"You should be more careful next time. I hate to see you hurt," Timothy urged, hugging George tightly; tears were forming in George's eyes, trying valiantly to hold it together.

"I... love you, Timothy," he breathed, fearing someone would hear.

"I love you too," he replied, kissing the top of his head softly.

George backed away, wiping his eyes with his shirt, then recollected himself. "So, I was thinking maybe we could do something together for the Fourth of July after work. Set off fireworks? My parents wouldn't mind all of you coming to the house, and I was going to invite you, Hannah, Becca, and Meagan. Are you up to it?"

Timothy's grin faded, and a frown took its place. "I'll ask my mom later, but yes, that sounds like a great idea. I'm in!"

A small weight seemed to have been lifted from his shoulders, as if being weighed down by fear, paranoia, and doubt wasn't enough. Though it seemed George was making headway, trying to hint at Timothy spending more time with him.

"Did you have fun last night?" George blurted, unexpectedly.

"What do you mean by 'fun?'" Timothy glared suspiciously at him.

"You went to the movies last night, right? Your mom posted about it. Which movie did you go see?"

Timothy stared out the store window absently, "*Jargon*."

He went to see the movie you've been waiting to see for the past year without you. You wanted to go with him, and the two of you were planning on going sometime this summer...

Anger began to rise throughout his body, and for the first time, George wanted to slug Timothy in the face.

"Did you know your friend Michael sent me a friend request? Don't worry, I didn't accept it. All I can say is you'd better find some way to make it on the fourth of July." George turned away, isolating himself from Timothy.

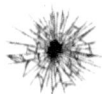

After two hours of silent, subtle glances at each other from across the parking lot, George finally decided to go back inside. He wiped the sweat from his forehead, glancing over to the registers. He needed someone to talk to. Someone to let all of this emotional baggage out to. He wanted it to be Meagan, but his heart shattered into fragments every time he thought of her reaction.

Besides, would she understand my predicament? Dom is bagging for her...I'll just wait.

But then there was Becca, muttering to herself, because she didn't have a bagger. Items were starting to pile up on the counter and drop to the floor.

You're wanting to pour your whole life onto one person you haven't met yet. You've kept who you are a secret this long; why say anything now?

George rushed over to her aid, grabbing the packs of drinks and the dog food from the relentless conveyor belt and moving them to the customer's empty cart.

"At least someone has enough courtesy to help me. The others literally stand there drooling!" She batted her eyelashes over toward the next register, signaling to the older man standing lost in space.

George, glad he could escape the tension with light humor, managed a feeble smile.

"Thank you, hun. I appreciate your help," Becca frowned. "Are you okay?"

"Hmm?" He bit his lip, noticing his hand trembling while placing the last bag filled with eggs and bread into the cart.

"You seem to be on another planet. Do you need to talk?" Becca offered.

"I did forget to take a bottle of water with me. I'm probably dehydrated from being out in the sun."

"We can't have you passing out on us, now, can we, cutie? Here," Becca handed George an unopened bottle of water.

George tossed the water bottle cap on the counter and chugged. His stomach growled in hunger, and his knees burned in anger at him, noticing he'd been neglecting his body.

Becca gave the receipt to the customer and wished them a wonderful day before leaning over the counter. "Sweetie, that's not the best approach when you're dehydrated."

George lowered the bottle. "It's not?"

Becca shook her head. "You'll be making yourself go to the bathroom more. If you want to rehydrate, take small sips."

George nodded.

"You're too adorable," Becca said.

George felt his cheeks flush as he began to relax.

"Are you only here for the summer?" Becca wondered, her blue eyes still fixated on him.

"During college, too, after school." George rolled his eyes.

"What are you going to school for?" Becca seemed invested in what George had to say.

George began to reply when a hot breath ran down his neck.

"George, go on break," Timothy commanded, appearing behind him, silencing George.

"Before you go, Hannah told me about setting off fireworks on the Fourth of July! It sounds fun, I'll be there!" Becca retorted enthusiastically.

"At least I know you'll be there," George rasped in a gravelly voice.

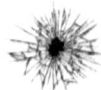

For the next couple of weeks, George reluctantly didn't message Timothy, knowing he wouldn't respond. Finally, he decided to message him on the Fourth of July, giving him his last chance to prove to him he still cared.

Morning, wanted to make sure that you're still coming over. Did you ask your mom yet?

He glanced down at his healing cuts, wondering if they would turn into scars. He lightly pressed down on his skin, then ran down through all the cuts.

The stinging feels...great.

BZZZZ! George opened the text from Timothy.

She said it was fine. I'll be there. Don't act cold to me today.

George cackled cynically, not believing him until he was actually there with him. That moment would be perfect; it would also prove he still cares enough about him to consider his feelings.

George jumped out of bed, grabbed his wallet, and counted how much he had saved.

Twenty dollars in total, at least we will be splitting the firework costs five ways! The rest of the money I gave to dad as an attempt to make peace for the suit I ruined.

He didn't mind spending money to have a good time; however, he was also looking forward to saving up for his first year at college, and he wanted to be ready. *Better start being a little more frugal if that's gonna happen.* It wasn't like he got out much to begin with, and every day during the last school year, he was participating in after-school programs and homework. *I have to be the best. To be a role model to my siblings.* George snapped out of the thought. To show his appreciation, he decided to message Timothy's mom on social media.

Hello, this is George. Thank you so much for allowing Timothy to come over to set off fireworks! This will be a blast for all of us!

Before dusk, the whole store was nearly empty, and the supervisor called up employees one by one to see if they wanted to keep working or go home early.

"George!" Meagan called from up the aisle, rushing to him. "You can go on your break, but they might call you down afterwards to let you go." She took the cart from him and began running down the aisle, the wheels squeaking, before disappearing around the corner. "It's amazing that we might have three whole hours of fun tonight!"

George walked upstairs, heading to his locker to check his phone. He sipped his water while reading Timothy's mom's response.

Timothy never asked me about this. This is the first time I've heard about the idea. I'm going to have a talk with him when he gets home.

George spat-sprayed water onto the table when Timothy walked out from the men's restroom.

"What happened!?" Timothy rushed over to George, who was coughing in disbelief.

"You lied to me! You said it was fine for you to come with us tonight! You didn't even ask your mom! Stay away from me…" George was backing away as Timothy stepped forward.

"Let me explain…"

"You don't need to explain." George ran down the stairs and outside to a bench. A mixture of fury and numbness flooded inside him. Timothy followed him, sitting beside him.

"I had to wait for the perfect time to ask her, and now I don't know if I'll be able to at all. I was going to ask right after my shift, but now that I'm going home early, I can talk to her face-to-face."

"All I did was thank her for letting you come…how was I supposed to know!? You don't even text me anymore. I purposefully didn't text you for weeks to see if you would text me first!" George turned his head away, not wanting to talk to him any longer.

"I'll let you know if I can or not later. You need to stop being paranoid and trust me for once." He walked away towards his car, leaving George feeling even more abandoned.

I can't trust you when you don't even try for me. I try for you all the time. My heart is aching, it hurts to breathe, to live.

His excitement and sprightly mood vanished into the humid summer air as the fifteen minutes slipped by aimlessly. He clocked back in, and within twenty minutes, he was called to the customer service desk.

"We're dead, and we still have too many people working. Would you like to go home early?" The manager glared at him sternly, trying to intimidate him to leave.

"Are you okay? You seem flustered," George asked.

The manager's eyes softened. "I'm concerned. Compared to last year, we have five less female associates. It's weird that for the past month, I've seen them not show up or give two-week notices. Can you believe it? It's a small town. Where else could they have gone to work? It just bothers me."

"It is weird. Maybe they went to work at the movie theater? But I know you care about your associates, so I get it. Anyways, I finished the go-backs, so there is no point in me sticking around. Thanks!" George rushed upstairs to grab his belongings. Meagan, Becca, and Hannah were waiting for him at a table.

"Are you okay, hun?" Becca stood up and bear hugged him.

"What happened on your break?" Meagan asked, a little concerned.

"Nothing, don't worry about it. Let's go buy the fireworks. I'll text Timothy afterwards."

"Did anyone think of what we would be lying on? I don't exactly want to lie in the grass the whole night," Hannah inquired from behind. George and Becca gave a puzzled stare.

"I brought an old blanket," Meagan replied, laying her share of fireworks on the conveyor.

"Great! What about flashlights?" Hannah asked.

"I didn't bring any…" Meagan replied.

"I have flashlights in my car." All four of them turned around to face Dom behind them.

"Why do you have flashlights in your car…?" Meagan asked suspiciously.

"In case of an emergency, I'll let you borrow them if I can join you and if you come over after." He glared back at Meagan. Meagan exchanged a hopeful glance at George.

"Fine, only if you pitch in." George dumped his pile on the conveyor belt, giving the cashier his share of twenty dollars.

"Sounds fair," Dom said, slipping a ten into the cashier's hand.

George flipped through his phone while everyone else began pitching in their share, sending a text to Timothy.

Are you coming or not? We'll be at my house; we have the fireworks ready. You know where I live. I expect you to be there.

George strained a smile to all four of them, "Alright, let's have some fun!"

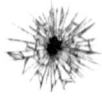

"Betcha can't catch me!" Meagan yelled at Dom, racing around the field with a sparkler in her hand.

"Wanna bet!?" Dom lit a sparkler and began chasing her around, laughing like a maniac.

"Hey, Hannah, you want to help me light this one?" Becca grabbed a pack of fountain fireworks and began walking out into the field.

"Sure, wait for me!" Hannah said, running after her, and they disappeared into the darkness.

They're all having fun…and I'm sitting here worrying when he'll text me…why am I so worried about him? I want to have fun.

George grabbed a sparkler, then sat at the edge of the blanket and lit it. The white light sparkled into his face, staring as if in a trance.

"BBBBBZZZ!!!" George's phone vibrated against his leg. Grabbing it quickly, he viewed the message from Timothy.

My mom agreed to let me come, only if Michael could come with me.

The white sparkler burst into a red flame before dying into ash. The smoke rising above George's head. Jealousy had fully overtaken him.

Chapter 5

You're still in the way.

I don't understand. I'm not in the way.

Take a look around. What do you see?

George glanced around only to see red in every direction. The crimson void consumed him, and all he could see was himself.

Red, I see red.

Look closer, in front of you.

He stared straight in front of him as the voice directed; a small green dot was amidst the red.

A green dot, what is that supposed to mean!?

You must answer that yourself, find the way. The answer lies in front of you.

All I know is I'm done with Timothy; I cannot go on being the second choice, and I know I'm his second choice. Why else would he have wanted to bring Michael?

If that's what you feel, then cut loose the dead weight and move

on.

I want to but—

The only person who is stopping you is you.

Do I have the strength to do this?

Yes.

How do you know?

That's not important.

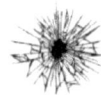

George awoke with a throbbing pain in his arm, and his head was pounding. He thought he saw stars, but it must've been his imagination. He checked the time: it was only seven am. He lay back down, then put his arm on his forehead and thought about last night.

I dropped the sparkler, then fled to my car and began to cry. I don't know how long it fucking took for the others to realize I had disappeared, but I was too busy sobbing to care. Meagan was the first, then everyone else piled into the car. I told them I was fine, but they insisted I tell them the truth. I told all of them about myself and Timothy. Of course, they knew by the tension between us, but they were all silent by the time I was finished.

I sat there emotionless, my sobs breaking the utter silence. My feelings were coiling up into a spring that could erupt and lash out at anyone and everyone. My heart cried, but my face was expressionless. My brain screamed, but my body was still. My bones cracked, but my skin was icy. My teeth clenched, but my tongue was resting in place.

That's when the wind whipped and whooshed outside, lightning blazed across the sky, and thunder pounded above the car. A thunderstorm began to form, and everyone agreed to pack things up and call it a night.

George's lip curled, and his chest tightened.

What were they thinking? Did they care? Do they hate me? It's my fault for talking about my problems and explaining myself, which turned out to be a total mood killer. But Meagan... she helped me inside my house. We managed to make it to my room without waking the rest of the house. A burst of white light flashed in my window, my backyard lit up for a few seconds, and my eyes met those shimmering eyes once more. A black silhouette stood at the edge of the woods. A booming thunder made both of us jump, and we exchanged looks. Fuck! Did Meagan see it too? She did say the thunderstorm ruined the night, but that didn't comfort me at all. I'm tired... emotionally exhausted. I can't stop thinking about last night; the thought of something or someone watching me, and not knowing where my friends stand when it comes to my sexuality feels like a centipede with hundreds of legs crawling over my brain, itching and eating away at me from the inside out.

The next morning, Meagan's thoughts raced while brushing her hair back in a side high-up ponytail.

Am I mad? No, there's no reason to be. Am I surprised? A little, because he wouldn't come to me and tell me. He didn't feel comfortable enough, though I thought we were friends...it's awful...I hate he's experiencing another toxic relationship. It doesn't make sense: he's sweet and adorable, and he tries to be whatever you want.

I hope Dom is okay with me going out with George today. I want to help him get his mind away from Timothy before he gets too depressed. Crap... what if he is, and I didn't notice? What I did notice was those creepy eyes last night... or a dark figure standing between the trees? If it hadn't been for the lightning... had it been there this whole time? Watching us? George. Need to focus on George...

Combing her fingers through her ponytail, she paused.

The arcade and pizza would put a smile on George's face.

She texted George, hoping he would agree.

Meagan's mouth watered thinking about pizza, slipping on mid-rise jean shorts, and sneakers.

George…please…don't let a psychopath ruin you. You're strong and determined.

Then abruptly, her phone buzzed from the side of the sink. She grabbed it and read slowly:

I asked my mom, and she said I could go. Meagan…I haven't been hungry lately. I hardly eat at all anymore. I've been eating maybe once a day, where before I usually eat four to five times a day; This has been going on for a couple weeks. Now I'm scared; I was at 140 pounds just two weeks ago, and now I'm at 128…

Anger and frustration bubbled up inside her, but she took a deep breath before she answered.

We are getting pizza this afternoon, and I will make you eat. Otherwise, I'll kidnap you and you will have to stay at my house until you feel better.

She stared at her face in the bathroom mirror. Her cheeks were full of color, her skin was pale, yet soft, and her dark mahogany hair gleaming, surprised it had been styled. The minutes ticked by. She was admiring her angelic face, and her worries seemed to disperse momentarily, before a vibration startled her.

I'll try, but every time I try to eat, I get sick to my stomach. I threw up earlier this morning just trying to eat some eggs; my nerves are tearing me apart.

Meagan didn't know how to respond.

He's falling apart, and I'm watching it happen. He needs to relax.

Another message popped in front of her eyes, this time from Dom. Her heart skipped a beat.

I was going to hang out with you today, but I was called in, unexpectedly. I wanted to take you to the movies. Please forgive me.

Meagan felt an uneasy sensation flow over her body, and she held her stomach. Whether it was butterflies or nerves, she couldn't tell.

"Have you two decided what kind of pizza you want?" the waitress asked, clicking her pen vigorously.

"What would you like, George?" Meagan asked.

"It doesn't matter, whatever you want," George replied.

"One pepperoni pizza, please." Meagan gave the menu back, and the waitress walked away.

"... George... I wanted to ask you, since we're friends, what made you feel like you couldn't tell me about your relationship? I want to understand from your perspective."

George stared at the glossy wooden table as he talked. "It's not easy. I didn't know how you would respond. I don't want to lose what few friends I have, and I can't tell my parents. It's a struggle keeping a dark secret hidden all these years."

Meagan held his hand and gasped, "You don't need to hide yourself from your friends anymore! If you need someone to talk to, talk to me! You don't need to tear yourself apart. You're destroying yourself for a love I don't think exists anymore. I know you don't want to hear this, but I think you should break up with him."

Tears swelling in his eyes, George gazed into Meagan's concerned face, "All I wanted was for someone to listen... All I wanted was for someone to show me compassion, to give me love. My whole life has been filled with malice, with coldness. I never felt like myself at home. I'm a puppet. I please my parents, stringing along with anything they want. I have to be the best, and I'm never good enough. Not for them, not for Timothy..." George realized he was pouring his wounded heart out to her, and it scared him. Trying to quickly change the subject, he said, "My hands are always freezing. I can tell you're uncomfortable by the touch. I'm sorry, I forgot," withdrawing his icy fingers from her twitching hand.

The waitress appeared with a large sizzling pepperoni pizza. "Enjoy!" she called, hurrying to another table.

"I want you to eat, if not for yourself, for me…please…," Meagan pleaded.

She's worried about me.

"I will." He took a slice and nibbled on it. For a few minutes, they ate in silence until George spoke up, "Don't worry about me, I'm used to it." He smiled weakly as he managed to finish off his first slice of pizza.

"No one should have to go through any of this, including you," she said, grabbing another slice and slipping it onto George's plate, adding: "Eat."

George picked up the slice but hesitated. "Please, I want to make today all about fun. Let's talk about something else. Alright, how are you and Dom?"

I'm already full…I'm going to have to make myself eat.

"He wants to take me out to a movie soon! I think we can make this work…. But enough about me. I've always wondered what exactly you're going for in college?"

"Well, I've always wanted to start my own business…I want to be an entrepreneur."

"Quite fascinating, in what kind of business?" Meagan was intrigued, sprinkling parmesan cheese on top of her pepperoni.

"I want to open my own book and game store. I'd have all different genres of books as well as manga. Also, I'd have every single game for every console. It sucks. The only game store in this town only has the newer consoles."

Meagan's eyes lit up, and she dropped her pizza. "No way! You seem like you have everything mapped out! That seems like a great idea. You want to know what my all-time favorite game is?" she scooped up and bit off a huge chunk from her pizza.

"Well, you know mine is Resident Evil, but I have no idea what yours could be." He admitted.

"Jet Set Radio Future!" she giggled.

"Here's the bill," the waitress interrupted their shared moment, handing the receipt to George.

While reviewing the bill, Meagan snatched the receipt away, shaking her head. "No, this was my idea and your treat. I'll pay for it." She pulled out a twenty-dollar bill and gave it to the waitress, and added, "Have a nice day."

"You know what? Let's go to the arcade so I can kick your butt at skee-ball and air hockey!"

"I bet I can win at both," Meagan teased at the door.

"Yeah, we'll see," George muttered, rolling his eyes. "Just go in."

Meagan opened the door, then immediately shoved George back

outside. "Umm, maybe we should go get ice cream first, heh."

George raised his brow. "Do you have multiple personality disorder? Let's go in and have fun." He pushed past her and walked in.

"George, please …" but her words faded out when George stood still, gawking at Timothy playing skee-ball with Michael.

George's hands balled up into fists as he tried not to march over and knock the lights out of him. Meagan tapped his shoulder, and he took a deep breath. He spun around laughing, "Let's go have fun! I can beat you at air hockey!"

Meagan's lips moved, but no words or sound came.

"Let's go!" He grabbed her hand and pulled her toward the air hockey table. He forced a dollar into the machine, and the surrounding neon lights flickered on and off. George grabbed the puck, saying briskly, "Are you ready?"

"Y… Yes," Meagan replied uncertainly.

Concentrating only on the puck, George hit it forcefully.

Lies, all lies! He's not sick, he's on a date with him! How could he? Was I just a pawn in his game? Did he just use me to pass his classes? THIS IS THE LAST TIME I GET USED.

"GRAHH!" George shot the puck straight into the pocket. "Ha! One to zip!" Each time the puck was hit at him, he slammed it back into the goal with ease. "Seven to zip, I win!" George hopped up and down triumphantly.

Meagan watched George jump up and down.

What's happening to him...?

She leaned her head slightly and saw Timothy had noticed they were there. He stared emotionlessly, his eyes dull in the dim lighting of the arcade.

He honestly doesn't care for George...I want to help, but how?

"George, let's go play Deal or No Deal," Meagan said hastily, hurrying over to the game at the back of the arcade and slipping in four quarters. "I'll pick the suitcase we want to keep, and you eliminate the ones you want." She pressed a button at random, then allowed George to play while she peered back at Timothy.

Her heart jumped. He was still facing her with a cold, dead stare.

He really is a douchebag! It's taking all I have not to bitch slap him. I have to keep him away from George...

An hour passed incredibly slowly, then Meagan pulled out her pockets, lint falling to the ground. She checked her purse. "I'm out of money, let's go cash the tickets in." She glanced quickly around the arcade, noticing Timothy had left.

"The ice-cream shop is next door, let's go get some. We can just keep how many points we earned here and cash them in next time." George grabbed the ticket receipt, stuffing it into his pocket. "Oh, wait. That sounds delicious, but I don't have any cash on me."

Meagan smiled, saying brightly, "Alright! Well, it's time to break out the emergency funds credit card. This totally counts as an emergency!"

George opened the door for her, but her chest was already tightening with hatred. Sitting in the corner, she spotted Timothy and Michael sharing ice cream. Meagan felt a blow to her back when George flew past her.

He scurried to the register, "Two chocolate single cones." Meagan was lost for words as she stepped up to the counter to pay.

The cashier handed George the two cones.

"Here you are." His mouth twisted into a malicious grin, handing one of the chocolate cones to Meagan.

George scampered over to the vile couple sitting in the back and plunged the cone into Timothy's face, smearing the chocolate over him.

"You're welcome, fuck face," he snarled, his voice was deep. He swiveled around, then darted out of the shop, hiding his face.

"George!" she called, dashing off after her friend. She burst through the entrance and immediately stopped. George vanished around the corner, but through the glass pane, she could see Dom in the arcade with another girl. Not just any girl. It was the new hire, Amanda, who started a week ago. The cone slipped through her fingers, and the sweet dessert splattered on the sidewalk.

Chapter 6

George's mind reeled in a thousand directions after he rounded the corner of the arcade; his vision became blurry with tears flooding down his cheeks.

This is what happens when I trust people; this is what happens when I give them my heart; this is what happens when I love.

On one hand, he was proud he'd taken a stand for himself. On the other, George still felt sick, weak, powerless, and embittered. His vision began to black out, but he kept running. That's what he did best. He ran from his problems. Tripping over his own feet, he hit the ground; his thoughts overtook him, and his world turned dark. A familiar voice rang inside his head.

George, you must calm yourself.

"Leave me alone, I want to die here."

It's not your time to die. Calm yourself.

"How can I!? I have a constant fear every day; I feel like I'm never good enough for anybody, and I try so hard. Do you not understand!? I'm caving in!"

I understand, but do you? This fear and paranoia shouldn't be controlling you. Instead, you should be controlling it. It's alright to cry, but it's not alright to give up. You have so much before you, you cannot comprehend yet. I want you to dig deeper and fight the demons.

"Timothy is the demon; I have to break up with him."

That's the first step to recovering. Remove the toxicity in your life. But you cannot remove him just yet; you have to wait for the right time. Make it hurt, like ripping off a Band-Aid all at once.

"When?"

You will know when the time is right. Listen and discern the lies from the truth. Wake up, she's calling for you.

"George? George!? GEORGE!!!!" Meagan screamed and shook him awake. George's eyes fluttered open only to see pavement.

"I... I blacked out... sorry, Meagan...," he said, sitting up.

Falling to her knees, Meagan's eyes were watering. "D... Don't scare me like that..." she began sobbing, shoving her head into George's chest without the caution her haphephobia would have normally presented.

"I... I'm sorry... I didn't mean to... I've held my emotions in for so long... but I..."

Meagan sobbed louder. George fell silent and rubbed her back softly.

"Please don't scare me like that!" her words slurred, backing away, shuddering from George's chest, trying to get ahold of herself.

"We should go. Are you able to drive home?" George asked, staring up at the clouding, gray sky.

"Yeah, I'll be fine. What about you?" she whispered.

I'll be fine, don't worry about me." George helped her onto her feet. His surroundings were still spinning, but not enough for him to fall. Meagan wiped away her tears, then both friends went their separate ways in silence.

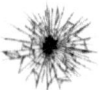

George stared at the penguin necklace that Timothy had given him.

You gave this to me when I first met you. I tried to wear this everywhere I went. I thought this would be my good luck charm, but all this is… is nothing. Nothing special about it at all. It's a symbol of the burden you are.

George threw the necklace at the wall. "You promised me three things, Timothy." His eyes were swelling up, snatching it from the floor. "You said you would never cheat on me, you said you would never leave me, and you said you would never break your promises. You broke all of them to please yourself." George scoffed, then, without hesitation, tossed it into the trash.

No one will love you fully. They will just use you and your strong compassion, George. Why not end it? Your pain? Why not end the suffering you've endured for so long? It's easy, and it won't hurt for too long. What do you say?

George nodded to his thoughts, answering aloud, "What's the point of living anyway?" he asked himself. "True, you have to struggle through life, but what comes out of it? Death. I've made my decision."

"George! Get ready, we are going out to eat tonight!" his mom called from the stairs.

George coughed loudly, "I don't feel well, you guys go, I'll stay home tonight."

"Whatever," his mom said.

"You won't have to deal with me anymore after tonight," George whispered and locked his door, waiting until his family left.

"I'm sorry, Meagan, Becca, Hannah…" he smiled weakly at his phone, sending one last text to Meagan.

Thank you for trying so hard to make me happy today. I truly enjoyed it, but I only feel as if I get in everyone's way. I don't even know why I'm still here, why I'm still alive. I've made my decision…you'll be fine and better off without me. I'm glad to have called you my friend.

He headed downstairs to the garage. He grabbed a rope from the shelf where his dad stored his tools and began making a noose.

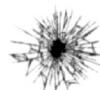

Meagan pressed the buttons on her controller furiously, taking out her rage on her game.

Is he a player, like Timothy? I can get over it easier than George, yet earlier…I fell into his arms. I couldn't help it; my knees caved in. And I didn't once think about the fear of touching someone.

She paused her game and checked her phone. A notification from George was on the screen. Terror struck as she read the text.

"George…no!" She threw her controller down, raced to her dresser to grab her keys, and flew out of her house. "I said I'd be there for you, George!" she screamed— scrambling to her car— tried calling him.

"Hey, it's George. I'm too busy right now. Please leave your name and number, and I'll get back to you!"

"Damn it, George!"

His ringtone went off while he pulled the rope tightly through the loop one last time.

George let it ring until it went to voicemail, murmuring, "I'm sorry Meagan, but this is my decision." He grabbed the noose and headed for his room.

Meagan's heart raced. She'd never been in this type of situation before. She pressed the gas pedal to the floorboard, watching the speedometer reach sixty miles an hour. It took five minutes to get to George's house, but every minute counted to save her friend.

Where is his family? Do they not know he's been acting strange? Shit, I don't have their number!

She pulled into the driveway and busted through the door, yelling: "George!?" There was no reply. She found it hard to breathe, but she stumbled up the stairs and found his door open. Her heart weighed a thousand pounds when she stepped into his room.

Chapter 7

She heard weeping. A rope was hanging from the ceiling fan, but nothing was dangling from the noose.

"George..." She walked to the other side of the bed to see her friend, his knees tucked under his chest, and his face hidden from the world.

"I feel like such a coward, I can't even go through with it!" he managed, inhaling deeply, then wiping his swollen eyes.

"You're not a coward! Your intuition knows this isn't worth killing yourself over. You're so much stronger than that, and you're fighting the demons in your head!" Meagan sat down beside him, leaning against the bed frame.

"That's not the only reason," he said, shaking his head.

"Then tell me what else there is?" Meagan asked, rubbing his back soothingly.

"I can't be myself around my family, I always have to be someone I'm not. Any relationship I'm in, I give a full 100 percent, but people don't give a shit about me. Something bad always happens. They leave, cheat, lie, or ghost me, and I'm sick of it! I'm so scared to go to work tomorrow, then the scholarships I've applied for... I've heard nothing. My anxiety, doubt, and stress are through the roof. I don't know what to do anymore." George sulked, tears streaming down his face.

"I can't imagine how scared you must feel, the fear of being rejected, but what Timothy did to you, you deserve so much better. All these trials from these relationships are making you stronger as a person. This is life, life tries to break you, but you can't give in. Keep trying and you'll succeed. In my eyes, people are dealt crappy cards in life. It's up to us to figure out what to do with them."

George lifted his head, pleading, "How do I get over this wall when my mind can't think logically? I don't know what to do."

"Focus on yourself, time will heal you," she said, thoughtfully.

George responded with a nod, then stared at the floor. "Please, don't tell my parents about this," he sighed in anguish. "And, honestly, I don't want to go to work tomorrow."

"You have to show him that you're better off without him. You have to show him that he can't control you. I don't want to work either, but we have to. At least we'll have each other." Quivering, Meagan gently traced her finger in George's sweaty palms.

Am I becoming more comfortable with him?

The two friends enjoyed being on their own for the moment before Meagan retracted.

It's not so nauseating...

"I guess I should take the rope down... you'll have to go before my parents get back or they'll think we..." George flushed slightly.

Meagan nodded, understanding. "I'll see you tomorrow, okay? We'll get through this together." Meagan stood, then proceeded out of his room.

I have to mentally prepare myself not to murder Timothy or Dom tomorrow. I'll be straight up with them, and they won't like it.

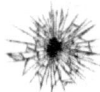

Meagan knew she didn't have it in her to bottle her emotions away in a chest and throw away the key. Talking to Dom about her discovery would be the only way to clear her mind. For a moment, her eyes shifted to George, who seemed paranoid; Timothy was supposed to work today, but he hadn't shown up yet.

Coward! He probably was afraid George would kill him.

"Amanda, you can go on your break. Meagan, will you bag for Dom?" She heard the manager say, breaking her train of thought.

Damnit! I don't want to bag for him, but I need to confront him somehow. This can't wait; it's eating me alive. This could be my chance since Amanda went on break.

Dom beamed at her.

"Yeah," her voice turned soft, which annoyed her.

"How was yesterday?" Dom asked as she slowly approached the register.

"We had fun," she responded. "I actually need to talk to you."

Dom's eyes lit up with excitement. "Oh? What do you want to talk about?" His voice was soothing, and his charming smile lured her in.

Meagan gulped, realizing this would be harder than she thought. "We went to get ice cream, and when we left, I saw you with..."

"She's just a friend. Someone I can talk to," he interrupted.

"I thought you were interested in me. Interested in helping me with my phobia," she stated glumly.

"I am interested in you, and she's just a friend. But while we're discussing friends, I can't help but be jealous of George. You were supposed to come over after the fireworks the other night so I *could* help you with your phobia, but you stayed with him. Then you two went for ice cream yesterday. Seems like a date to me."

"I was helping a friend. Are you seriously blaming me? You heard George explain himself and his relationship to us. I thought you were called into work. What were you doing there with her?" Meagan glared at Dom, crossing her arms over her chest.

"The manager did call me in, but when I got here, they said they didn't need me, and I was out. She wasn't busy; you were. We were just having fun, but you made it clear we were only friends, not dating. Why are you so concerned with who I hang out with?" Dom explained, his hands slamming the counter.

"Friends? I'm not fucking dumb, Dom. I told you I see you with nearly every girl who works here. But just so you know, I was actually considering being your girlfriend!" Meagan stormed off, abandoning her post.

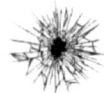

Two registers down, George eavesdropped on Meagan and Dom quarreling.

Amanda? Dom did the exact shit to Meagan as Timothy did to me. And what? He's jealous of me?

"Tch, women!" Dom muttered as George walked up. "Let me guess, you overheard."

George watched him cautiously, "I did. We're friends. There's nothing between us. Maybe you two need a break from each other, and I don't mean talking to other girls like Amanda. It might be your last breath you take. After things have simmered down, why don't you two try talking about it outside of work?"

Dom stayed quiet.

"You might not see it, but she does have feelings for you. She's being careful after seeing what has happened to me." George explained.

A sharp sting dug into George's shoulder, and Amanda appeared beside him, releasing her cat claws. "You should let me bag there, George," she insisted.

"Umm, there are other cashiers that need your help," George pointed out.

"George, you can help Meagan," Dom replied. His eyes had turned hollow.

"I wouldn't do that if I were you," George warned.

Amanda laughed and pushed George away from the register.

"Don't say I didn't warn you." George spun around and headed toward Meagan, who was now covering yet another break.

A young, fit man roughly the same age as them approached Meagan's register.

"Where's George?" he asked rudely.

Meagan, confused, pointed at him saying, "He's right here."

"Hey, buddy, long time no see! I'm back in town!" the newcomer grinned, walked over, and smacked him hard on the back, nearly knocking the wind out of him.

George coughed, "Who are you?"

The boy frowned, "You've already forgotten your best pal, James?"

George's insides cringed at the name.

Chapter 8

"Earth to George, are you going to respond, or am I going to have to embarrass you in front of your co-workers?" James' deep voice boomed with a commanding force, and he smiled broadly, lifting his chin slightly toward Meagan, who was scanning items.

"I haven't forgotten you, James. You've changed since ninth grade. I thought you left and you were never coming back?" George's voice turned cool, sliding James' groceries to him.

James, now a head taller than George, had a toned body, with short, black, spiked-up hair, and broad shoulders. "I was dumber than a box of rocks. My parents are a town over, and I decided to move back for college. And rent with a couple of my high school friends. I stopped by your house earlier— your folks said you worked here— had to restock on groceries, but maybe we can catch up after work!"

Reconnecting with an old friend? Rekindling a flame. Should I?

"That'll be fifty-seven-thirty-three," Meagan interrupted.

James paused to gaze at her for a moment before passing over wadded-up cash. "Meagan, is it? You're pretty hot. Maybe we should get to

67

know each other sometime?" He winked, holding his hand out for his receipt.

"In your dreams… Here's your change. Have a good day." Meagan rolled her eyes.

"I get off at nine, but—" George started, but James cut in.

"I won't take no for an answer. I'll see you tonight, bud." Grabbing all his bags with one arm, James walked out, exuding charisma.

"Alright, care to explain who the jackass is?" Meagan demanded.

"James has been a friend of mine ever since we were five. After the eighth grade, he moved to the next town over because his dad relocated for a better job opportunity. During the summer before ninth grade, he began hanging around the wrong crowd; the stoners and alcoholics," George explained. "His attitude changed drastically, and before I could even ask why, he moved away. He tried pressuring me into smoking weed from a bong one night, but I left before we had an argument. He never intimidated me, but it seems he doesn't remember we didn't leave on good terms."

"Well, I don't think you should hang around him. It sounds like he hasn't changed a bit." Meagan instructed, sounding a bit tense at the situation.

"He seems to be in a better mindset and could be a distraction. I want my mind on other matters. If he hasn't changed, then how about I ditch him, and we watch a movie instead?" George suggested.

"Sure! Sounds like a plan," she replied, color rushing back into her cheeks.

George noticed the tension in her body releasing, and her brown eyes sparkling in the overhead lighting.

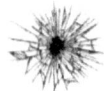

"Lookie here, it's George! You came through! I thought you weren't going to show up!" James' husky voice taunting and echoing throughout the parking lot.

"Uh…yeah, I kinda have to get to my car," George muttered.

"Have you asked your folks if I can come over? We could have a sleepover just like old times," he pulled out a vape and sucked in, holding it, then releasing a cloudy exhale.

"I haven't asked them. Let's catch up and see where it goes first. Also, my parents are strict, you know this. When did you start smoking?" George asked, raising a brow.

James puffed out a cloud of white smoke, tickling George's nostrils, filling them with blue raspberry.

"Chill out, I won't vape in the house. I quit the weed and smoking cigarettes. I got it from a friend to try. It's not for me." He stared up into the black, twinkling sky.

"Ah, a friend. Vaping still isn't good for you, but I see you're still trying to fit in." Before George could reply to James, he heard Timothy's voice. He glanced back to see Timothy and Michael enter Arcae's.

"Let's go, now!" George commanded and threw his name tag into his car.

"Why do you have your underwear in a twist suddenly? We're not done with our conversation," James declared, breathing out another puff.

"Do what you want to do, but I'm not staying here any longer." George practically dove into his car.

"You're a pain in the ass sometimes, ya' know that?" James said, slamming the door to his truck in frustration.

George rolled his eyes, pulling the door shut and speeding off out of the parking lot with James in tow.

"Hmm, that's weird…I have no idea where my parents went." George stepped into the kitchen, adding, "My siblings aren't here either." A note lay on the table:

We decided to go out to eat. We won't be back until late. Your siblings are with the babysitter. Heard James moved back into town. We told James it was fine to come over for a couple of hours so you two can catch up. Close and lock the door.

"I guess we'll be catching up tonight." George watched James slump down rudely as if he were at home.

"Did you want to play video games?" George asked, thinking that killing an invasion of zombies sounded relaxing right about now.

"Video games?" James repeated, confused. "I haven't played video games since you and I did back in middle school. Do your parents have beer in the fridge? We could play beer pong! That sounds exciting!"

George rolled his eyes and snorted, "Yes, there's beer in the fridge; and no, you can't have any. I'm not risking getting my ass burned because you want to drink."

James sighed heavily, "You're a buzzkill, ya' know that? Video games aren't fun anymore."

"What happened to you? I never got to ask before you left, but you've changed. Why? Was I not a good enough friend? When you left to go hang out with your druggie friends, I truly felt abandoned. I was all alone most of high school." George watched James carefully, his chest burning and knotting.

"So you think I'm a 'druggie' now? You want me to be genuine with you? Excitement is what I crave, and what we used to do didn't feel exciting to me anymore. I knew you'd get upset if I told you back then, but I'm here now, and now is our prime time. We're about to start college. You need excitement in your life! You can't be boring forever," he sneered.

Fury quivered on George's lips. "You're a complete idiot! You think this is excitement? Getting high, drinking, and smoking? You only feel a rush for what? A couple of hours, then the aftermath is shit!"

"Not every time, and we ARE going to do it whether you want to or not." James scowled, heading for the fridge.

George sprang into action; adrenaline, hatred, rage, fear, and worry surged through his veins as he seized a kitchen knife and held it to James' chest.

James chuckled in delight, saying, "I didn't know you had it in you." He walked up to the butcher's knife, letting the sharp tip rest on his chest.

"If you don't get out now, I *will* stab you!" George yelled – trembling at the thought of what he'd just said.

"You know what, this was a mistake. I'll leave," James lowered his head behind George's ear, whispering, "I'm not scared of you, George." He slammed the front door on his way out, and George dropped the knife to the floor.

What is wrong with you? You weren't actually going to stab him? Were you?

"You did what, George!?" Meagan exclaimed in disbelief.

"I threatened him with a knife...I could've killed him, but I didn't... Can we just watch the movie?" He diverted, explaining further, and pressed play.

Meagan observed him carefully. She frowned when she saw his eyes were no longer as innocent as she'd known. Instead, a bit of darkness had taken its place.

The other day, when my face felt his chest... something sparked in me. And for once, it wasn't fear. I wonder if he felt it too?

"Wait, pause the movie," Meagan replied.

"What is it? I didn't want my parents coming home to two drunk boys—"

"No," Meagan shook her head, "it's not that... It's the other day. When I fell into your arms, I sensed a spark between us. Did you feel it too?"

George frowned and thought for a moment. "I didn't feel a spark, but I did feel whole... now that you mentioned it." George blushed slightly and stared down.

"What if," Meagan went on slowly, "we're the ones who are supposed to be together?" Her heart thumped a thousand miles per second. *Was this actually happening?*

"How would we know?" George asked.

Meagan bit her lip, then found herself leaning closer to George, holding her breath.

What are you doing? Stop! I can't stop...

She pulled back. Her phobia was kicking into overdrive, and her breathing was ragged.

"It's ok," George whispered. "I won't hurt you."

The reassurance was promising. Not the same respect she'd gotten from Dom. Something about this was different. She felt George slowly slide her hair behind her ear, and she jumped a bit at the touch. He comforted her again, letting her know she was in control. Her breathing slowed, her eyes closed, and she forced herself to give way to the moment.

Chapter 9

It felt like it lasted for hours, but it was only a few seconds. It was softer and much more tender than Timothy's kiss. My mind is going in every direction. It's hot in here, my palms are sweaty, and my heart is throbbing— no, pounding.

George's breath grew quick and sharp after Meagan pulled back.

Avoiding his gaze, her face shifted towards the living room window, murmuring, "Sorry, was that not what you wanted?"

George stared hesitantly at her. He didn't speak for a moment, his eyes locked on her arms retracting inside her hoodie like a turtle. "If I didn't want to kiss you, I would've turned away, and I wouldn't have told you it was ok. I honestly didn't expect you to last even for a few seconds. How do you feel?"

"I don't know. It's confusing. This was my first kiss. All I feel is my heart on fire." She turned toward him, clutching her chest. "It kinda gave me butterflies."

"Of course, this was your first kiss. I never had the chance to kiss Kat. This was my first kiss with a girl. It felt different, but in a good way. For your first time kissing, you're a better kisser than Timothy," he admitted.

"I don't know how I feel… All I know is it didn't feel wrong. What does this mean?" Meagan asked, rubbing her arm. "I'm a little confused. I thought you preferred guys over girls."

"I don't think I prefer one over the other, I just want someone to give me unconditional love, to be goofy with, and to cuddle." George pressed play on the remote, returning to the movie.

He felt warm, clammy fingers grab it from his grasp. Meagan pressed pause again, staring at him. "I want the same, unconditional love. So, what if we gave that to each other? Or do you think we should remain friends?" Meagan gripped the hem of her hoodie tightly until her knuckles turned white, and her eyes waiting for George's response.

TCH TCH TCH— a fingernail tapping the window ceased his answer. George and Meagan fumbled off the couch and onto the floor. A black shadow faced George with the same eyes they'd both seen before.

"What the fuck!" George reached and picked up the first thing he could grab— the TV remote.

"I told you not to throw bread at them!" An angry female voice burst through the house. George and Meagan stood with a puzzled look on their faces – fear in their eyes at the shadow they'd just seen.

"What in the living devil is going on!? Where's James? Did you lie this whole time just to smooch with your girlfriend?" his mom yelled, walking into the living room.

"I… It's not what it looks like," George croaked.

"I think I should leave. My grandma doesn't want me home late." Meagan scrambled up her belongings and sprinted out nervously, without another word.

"Explain!" his mom snapped coldly at him.

"Mom, what the hell! I told you we didn't..."

"You know what? Don't explain. I'm disappointed in you. I don't want to hear another sound from you." His mom threw her coat down on the armchair and disappeared into the hallway.

I always abide by the rules, and when I want a little excitement in my life, it's always crushed. Like I can't even have a girlfriend — or even a friend that's a girl. It was worth it...she was worth it, but what the hell was outside the window watching us? She had to have seen it too.

With each step up the stairs, he thought about the kiss.

Despite her phobia, Meagan could still feel George's lips pressed against hers when she crawled into bed. Her mind filled with thoughts as she lay there.

His mom blew everything out of proportion; if she knew what James was trying to do, I think he would be in far worse shape than if I hadn't been there. Who knows what could've happened?

I'm just not ready for a relationship yet, and the kiss was probably in the heat of the moment. I don't know anymore! Then there was the figure. It vanished when his mom came in, and I didn't see anything leave. It had to have been our paranoia, right?

Meagan rolled on her stomach. Slamming her face into her pillow, she let out a, "Ugghhh!"

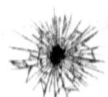

George squinted. He blindly moved his hand around the dresser, trying to find his phone. He finally felt the vibration underneath his fingertips, sliding up to answer the call.

"Hello?" He asked woozily.

"Hey, George. Sorry if I woke you, but I was wondering if you could come in today?" a female asked.

George wiped his eyes, realizing it was his manager. "Did someone call out? What time?"

"Not a call out, someone quit. Their shift was at noon."

His manager's voice rang in George's ears. He asked, "I'll come in. May I ask who quit?"

"Timothy. Thank you, I'll see you then!" She hung up before George could respond.

Coward! At least I won't have to see his stupid, cheating face again. I'll take all of his hours.

George kicked the covers off when his phone vibrated again. He didn't recognize the number, but answered anyway.

"Hello…?" he inquired slowly.

"Hey, George, it's me, James."

"What do you want?" George scowled.

"I want to apolergize fer last night, I didn't mean to be disrespectful, I just wanted ya to see things my way. I'm coming back into yur store today. I forgot somethen'. I'll make it up to ya later." The sound of his voice was back and forth between a sincere apology to still drunk from the night before.

George laughed, "You've got to be kidding me! You're fucking drunk. How did you get my number?"

James burped and sighed, "I'm not drunk, just a little bit a' tipsy is all. Trust me, I'll make it up ter ya'. Don't ya worry about that, buddy, heh." The line went dead.

"Great, now I have to deal with an alcoholic teen walking into the store. God knows what he might do," George grumbled.

"George, come here, hurry!" Becca scanned items frantically, "Hurry, before my bagger comes back!"

George had been on edge since he started his shift. His eyes darted this way and that, trying to see if James would zig-zag into the store.

"What is it, Becca?" He asked.

"So, my birthday is in a couple weeks... Your total is thirty forty-seven."

"Oh? What about it?" George smiled.

"Hope you have a wonderful day, sir." She turned back to George. "Anyways, I wanted to invite you, Meagan, and Hannah! It's the first week of August, and I would love for you to come. I'm twenty-one, so I can spot you all some special drinks if you know what I mean."

"A party!? Imma' in!" James walked to the register with a thirty-two pack of water.

George's left eye began to twitch. "How did you...when...James!"

"Only friends are invited, sorry," Becca informed him.

"I'm George's friend. I was going to, er, make up to him with video games, but this sounds way better."

George shook his head, "Absolutely not, James! You're drunk right now!"

Becca stared at George, then at James, saying, "Maybe sober up a little first, and I'll invite you. Any friend of George is a friend of mine."

James' drunken eyes lit up, "George, scratch the video games, yer going to that party!"

Chapter 10

"Who the heck was that?" Becca asked, keying in produce numbers after James had staggered off.

"An old friend," George muttered.

"Does he always show up drunk in public?" She typed in the numbers more quickly.

"It's quite possible. And after last night, it doesn't matter what I do, I'm still a disappointment. Fuck it, count me in. Oh!" He nearly dropped the bag, turning red. "Did you hear about Timothy quitting?"

Becca rolled her eyes. "Don't worry about him, just focus on yourself."

George nodded in agreement. "I know, but I think he's trying to make me jealous."

"Speaking of the devil," Becca nudged her head toward the sliding doors.

Timothy and Michael walked into the store hand in hand. Timothy locked eyes with George and immediately began mouthing words and straining his laughter.

"See what I mean, Becca! You're right... Focus on myself." George said, shifting his focus to Becca.

Becca's voice lowered. "Listen, it's been a rough year since my mom left. This is the first time I've been able to celebrate anything in a long while. Finances have been really tight and I try to distract my dad..."

"Need to look all fresh for our date tonight, babe." Timothy broke Becca and George's conversation. "This is all," he continued, handing her the cologne.

Ignoring both of us now?

Becca appeared unbothered when Timothy slapped his lips together with Michael's, but inside, George's stomach lurched in anxiety.

She slapped the receipt in his hand. "Asshole."

Timothy shrugged, dragging Michael out of the store.

Tears swelled in George's eyes, his heart still refusing to beat properly.

I can't do this. I don't want to be here when he comes in. My stomach...

"George—?" Becca started.

"I'm focusing on myself. Excuse me." George fled to the bathroom.

His stomach roared in anxiety, slamming the stall door. He fell onto his knees and hovered over the toilet as bile charged up his esophagus. He clenched his stomach then closed his eyes, trying to think of other things.

I feel weak and lightheaded. I can't go back out there knowing there's a chance I might vomit on the floor. Happy thoughts, think happy thoughts.

He pictured him and Meagan kissing.

"George, you're needed at the front. George, you're needed at the front!" His manager's voice was sharp and booming through the intercom.

George managed to wobble his way back to the front-end, trying to keep calm in the process.

The manager rested her hand on her hip.

"I felt queasy, so I ran to the restroom and I threw up twice," George lied.

She sighed, "Is it that bad?"

George nodded, "Must've been something I ate."

"Alright, go, I'll clock you out." The manager instructed.

"If you need coverage, I'll stay." Becca offered from behind.

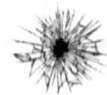

George clutched his stomach, proceeding to his car when he felt a nudge behind him, "Are you okay?" Meagan's worried voice flooded behind him.

"No. I'm not... I couldn't handle seeing Timothy and Michael kiss, my childhood best friend is an alcoholic, my parents are up my ass, and something was watching us last night. Then there's our kiss. I'm confused and overwhelmed. I want to be by myself." George sighed.

Meagan studied him for a moment, "I understand you're overwhelmed, but don't think you're the only one with processing shit." Meagan's eyes softened. "I'm confused too, and this is the second time I've seen this thing watching us. The other was in your room on the Fourth of July. I—"

"I'll be fine. We'll talk about it later," George said with a half-assed smile as he jumped in the car, slamming the door behind him.

George went straight to the medicine cabinet. His parents were still at work, and his siblings were at the babysitter's.

If I'm going to sleep, I'll need a little help.

George slipped a Benadryl into his mouth and swallowed. Within twenty minutes, he became extremely drowsy, nodding off in his bed.

Escaping again, I see?

"I was helping myself go to sleep faster. I am not escaping," George breathed to the voice inside his head.

You know as well as I do, Timothy will be popping up more frequently. You need to let him go. Yes, it will hurt. You'll have to show him you're better off without him. You have friends who support you!

"Why are you always right? I don't want to seem weak anymore. I don't want this anxiety."

Forget him and focus on yourself.

"How am I supposed to forget this cheating monster when he rubs his new boy toy in my face!"

You need to begin a healing process. Focus on you.

"I have to give myself some space away from him. I can't do it when I'm constantly seeing him every day."

Give yourself a break. Now... go to sleep.

George drifted off to sleep, dreaming of landscapes, stars, sunsets, forests, and those mysterious pair of eyes watching his every move.

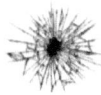

The next morning, George had the perfect idea. He could feel his heart healing, instead of the shattered glass it had become, he started picking up the pieces. He decided it would be best if he didn't bring up the kiss conversation to Meagan until he'd successfully given himself closure from Timothy. George sat down at his desk and ripped a page from his notebook, scribbling his heart on the page.

Dear Timothy,

We haven't spoken since I found out, but I wanted to tell you that even though you made me three promises: you would never leave me, you would never hurt me, and you'd never break your promise. You broke all three. Even if you don't see it, you did. This is not why I'm writing this letter. I wanted to tell you I have goals and ambitions I want to uphold, and you will not hold me back. You don't deserve anyone, yet you have someone. I'm not sure if I'll ever forgive you for what you've done. This letter doesn't mean we are friends. I will not even consider being your friend. I hope you can treat Michael better than you did me. Good luck and goodbye.

— George

George folded the piece of paper in half and stuffed it into his pocket. He felt determined. This was on him and on him alone. He didn't feel the need to share the idea with anyone, not even Meagan. He could hear her now, berating him about giving Timothy a letter. He couldn't let the relationship they once had remain open; he deserved closure.

George hurried down the steps, out the front door, and out onto the sidewalk. Staring up at the crystal-clear sky, he felt a ton of weight had lifted from his shoulders. He felt free from worrying, free from fearing what might have come. He'd learned his lesson and deserved to focus on himself, to better himself. With the weight lifted, he started to run – a slight jog at first, then faster and faster.

I want my closure.

He found himself stopping in front of Timothy's house. Without hesitation, he walked up to the door and rang the bell. To his surprise, Timothy answered the door. This time, his boytoy wasn't attached to his hip.

"I wanted to give you this." He slipped the note into Timothy's hand.

Timothy raised an eyebrow, then unfolded the piece of paper to read. Before George let him begin reading it, he swiveled on his heels and took off back towards his house, leaving him standing in the doorway.

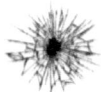

Dusk fallen. George clocked out and headed to his car, swiping up to read his messages.

I didn't give him any time to reply, but I can feel he wanted to say something after reading the note. I want to get over this wall, so I know that I can be free and focus on Meagan.

Confirming his thoughts, Timothy had texted him.

I need to talk to you after work. There's something I need to tell you face-to-face. It wouldn't be right to text it; besides, I don't want you going around showing it to people.

George scoffed in disbelief.

You better not be pulling anything funny because dumping you was a big step for me. I should've dumped your ass long before, but I didn't. I'm off now. Where do you want to meet?

He sent the text and peered around the car, feeling as though he was being watched. He waited for a few minutes for him to reply, his paranoia making his heart jump out of his chest. Finally, Timothy responded:

Meet me at Frozen Froyo.

George fidgeted, slamming his car door shut. He was nervous. He didn't mention the text messages to his friends; they would have stopped him from meeting with him. He stepped into the shop and looked around for Timothy. He was sitting in the back alone, watching the door like a hawk. He raised his hand to motion toward him. George took a deep breath and courageously went over to the table.

"If you're in the mood for frozen yogurt, I'll buy it for you," Timothy offered warmly.

George shook his head, "I'm not five. What did you want to talk about?" He sat directly across from Timothy, his mind preparing for what was about to be said.

"Well," he stared down and twiddled his thumbs, "I should start by saying that I miss you. I never intended to hurt you," he said, staring up at George with puppy eyes.

"If you didn't intend to hurt me, you wouldn't have done it, so why?" George's tone was icy.

"He didn't have anywhere else to go; his parents kicked him out of the house that day he spent the night. I don't know. It just happened."

His staying with you because his parents kicked him out didn't faze me. I was proud of you for letting him stay, but sleeping with him? I felt so alone, and you know that I can't just come out and say that we are dating because my parents would kick me out. Then where would I have gone? I doubt your family would allow me to stay with you if that'd happened." George clenched his jaw.

"I would have let you move in with me. I know I fucked up, sweetie. I still love you! I miss cuddling and kissing you. If you want my honesty, Michael is horrible. He smacks me, isn't as cuddly as you, and always has an attitude." Timothy stared down at the table. He couldn't bear George's eyes.

"How can I trust you again after what you've done to me? I gave you plenty of chances, yet you kept lying. As for Michael, it sounds like that's what you deserve." George crossed his arms.

"I don't deserve to be forgiven, and I don't deserve your trust. I wanted to bring you here to tell you that I miss you." Timothy reached across to hold George's hand.

George pulled back. "If you want my honest opinion, I'm not giving you any chances because we are never getting back together. You're not messing with my head again. You are a fucking narcissist and you know it. You're just trying to make me feel guilty so I'll give you another chance."

Timothy shook his head, "I'm not trying to…"

George had heard enough. "I didn't come here to listen to your pity lecture, I came here so I could get the right closure I need to move on. You're with Michael now, so treat him better than you treated me. I don't want anyone to go through what I went through with you." George scooted his chair back. "I'm finally free. I guess this is goodbye."

Timothy's mouth fell open as George turned around and left his past, looking forward to what the future held.

The bright sunny morning brought solace to George as he considered replying back to a message Meagan had sent him. However, when he picked up the phone, Timothy's name appeared on the screen, calling him.

He's never going to leave me alone!

Eyes bloodshot, George answered anyway: "What?"

"Please don't hang up…" Timothy seemed to be sobbing in the background.

"What do you want?" George asked bluntly.

"I couldn't sleep at all last night. I couldn't stop thinking about you. I miss you. I miss us! It doesn't feel right with Michael." He sobbed loudly through the phone.

George, lost for words, didn't know how to respond. He was quiet, pushing down any sympathy for him. "The ship has sailed. Enjoy the grass on the other side." His heart didn't ache. He'd healed himself, but he wanted to make Timothy suffer more by listening to him gravel.

"Can you give me one more chance?" Timothy pleaded, waiting patiently for George to respond as the sound of his heavy breathing came through the other end of the phone.

"You know what I've been through. I opened my soul to you, and you used me. I gave second chances to everyone. I even gave you a second chance when I knew he was living with you, but you blew it. You're just another ex now. If you'd excuse me, I have better things to be doing than sitting here listening to you whine." George felt vomit rise into the back of his throat from his nerves. He quickly swallowed it.

"You have to let me prove it to you." Timothy's voice grew hopeless.

"Oh, you have proved something to me. You showed me that I deserve better, and I have someone better. You shouldn't cheat on anyone else ever again. Even Michael deserves someone better than you. He probably doesn't even know what a horrible person you really are. Oh, and what you did last week; I know you purposely came into the store and kissed him in front of me just to tear me apart." George began doodling on the back of his notebook.

"I only did it because when I looked at him, I saw you. I'm not saying he looks or acts like you. I saw you in his face and immediately kissed him. I'm not even with him—"

"Like I said before," George butted in. "I'm done. I don't want to go any further with this conversation. Bye." George pressed the end button and began texting Meagan.

I was exhausted yesterday, so I fell asleep when I got home from work. I think I might need a little more time to think about things. Are you still going to Becca's party in a couple of weeks? If so, maybe we can chat then?

George set down the phone and stared out his window, worrying.

Timothy will stop at nothing to get me back, and Meagan wants to know the answer to giving us a chance…I don't know what to do. Obviously, I'm not getting back together with him, but what do I tell Meagan? I need a while longer? Can we give it a chance? Or would it be better to remain just friends?

George was slightly startled when his phone buzzed again.

Yes, I'm still going. I'll give you some space and see you in a couple of weeks.

"I'll talk to her at the party," George told himself.

Chapter 11
(Two Weeks Later)

Meagan puckered up, lathering a coat of salmon-colored lipstick on her lips. She felt she was putting on too much for the party, but this was the first one she'd ever been invited to. It was a birthday party, nonetheless, and she wanted to impress.

Face it. You only want to impress George. Hoping he finally talks to you.

She stared in her full-length mirror at the sparkling baby blue skirt and open-toe flat black sandals.

It's only a birthday party? Why am I dressing up like I'm going to a homecoming dance? Stop, just focus, it's Becca's day, not yours.

Meagan grabbed her keys, stepping out of her room.

I'm ready to tackle the night.

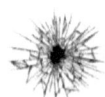

George walked out onto the driveway, unlocking his car door. As he lifted the handle, a powerful, low-pitched blast blasted through the muggy air.

James pulled up in his truck, causing George to almost drop Becca's present.

"Fuck." George breathed.

"George, let's go get this party started! You're riding with me!" he yelled and motioned for <u>him</u> to get in.

"You've got to be kidding me. Becca invited you, didn't she?" George shook his head and unwillingly hopped inside James' truck.

James backed out of the driveway and drove slowly up the road.

"Do you even know where she lives, James?"

"Of course! She sent me her address." James chuckled softly.

"Becca didn't give you her address! Did you stalk her?" George glanced over, and James' expression turned serious.

"She did give it to me. All I had to do was be a little flirt and she wrote it down for me. It should be about fifteen minutes away from your house. Don't doubt what I can do."

George turned his head toward the window and watched the scenery roll by.

He's up to something, and I don't want to be part of it. Since he has Becca wrapped around his finger, I have to be because I know now how he can be. I don't want my friends to get involved in this.

"Did you bring alcohol, James?" George asked as houses rolled by, the sun was setting.

"That's for me to know and you to find out. I want you to have a good time. I don't want you worrying about anything tonight. You're in good hands." James took a left and continued cruising down the street.

"I'll have a good time, don't get me wrong, but I'm not getting drunk.

Someone is going to have to drive us home." George snapped.

James sped up, "What did you get Becca?" he asked, abruptly changing the subject.

"She wanted to remember everything, so I bought her a Polaroid camera. Did you buy her anything?" George avoided any eye contact.

"I did. Have it in the back of the truck. If she's a friend of yours, she's a friend of mine." James turned around a sharp curve.

The conversation dropped after George couldn't figure out why he was acting strangely sweet. James pulled into a narrow driveway with pink flamingos and frog statues scattered about the yard and a rustic white single-wide mobile home set nestled at the end of the driveway.

"Wow, Becca, someone needs to pressure wash..." George breathed absent-mindedly, forgetting James was beside him.

"You go on in. I have to get the present ready," James instructed, shifting his truck into park.

George hopped out and walked up to the front porch, pressing the doorbell, gripping Becca's present. Thumping sounds came from inside, and George turned back to James, who was rummaging in the back seat.

Becca opened the door. She wore denim jeans, a faded purple shirt, and black eyeliner. "Come in, come in! I was worried no one would show up. You two are the first ones here. My dad's at work tonight, he told me to enjoy my night."

"Oh, that's nice. What does your dad do?" James asked.

"He's a paramedic. Works overnight most of the time. You know, twelve-hour shifts all the time," Becca responded.

George studied the living room – a two-person chocolate sofa now layered in confetti faced a roughly forty-inch flat screen TV, and balloons resting on a gray armchair.

"I have pizza and homemade jungle juice I concocted in the kitchen, and karaoke hooked up to the stereo," Becca said.

George walked over to the sofa and sat down. He looked around, admiring the Halloween lights casting an orange and purple hue against the walls, and figured they must have either left them up all year or were getting a head start on decorating for the year.

Jungle juice— sounds sweet and exotic.

James stepped in with a black plastic bag, demanding, "Where are your refreshments? I'm thirsty!" Becca gave him a sharp side-eye before escorting him into the kitchen. A few minutes later, the doorbell rang, revealing Meagan and Hannah.

George's face froze, and his eyes gawked at Meagan. She was absolutely stunning.

She didn't have to dress so fancy!

Meagan stepped into the living room slowly, staring down at the floor— ignoring George's gaze. She was holding a present wrapped in purple, with a bow elegantly placed on top.

James strolled over to the sofa, sat down, and said, "Can't be a party without music. How about we get the stereo started?" He took out his phone and plugged it into the audio jack, scrolling through the music. His eyes lit up when he took a sip of his drink. "This juice is dangerous! I didn't know ya' had it in ya', Becca! Did you use guava juice instead of pineapple? And this rum is the shit!" The room began to fill with rave music.

Hannah's eyes widened, "I want to try some!" she said eagerly, laying purple cupcakes on the counter.

94

Becca laughed. "Thanks, James! Hannah, let's go get some."

"Here, let me show you what I brought," James grinned, following behind them.

"You are stunning, Meagan!" George complimented after the others left the room.

"Yeah? I don't know why, but I felt I should get dolled up every now and then. I felt tonight was as good a time as any, but now, seeing everyone else in normal clothes, I'm second-guessing that choice," Meagan admitted and moved closer to George.

"You don't have to dress up to be beautiful," he said.

Meagan nodded. "I tried to give Becca her present yesterday, but she insisted on waiting until today to open it." Meagan frowned in disapproval before saying, "I'm surprised to see you brought James along."

George shook his head, "Becca invited him. I didn't want him here. I knew if he came to this party, it would turn three-sixty in seconds. I think he's trying to pull some shit tonight, honestly. Put your guard up."

Meagan's eyes widened. "Becca gave in to that prick?"

"It seems that way, but before we get into the kiss, how are you and Dom?" George asked.

Meagan rolled her eyes. "I've gotten over him. You know I caught him with Amanda at the arcade, right?"

"No! You never told me that!" George said.

"Oh my God. With everything going on between the two of us, it must have just slipped my mind. Anyways, he's a moron and a man whore. Now I see him trying to flirt with Hannah when Amanda's not around. I'm sure she knows better than to let him in with his charm, but who knows."

She sighed. "Besides, Dom gives me the cold shoulder, and Amanda is a total bitch! I hope she gets fired with that nasty attitude of hers. I don't want anything to do with either of them. What about you?"

"I needed to deal with Timothy in my own way. I dumped his two-faced ass, and I'm processing my feelings. The kiss was..." George was interrupted by the doorbell ringing for a third time.

"I got it!" Becca called from the kitchen.

"Happy birthday, Becca!" Dom, thrilled with joy, shoved a present in her face.

"Happy birthday..." Amanda announced unconcerned.

"Thank you both, come in," Becca ushered.

George and Meagan both exchange horrified glances. "Did you not tell Becca about what happened between the two of you?" George asked worriedly.

"You're the only one who knows besides the two of them. I didn't know how Becca would respond, so I left her out of it. Maybe I should leave..." Meagan gripped the sofa's arm, pulling herself up, but George yanked her back down.

"Don't leave. I want you to enjoy this party," he whispered.

"How? I'm ready to beat both of them in their smug faces!" she huffed, pulling her hand from George.

George cautiously put a hand on her leg, "Because you're here with me. Besides, we need to discuss whatever that thing was in the window. Do you believe in ghosts?"

I have mixed and confused feelings, but I know I can't leave her without any answers— but I don't want to tell her that. It might upset her more.

Dom and Amanda walked into the living room, their expressions hardening as they saw George and Meagan sitting on the couch. They were silent, the tension thickening when Amanda planted herself in Dom's lap.

"I believe in karma," Meagan replied. George thought her eye twitched.

Becca came out with a tray full of jungle juice, with James close behind, following her like an obedient puppy.

"These drinks are delicious! Everyone, try some!" James passed out the blue solo cups, winking at George.

"What did you put in it?" George inquired, swishing the pink liquid in the plastic cup, wondering what it could possibly be mixed with. He took a sniff to see how strong it was.

"It's Becca's jungle juice. It has vodka and rum. Come on, try it. One cup will not hurt you. Try some too, Meagan," James urged as he shoved a cup in her face.

They both hesitated, then sipped simultaneously. George's eyes widened, and he looked taken aback. "Wow, you can make a punch!"

George watched as Meagan chugged the rest of hers.

"Well, I don't want to open presents right off the bat, but I thought we could eat some pizza and play something daring. Since it's my party, I think we should play the game James brought." Becca grinned, taking a card box out from James' black bag. "After we play the game, then I'll open the gifts and have one of Hannah's delicious-looking cupcakes!"

"Sounds like a plan, Stan," Hannah quipped.

George and Meagan went quiet, Dom and Amanda were sipping their spiked punch, and James sat on the floor, all ready to play.

"The pizza's in the kitchen, nothing fancy, but you guys can help yourselves to as much as you want. Everyone, sit in a circle." Becca commanded. "Make sure you use a paper plate!"

Everyone made a circle, pizza in one hand, drink in the other. Meagan sat a bit closer to George than the others. He could hear her breathe, trying to calm herself.

"We need to amp this party up! You guys need to get hyped! This is what we're playing," James grabbed the game box from Becca and opened it. The box read *Do or Drink*. "You either do what the card says, or you drink. Simple right? Birthday girl, you draw first," James shuffled the cards before giving them to Becca.

"Here it goes," Becca smiled, pulling the card on top. Her eyes widened. "Sit on the lap of the person to your right for the next round or drink twice." She turned to James.

"Oh, lookie at this! The first victim is the birthday girl!" James chortled, patting his lap.

George raised his brow at her.

Becca shrugged. "I'm here to have fun," she said as she sat down on his lap. "Here, Hannah."

Hannah picked up a card and read aloud. "Choose one other person to flash a body part of your choice privately or drink three times."

George stared at his cup, not wanting to be caught in Hannah's crosshairs.

Dom, she's going to pick Dom.

"George," Hannah said, with a buzzed giggle.

"Wow, I don't know if I want to do this..." his mind drifted off, feeling like the buzzkill of the party. The others sat in silence, staring at the clock. George tapped his fingers nervously.

"I'm not asking, I'm telling! Actually, screw it, let's go!" Hannah growled, jerking George up impatiently with their cups still in their hands.

"You guys can use the bathroom, first door on the left!" Becca yelled as bouts of laughter followed.

George sipped his drink.

At this point, I'd rather be drunk...he considered Hannah a friend, nothing else.

George's sip turned into a gulp when Hannah slammed and locked the bathroom door.

"So, are you really wanting to do this?" George asked. He noticed her eyes were distracted.

"Damn it," she whispered.

"Hannah, I'm not doing anything remotely sexual with anyone tonight, are you..." George burst.

"I know you're not! I had to pick you. Dom is with Amanda, fuck..." Hannah balled her fists.

"You're still head over heels for him?" George's lip curled in disgust.

"Never mind!" Hannah snapped. "Here, this is harmless," she turned, lowering her black shirt to reveal a two-headed serpent on her right ass cheek.

The color drained from his face, and his mind went immediately back to the dream that had him surrounded by snakes. He felt the blood rush from his face, noticing his pale skin in the mirror.

Hannah howled. "Damn, boy! I at least thought you were an ass man!"

George— lost in his own mind and unaware of what she'd said— took another swig of his drink.

"Sounds like they're getting it on in there," George heard Dom say.

"We should go," George said, scrambling to unlock the door.

They walked back into the living room. Hannah giggled behind him, and George rolled his eyes.

"Oh, Dom, we'll be louder than anyone here when it's our turn!" Amanda snickered with delight as Meagan's face turned scarlet.

"George, you're not throbbing yet?" James teased. "I know I am."

"That's none of your damn business," he snapped back.

George looked over at Meagan, and her eyes diverted to her empty cup, "I need a refill."

After a few rounds, he pressed the back of his hands on his cheeks, realizing they were warm. He'd have to slow down on the Jungle Juice if he was going to drive them home.

Dom pulled a card. "Choose a player to play 7 minutes of Heaven or finish two drinks." Dom grinned and smoothly pointed to Meagan.

"Meagan, let's go." Dom ushered her as she side-eyed him. Meagan could feel all eyes watching her.

I'd rather die. Why couldn't I get this card so I could pick George? We could use the alone time to talk. Why the hell didn't he pick Amanda? Fate chose me.

Amanda began to protest, but James interfered. "Let's keep the show going!" James said, grabbing both Meagan's and Dom's wrists, dragging them into the bathroom, and turning off the light.

Meagan huffed as darkness filled her world. She heard a click as Dom turned the lock. The seconds ticked by without a word.

Meagan slid her hands blindly up the wall, trying to feel for a light switch, but ended up touching skin. It was Dom's chest. She quivered and started to panic.

She heard Dom snort, "It's best if we didn't see each other."

Meagan stopped feeling for the light switch, dropping her hands. "For once, you're right. We just have to bear each other alone for seven minutes." She pushed herself against the wall, trying to get as far away from him as possible.

"Oh, no, you don't. You two have to kiss, or else you'll be locked in there for eternity," James' cackle stirred up the blackness, and Meagan began seeing blotches of red in the darkness.

"I chose you for a reason," Dom whispered.

Meagan heard him shuffling toward her as she backed up as far as she could— her anxiety rising.

"Meagan, stop resisting. You know as well as I know that you've always wanted to kiss me, so here's your chance!" Dom found her arms and pinned her against the wall.

"I don't want you anymore!" she cried, thrashing to break Dom's grip, but he was much stronger.

"Oh, but what if I still have feelings for you?" he admitted and pressed his lips firmly on Meagan's.

Chapter 12

Meagan was stunned, panicked, and tears streamed down her face. She couldn't speak. Then she heard Dom's scathing voice out of the darkness, "So, was that kiss everything you ever wanted?" His deep laughter echoed, making chills run up her spine.

He wanted to kiss me to deceive my perception of him. I feel sick. Why didn't I leave when I saw both of them walk through the door? I wanted to be strong, to prove to myself, and them, I was over him. I should have listened to my gut.

Meagan uttered a squeaky cry and a gasp for breath, but it was as if the darkness had swallowed every bit of oxygen available.

"I think I should be genuine with you this last minute here since we're alone. Even if Amanda wasn't in the picture, I would've used you. You're an intelligent bleeding heart who would be easy to take advantage of. I wanted to charm you into falling for me so that I could get anything I wanted from you. It was that simple," Dom informed.

The red blotches— now fuller in size— dotted Meagan's vision; her mouth quivering with disgust, fear, and rage. The bathroom door unlocked slowly, as adrenaline burst in her veins. She thrust her body into the open door, using all her strength to knock down whoever was in the way.

"Agh!" Meagan shoved James to the floor as her mind told her to scram to the front door.

"Meagan, what's wrong?" She heard Becca's voice somewhere behind her. Ignoring her, she scrambled out the front door and behind the trailer.

Meagan couldn't think. All she told herself was to keep running, don't look back. Flee.

She pushed through branches and briars as she ran into the dusk-covered forest, wanting to flee from reality.

"MEAGAN!" George's scream pounded through her ears as she sprinted further into the forest.

Run. Don't stop, throw yourself forward, and don't look back. Get yourself lost.

"Get myself lost?" she asked herself, the intriguing thought replaying through her head.

As she left her friends and enemies behind her, her thoughts began to impel her forward.

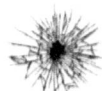

Heat rose in George's cheeks as he swiveled around towards Dom.

"What the hell did you do to her!?" George demanded, perplexed.

"I only told her the truth. If she can't handle the truth, then she's weak. Honestly, who would want to date her anyway?" Dom sneered

George's blood was boiling, from his temples, down to his toes. He lurched forward and shoved Dom to the ground as anger took him over. He began strangling him— his fingers wrapped tightly around his throat—

slamming his head repeatedly against the linoleum floor.

"Get off of him! Are you crazy?" Amanda squealed from behind. She dove forward, pushing all her body weight onto George.

"Get off of me, you skank!" George roared menacingly as he took his hands off Dom, then pushed Amanda off him. George growled, his mind racing with his actions, jabbing Amanda in the stomach with his elbow.

Amanda gasped and fell on her knees while Dom tried to throw a punch.

George recoiled, then dug his fingernails into Dom's chest, clutching his throat, and slamming his head into the floor again.

"Don't. Ever. Talk. To. Meagan. Like. That. AGAIN!" Blood began seeping from Dom's chest as he began to lose consciousness.

George felt Becca, Hannah, and James pull him off Dom. His eyes darted everywhere as he shouted, "Let me go! I'm not done yet! He deserves it!"

James held him down by the wrists, "Not cool! Calm down!" He restrained George on the floor, waiting for him to come to his senses.

"Let me go, I have to go after her! She needs me!" George pleaded.

"If you insist," he let go of his grip.

Why would she run out of the house like that? Something else had to have happened in there. I've gotta find out. But where did she go? I didn't hear her engine start—and surely, she wouldn't have left without Hannah?

George sprinted out of the house and into the driveway. Meagan's car was still parked there, and mysteriously empty.

Where the hell could she have gone?

He turned, looking behind the house.

Please no... not the woods... fuck!

George darted around the house, and a clamorous voice burst from him, "MEAGAN!"

The only response he heard was leaves crunching and rustling from the forest.   *This is crazy? Did she get that upset? This is serious...*

George dashed into the woods yelling, "Meagan, please stop! Where are you!? You're scaring me!"

Branches slapped his face, leaves flew into his mouth, and a brush attached to his legs, trying to stop him from catching up to Meagan. Ignoring the constant whiplash from trees, he whipped out his cell and turned on his flashlight.

The white beam poured into the dark forest, flashing it around in every direction. He waited and listened to see if he could hear any more leaves crunching, but all he could hear was footsteps in the distance.

"Meagan!" he called, following their sound. "If you hurt yourself, I'm never going to forgive you!" George's heart pounded more vigorously and rapidly, making his palms moist. He gripped the phone tighter; a small clearing appeared.

There.

Upon instinct, more adrenaline coursed through his veins, causing him to burst into a sprint. Once he was out of the woods and into the clearing, the moon shone out onto a cliff where Meagan stood at the edge, staring down. A gurgle and a low, deep rumble of water came from beyond the cliff.

"Meagan, what are you doing? This is dangerous, get over here now!" George took a few steps closer.

"No." She inched forward closer to the edge.

"Why? Are you giving up? You're giving up just like I tried to give up? I'm here, aren't I!? What did he say to you?" George pleaded for an answer— anything to distract her from the ledge.

"I was just another pawn in his scheme. He's a bastard for making me think I could even remotely fall in love with him. When he kissed me..."

"Wait, he what? I swear to God, I'll kill him," George interrupted.

"I didn't want it," she continued. "But he told me I was being used, and if I hadn't seen him and Amanda at the arcade, he would've continued to use me. He even said I was ugly. Even in that dark bathroom, I felt the tension and hatred from him. I couldn't breathe, and I was having a panic attack. All I could hear in my mind was, 'Run!' and that's what I did. Now that my mind and legs brought me to this cliff..." Meagan paused, her face turned away, looking into the moonlight.

George turned off the flashlight. "Why in the hell would you take the bullshit he said to heart!? I honestly expected better from you."

Meagan shook her head, "I'm always expected to be put up on a pedestal. Meagan has to be perfect all the time. Do you know how much pressure that is for me? You can't make mistakes, Meagan! You have to keep working, Meagan! You have to get A's, Meagan! Participate in more clubs, Meagan! Be more attractive, Meagan! Be more sociable, Meagan! Look at me, I'm wearing a fucking dress and make-up. I never wear this shit! I felt beautiful earlier, but now I feel like a mistake. Honestly, I hide all of this with my stupid jokes, laughter, and hyperactive personality. It's not the first time someone has been disappointed in me."

"I'm disappointed in you because you chose to believe him and not me. I want you to be open with me as you are now. I'm here anytime you need to talk. That's what we agreed on; we would be there for each other!"

George took a few more steps, inching closer to her. It was now clear her frustrations went back farther than what had occurred tonight.

"We did agree, but that's why I can't. You haven't mentioned our kiss to me. There's always some excuse as to why we can't have that conversation. I don't know what to think. I don't want to think. It hurts to think. I'm mentally exhausted, and honestly, I wouldn't mind falling into the riverbed right now." Meagan slowly turned to face George. "Why can't we be out here, George? What's so wrong with the woods? Why is it such a problem with this town? Maybe I belong out here."

"Don't you dare give up on me! You didn't give up on me, and I won't give up on you. You can't give up on yourself either! Get over here, please! You don't want this to ruin Becca's party." George took a few more steps toward her.

"Stop right there, or I'll jump!" Meagan's face seemed to slowly sink in, her skin as pale as the moon.

"Meagan…" George begged.

She closed her eyes, stretched her arms out, her heels inching closer to the edge of the cliff. "All I have to do is lean back and then I'll be free. Oh, beautiful moon. A glimpse of pure innocence, and then blackness. No more stress, and no more disappointment."

George was searching for words, but he couldn't find any.

She doesn't want to be here anymore. Rather than keep fighting, she wants to give up. How can I convince her otherwise? Why can't I think of anything!?

Meagan still had her eyes closed as a warm smile spread across her face, "A clear mind and body is a sound mind and body. Don't you agree?"

"You're not making sense to me! I want you in my arms, breathing, not in my arms, cold and lifeless! Who cares what Dom thinks? Do *you* think you're ugly? You admitted you felt beautiful walking into this party. I said you looked stunning! Do my words not mean anything?"

"I just want..." She started to say when a black silhouette pounced on her, leaning her farther back, losing her footing, and the two tumbled backwards.

Chapter 13

"Meagan, why can't you be like your sister? Michelle was flawless at everything she did! I wish she'd survived, not you!" her mom snapped brutally.

"I'm sorry, I'll try to be better next time, Mom," Meagan pleaded, staring down at the ground.

"You should get it right the first time!" her mom continued, "If you can't bring your grade up two points before the report cards come in the mail, then don't bother speaking to me." Before Meagan could apologize again, she stomped off in disappointment.

"A ninety-eight wasn't good enough? I thought she would be proud of me." Meagan said to herself, scrambling up the stairs and into her room, shutting the door softly and locking it.

I don't even know what my sister was like. I was too young to remember her. Every time I try to bring up the subject of how she died, neither of my parents would budge. I need to know what happened...I have to know what happened to her. At the same time, I envy her because she's the golden child I strive to be. If I screw up once, their love vanishes.

"Have they forgotten I'm president of five different clubs, I make straight A's, I volunteer, and I'm going to be doing an internship over Christmas break? Yet, it seems my sister has done way more than I have.

Don't they know how much stress I have, constantly worrying they'll stop caring about me?" She balled up her report card and threw it in the trash.

"Keep your head up, Meagan, do better next time..." Her voice trailed off into nervous laughter.

"I blame myself." The sound of her mom's voice could be heard from the room down the hallway. Meagan quietly cracked the door to listen.

Her mom continued: "The accident was my fault; if I hadn't upset her, she would've never left with Meagan that night. She would've still been here making us proud with all her accomplishments."

"I know, honey, but Meagan is trying," her dad replied soothingly.

"It's not good enough, Richard!" her mom hissed piercingly.

The corners of Meagan's eyes watered as she continued to listen.

"If only it had been Meagan instead of Michelle to die that night. After all, if it hadn't been for Michelle's fast instincts, Meagan wouldn't be here. I know she saved her." Her mom began sobbing, her words becoming inaudible, but Meagan had heard enough.

They would toss me out like an old chew toy if they could. They'd rather see me dead! What kind of parents are they not to be happy that both of their daughters hadn't died in a crash?

She tried to hold the tears in, but they kept streaming down her face as she pawed to dry them. "I didn't do anything wrong, so why do they hate me?"

Michelle saved me...but why? And why did she run off with me? Was it her fault or someone else's fault for the crash?

At dinner, Meagan avoided looking at her parents. Instead, she rolled peas around on her plate; her lack of appetite obvious.

"Have you thought about how to bring your grade up yet, honey?"

112

her mom inquired, sipping her glass of water.

Meagan peered up at her, asking belligerently: "Am I your daughter now? Or is this another trick question to try to downgrade me?"

Her mom nearly choked on her water, "I beg your pardon?"

"What I want to know is why Michelle took off with me the night of the accident?" Meagan's eyes darted from her mother to her father.

"If you insist on knowing the truth, fine, we'll tell you. Earlier that day, Michelle came home from school exhausted. We had looked at her grades, and she had barely received an 'A' on her last test. We were furious and fussed at her. She snapped and began cursing: we saw real hatred in her eyes. I tried to apologize, but she didn't accept my apology. Instead, she took you and promised you wouldn't be raised by parents who didn't appreciate a single thing you would accomplish. I beg to differ."

"She snuck you out with her, I think she was going to run away and raise you on her own— ha! Or at least live with your grandma. However, she must have been exhausted and drove off the road. Apparently, she tried to protect you from the impact of the car hitting the tree instead of regaining control of the car. The car nearly crushed her. At least that's what the police report said. Anyway, that's the reason why you're still alive and she's not. You took Michelle away from us!" Meagan's mom broke down into a sob.

"You mean, you pressured her so much, she actually had a breakdown, and wanted me to have a better life than she did? It's not my fault, you're pinning the blame on me! I don't want to hear another word either of you have to say to me! You two now have to carry the burdens of your dead daughter and your lost daughter." Meagan slid her chair back forcefully, grabbing her keys from the countertop.

Her father whipped his head toward her, "You step out that door, you won't be living here again!"

Meagan turned her head halfway back, "I guess I'll have to follow through with Michelle's plan and live a better life than here." With that heartfelt promise to herself, she closed the door on those who never truly appreciated her and pushed open one to a better life.

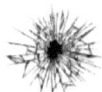

"MEAGAN!" George screamed frantically, watching his friend fall backwards into the dark river below.

He lunged forward, diving toward her and trying to grab her hand, but his reflexes were too slow.

She gave up on herself... no- the shadow pushed her. The one that's been watching us.

George landed on his stomach near the edge, his hand still outstretched, trying to swipe at the thin, humid air. He watched the blue skirt sink into the water. His heart felt like it had taken the plunge with her, leaving him hollow and breathless.

Chapter 14

The moon...it's beautiful. I want to be free like Michelle.

Meagan wanted to tell George, but before she could, the breath was knocked out of her as if she were being tackled by a football player. Her eyes locked with those of a shimmering, white presence, attached to a dark, unsettling form.

Her body descended into the darkness with the entity, the moon dwindling in her vision. As she closed her eyes, she felt an icy chill break into her skin. The frigid water felt like glass as her body hit the surface of the water.

"You're mine!" A guttural, low-pitched growl declared in a menacing tone.

Jolts of pain flooded her arms, back, and legs as she sank farther into the rushing muddy water. Her head slammed into the rock at the bottom as it dragged her along, and her vision turned blotchy red between the darkness and the thrashing current, her consciousness awash with the pain.

Am I dead? Is this what happens to people who die? They only see darkness, blackness?

A white light glowed in the distance of her vision, a human silhouette with long golden hair flowing in the freezing, murky water, the figure's hand motioning her to approach. Meagan obeyed, moving but not feeling her legs or arms.

Is my spirit floating? I don't feel anything, but I...

"I can read your thoughts," a honeyed female voice stated, bubbling through the water.

"Who are you?" Meagan asked, floating closer.

"You may say your savior, but I'm your sister Michelle." Her face glowed with beauty and radiance.

"Why are you here?" Meagan asked, now appearing only a couple of feet away from her sister.

The woman stepped in front of her, caressing her chin, "I'm here because you deserve to live, to fight. I'm not letting you give up so easily. I didn't give my life up for you to give up your own."

Meagan avoided eye contact, murmuring: "I can't handle it anymore, I'm ugly, I'm not as smart as you, and our parents disowned me! They always praise you. It seems I still haven't accomplished what you have. It seems they'll always love you more."

Michelle shook her head slightly, reassuring: "You have surpassed me and my accomplishments, and our grandma loves you deep down. I want you to keep fighting for me and grandma. You aren't dead yet, only unconscious. I'm here to give you a second chance."

Meagan watched her own pain in the reflection of Michelle's glossy eyes, realizing she was gasping for air.

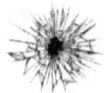

George's mouth quivered in shock, his eyes as wide as an owl's. Processing what he'd witnessed was inevitable. He heard an inhumane growl, then a splash.

"GAH!" The sudden crack of voice made him numb, his bones stiff as a board.

She's gone...I can't move! How far is the cliff? I don't want to see, oh God, please!

He dug his fingernails into the grass, pulling his face to the edge, his whole body numb. He could see water sloshing, traveling downstream, about twenty feet down from the cliff. Her body had disappeared into the slapping waves of the river. He frowned. Whatever pushed her had also vanished.

"Meagan!" he called out, hoping she could hear him.

She might still be alive! I have to get down there. I have to get her out.

George pulled himself to his feet, ignoring the thoughts of snakes and what lay beneath the surface, and leaped off the cliff. Immediately, the cold water from the river gave him goosebumps as it met his skin.

"I'm not giving up on you!" George exclaimed, fighting through the current, the high water slapping his nostrils. He plunged deeper into the water, the current ripping at his legs, hindering him from finding Meagan. He strained his eyes, searching as the current tossed him around like a rag doll. With a surge of adrenaline and letting his instincts take over, he let the current propel him forward.

Suddenly, he saw a pale shape drifting downward, her long hair swirling like seaweed. With a powerful kick, he reached her, his hand closing around her wrist. He pulled her toward him, wrapping his arm around her chest, and using the strength in his legs, the two broke the surface. As George placed her wet body on the closest embankment, he listened for any signs of breathing. There was nothing. He wasn't sure how to properly give her CPR. He felt useless, but knew he had to try something. He created a T-shape with his hands and forcefully pressed down on her chest.

I have to get the water out of her system! I'm blindly doing this, I just... have to... trust my... instincts...

"George! Meagan! Where are you?" Becca's voice interrupted George's rhythmic thoughts.

"Come on, spit up the water!" He kept pumping, breaking into a cry.

"Where the hell are you?" James growled from somewhere near.

"Down here, help me!" George screamed helplessly. "Meagan's unconscious!"

Muffled footsteps scraped across the grass; his friends rushed over to the embankment in the faint moonlight.

"What the hell happened!?" James asked, sliding beside them.

George kept pumping, "Something... pushed her! I think... she hit... her head... on the rocks. Now she's... unconscious."

Choking came from Meagan, followed by water spewing from her lips and out onto her dress.

"Meagan, Meagan! Wake up, are you alright?" George shook her briskly, then more vigorously.

"Quit shaking me..." Her words were slow, her eyelids fluttering open.

"Why were you...what pushed you, Meagan!?" Becca struggled to speak, kneeling beside her.

"Don't worry about me, I'm fine," she answered, lifting her head too fast, then wincing in pain.

"Tell them the truth," George stated firmly, his wet hair falling over his eyes.

"I guess it's apparent that I had feelings for Dom. We went out on a few dates, but I found out he was using me. He never cared about me. When he forced himself on me in the bathroom, I couldn't stand it anymore. I freaked out and ran until I got to the cliff, where George found me. We were talking until this creature came out of nowhere and knocked me off the cliff... and here we are." Her make-up dripped down her cheeks.

Then what we did the other night; did that mean anything? The kiss? Was it to make her feel loved? George thought.

"We need to get you back to Becca's and call an ambulance. You need to be examined for internal injuries. And if there's something out here, and we can't leave you. Plus, if anyone found us out here in these woods, we'd all be dead," George informed.

"So, what are we going to do?" James asked.

"We should pick her up and carry her out of here," George suggested.

No! You can't move her. Moving her could cause more damage if something is broken," Becca yelled as James and George moved in to try to pick her up. "My dad has an old emergency transfer board up at the house. We can use that to lay her on. Then we'll all have to carry her out of here."

"Great! I'm the fastest. I'll run up and get it," James said. "Where is it?"

"It's in the back bedroom," Becca answered. "Oh, do hurry so we can get out of here. I feel like something's out here watching us."

James took off in a hurry and was back in just a short time. George and Becca were sitting on each side of Meagan, both watching off in the distance. They jumped up to assist when he returned. Lying the board as flat as they could next to her, they slowly eased Meagan onto it. To keep her level, Becca took the front while the two boys steadied each side of the back.

"I'll call the paramedics on the way up to the house," Becca said. "Let's get out of here. It's getting really creepy out here."

Hannah jumped from the chair, shocked as the group entered Becca's trailer. "Oh! My! God! What happened? First, James comes in here rummaging through the house, now this?"

The group cautiously transferred Meagan to the couch while Becca searched for a blanket to wrap her with. The pain was visibly showing on Meagan's face.

"Meagan fell, and um... got hurt. We've called an ambulance already. They'll be here shortly," George said.

"Hannah, get a towel from the bathroom for her head," Becca commanded.

Hannah nodded, "I told Dom and Amanda to leave, George." But with all the commotion, her comment went unnoticed.

"We're all here for you Meagan, don't think otherwise. The ambulance is on its way. Do you think we should contact your grandma?" Becca dabbed the damp towel from Hannah on Meagan's forehead.

Meagan nodded, "My phone is in...my purse..." She winced in more pain.

Becca gave a worried glance at George, then at James, "Hannah, can you go call her, please?" She grabbed Meagan's purse, passed it over, and

Hannah stepped out of the room.

George turned his attention toward Meagan, "Try to rest until the medics get here?" She didn't answer, immediately drifting off to sleep.

Becca tapped Meagan's face, concerned. "Hey, sweetie, you can't fall asleep right now. We need you to stay with us. Meagan? Meagan! Wake up, wake up!"

Becca kneeled beside George, panicking. "I don't know what else to do! She's not waking up!"

"This is taking forever, waiting for the ambulance! I can drive us to the hospital, George," James offered.

"Are you capable of driving? I mean, you've had a few drinks...oh crap! We have to get rid of the alcohol! They're going to be asking what happened to her." George lurched into action, going into Becca's kitchen, seeing the pitcher of punch. "Down the drain it goes," George said hastily, pouring the green liquid down the drain.

"Chill out, George, you have time." James appeared in the kitchen, grabbing the rum, and heading back to the living room.

"Where are you going with that?" George inquired, leaning against the sink.

"Relax, I'm going to hide it. I didn't pay for it just for it to be poured out and tossed away. This will be my present to Becca; she's going to need it more than I will after tonight." He cackled.

"Listen," George said in earnest. "We need to think about what we're going to say when the responders arrive— like how the hell she managed to hit her head."

"While you figure it out, I'm taking this baby to my truck," James said, shaking the half-emptied bottle.

121

George began to protest, but James ignored him, walking out of the kitchen. He scanned the kitchen one last time before returning to the living room. "Becca?"

"Yes, George?" Becca stretched her knees, standing up from the couch.

"I'm sorry about tonight. It was supposed to be your birthday, and I should've known Dom would try to do something..." George hesitated when Becca put her hand on his shoulder.

"It's not your fault. Don't blame yourself, I— " Becca was interrupted by the door slamming open. Two paramedics rushed through with James.

"She's here on the couch," James directed from behind.

"Becca, what the hell happened here? I rushed here as soon as the dispatcher got the call with my address!" the older paramedic asked with salt and pepper hair and a light blue-collar shirt with the EMS insignia on his left sleeve.

"We were chasing each other with water balloons, and she tripped over her dress. I—" Becca was cut off by the other paramedic.

"Richard, we need to get her to the hospital now. Her head is bleeding, and she's not responding. Help me put her on the stretcher," the second paramedic informed.

George gasped, holding his breath while he watched them strap her to the gurney.

"We'll talk about this later," Richard said.

"Can we ride with you, Dad?" Becca pleaded.

"No one in the back of the ambulance, only immediate family

members. You know that. Do I smell alcohol?" Richard shook his head in disbelief as they wheeled her out the front door.

James exchanged glances with Hannah and George as Becca shut the door behind her dad.

"Water balloons, really?" James sighed, shaking his head in disapproval.

"If you thought of something better, then why didn't you speak up?" Becca said, shoving him into the back of the couch.

George stepped in between them. "Fighting isn't going to help. We need to make sure they don't suspect us of going into the forbidden woods. We'd be arrested if they found out!"

"Or skinned alive," James muttered.

"Why don't Hannah and I make our way to the hospital, you two go home," Becca proposed. "Hannah called her grandmother, so she should be on the way too."

"I need to make sure Meagan's fine, and what about the creature?" George protested.

"You'll be fine with me, I'll protect you." James teased.

"I'll keep you updated, George. Promise. Besides, we might need to switch out going to the hospital and keeping each other updated, right?" Becca pointed out.

George hesitated, but agreed, "... alright."

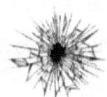

Primroses filled Meagan's vision: they were all around her. She crouched and stroked a stem, letting the sweet fragrance fill her nose.

"I accepted life, and now I might have life-long internal injuries because I wanted to leave everyone behind? Becca said they were all there for me; it was wrong for me not to listen to George." Meagan informed the primroses as if they were listening. One of the primroses closest to her seemed to nod in understanding. She blinked several times, trying to see if she was imagining it.

"So delicate and warm, sometimes I wish I had their personality..." She knelt down to the one she thought had nodded and caressed it on her cheek.

"Tibi ipsi crede..." it whispered into her ear.

"Wh... What does that mean?" she asked curiously, watching the primrose intently.

"It means believe in yourself, sister." Michelle appeared beside her, kneeling as the primroses swayed in the wind.

"I do believe in myself," Meagan turned her head toward her sister, "How do you know what they said?"

"They were my favorite flowers. Also, Latin is one of my most favorite languages. Little sister, how can you want to die one minute and the next you're totally ok with life?" Michelle's fingertips glided over the petals.

"Tibi ipsi crede! Tibi ipsi crede!" All the primroses chimed and chanted together, their leaves waving up and down in unison.

"I don't know if I would've jumped willingly. Something pushed me. A ghost? George tried to stop me—" Meagan gasped, remembering while the primroses chanted, "He said if I hurt myself, he'd never forgive me!"

As pain surged through her body, the primroses seemed to change from pink to orange. As her vision became blurred, she clutched her forehead. "What's happening to me?"

"I caused you to fall," her sister said, raising to stand next to her – her feet floating just above the flowers.

The primroses began to hiss and growl at Meagan. Suddenly, the roots rose up from underground and began wrapping tightly around her ankles, causing her to lose her crouching balance. She caught herself with her hand, which was immediately restrained by the roots. Having her pinned to the ground, her sister let out a cacophonous noise. "I marked you! You're mine!"

Meagan's eyes instantly shot open, a world with bright fluorescent light flooded her surroundings.

"She's awake," a woman in green scrubs ran from the side of the bed.

George, James, Becca, and Hannah weren't in the room. "I must've passed out on the couch. That's the last thing I remember," Meagan speculated.

A man in a white lab coat entered the room and studied the monitors, "Hmm, her signs are still stable here, but we ran a brain scan. We had to see if you sustained any internal damage. Your friend and grandmother are in the waiting room. Becca, I think that was her name, said they would stay a bit longer. Do you know where you are?"

Meagan rubbed her finger around a bandage on her arm, studying the needle they'd stuck into it. She lifted her head to glimpse at his nametag, "Judging by your nametag, 'Head Physician', I'm at the hospital. What happened?"

George... I need to tell him how I feel. Later. I need to know how bad my injury is. I hope it's nothing too serious. What will Grandma say?

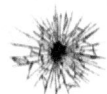

Leaving her before she woke back up was the best option; besides, my parents would kill me if I didn't come home. Meagan needed medical attention, and talking to her would have to wait until she was able to do so, or at least until the doctor sees what's wrong.

"Are you okay, bud?" James gradually sped up.

"Yup, just thinking," he replied mellowly, watching the trees blur past.

"She's going to be fine. Man, when you beat the shit out of Dom, I knew you had feelings for her. You can't hide your feelings from me," James pointed out.

"Why are you being so sympathetic towards me? You noticed? Where's your jokes?" George asked.

"I only get sentimental with the ladies; I can control my emotions with guys like you. Instead of panicking, I joke."

"So, in other words, you're a drunk asshole!" George accused.

"No, not drunk. Tipsy." James corrected.

"And you're driving us home intoxicated! What the hell's wrong with you?" George growled, grabbing his arm.

"What are you doing, man? I'm driving! Do you have a death wish or something?" James shoved George off him.

"Pull over and let me drive! I'm not tipsy!"

James chuckled light-heartedly, "I'm not letting you drive my truck! It's new and I've only had it about a month!"

George slumped into the seat, trying to stay calm, but his intuition kept screaming at him how this wasn't a good idea. At that moment, blazing lights shone around the bend, and the sound of metal screeching against each other rang through their ears.

I am going to die…

Chapter 15

I wish I could erase all the events from last night. How can I keep what happened a secret? Did we kill someone? Or was it their fault? What attacked Meagan? Why are the woods in this town off limits? George's mind flooded with questions. *I don't think I can last much longer.*

My parents think I'm innocent, but I'm not...they think I'm the perfect child. I'm clearly flawed; I hate being praised when I can't even be genuine with them. With what just happened, I buried myself deeper in the grave. I went into the woods, I was involved in a car crash, and an entity is apparently after me. And James. If he'd let me drive, we would've never hit that car. Was it my fault? What if everything was my fault? No. I told him he shouldn't be driving, but he wouldn't listen to me.

George rolled over on his back, wiping his eyes.

I can't get any sleep. I have too much on my mind. I wonder how Meagan's doing, or if Becca has an update?

He stared at his phone, reading seven am, and a new message.

George, this doesn't look good... the doctor explained she has a traumatic brain injury. I had to ask what it meant, but apparently, it's possible she's lost some of her past memories. Only time will tell. Her grandma and I are the only ones here. They want us to see if she can remember any of her friends. I've texted Hannah too... and Oh God, keeping up with this lie about water balloons... I'm not sure if her grandma is buying it or if she's disappointed.

"Are you up, hun?" George's mom appeared in the doorway, studying him. "I wanted to talk to you for a few minutes. Is that okay? Before everyone gets up." She walked in and sat down on his bed.

"Um, sure. What do you want to talk about?" George scooted up to the head of his bed.

"I've noticed you've been distanced from us lately. I want you to come with us later, we're going out for a family lunch. You don't have to work today, right? I really want us to have a family day."

George thought for a moment before responding, "I...can't today. I have to go see Meagan, she's in the hospital."

She was shocked, "What happened?"

"She hit her head hard. They want me to come in to see what memories she's lost. You guys would have more fun without me anyway," he admitted

"Your siblings miss you. You're always working. We never have time to get everyone together and go out like we used to. You have a different schedule to attend to, but I understand you need to be with your friend. Go this time, but next time is family day." She leaned across the bed and gave George a gentle kiss on the forehead.

Is this an alternate universe? My mom is never this delicate with me, even on her good days. It's not like her to care for me. It's always, "Get up, or else! Do this, do that."

His mom stood up, saying, "I love you, honey, don't forget that." She left the room, leaving George's mind spinning in circles.

"I won't forget," George replied in his empty room.

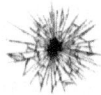

"Sure, I'll leave you two alone for about ten minutes. I'll be back to check up on her." The nurse closed the curtain.

George tapped his foot nervously on the floor while sitting in one of the chairs. "Do you feel any better?"

Meagan twisted her hospital gown, "So, Becca told you about the results? I suffered from a concussion and internal bleeding. They're treating me like a child. Seeing what I remembered about last night. I told them I didn't remember any of it. That's all I gave them. I'll have to go to a neurologist with this memory loss. I feel fine, just hungry— can't eat anything decent in here."

"Shit, Meagan... I was too worried, I couldn't sleep. Becca told me we could switch off on staying here, but I wanted to talk about us. I wanted to ask, do you still remember our kiss? If so, I wanted to ask what our kiss meant to you?" George asked gently, fumbling for the right words.

"Of course, I still remember. I realized I thought I wanted to be able to kiss Dom, but when he and I were in the bathroom last night, I didn't want him at all. Degrading me like I'm trash. When you came for me... well... I do know you make me happy. What I don't know is if the kiss we shared felt the same for you." Meagan said, staring outside the window.

"I see, the bastard! I slammed his head into the floor and almost strangled him to death when he told me he was going to use you. If James hadn't pulled me off, I would've killed him. Next time, if you don't feel comfortable, tell someone. You should've told Becca when you saw him and Amanda walk in the door." George's voice grew sterner as he talked.

She jerked her head around to stare intently at him, "If Timothy had come through the door, would you have told Becca you didn't want him there? Like I said before, I thought I was over him."

"Becca knew I wouldn't want him there; I didn't have miscommunication. We promised we would be there for one another. I tried to save you, but— wait, what's on your neck?" George asked, examining four claw marks stretching from the bottom of her chin to her chest.

The blankets ruffled underneath Meagan's legs, as she kicked them off in discomfort. "Must've been the doctors, anyway, you wouldn't have if she never knew you and him were a thing! I know I frightened all of you, but I'm tired of all this damn drama. I know spending time with you makes me happy, but you won't tell me how you feel, so... I need to get some rest. Can you please just leave?"

George began to protest when the nurse shoved the curtain aside, exposing the two of them. "There's a girl here, Hannah, to see you for a minute. I told her for only a few minutes since we have to check all the tests. Is that okay, Meagan?"

Puzzled, Meagan asked, "Who's Hannah?"

"She said she's your friend. Do you not remember her?" The nurse crossed her arms, narrowing her eyes.

"I don't know a Hannah…" Meagan hesitated, thinking, then shook her head in confusion.

She doesn't remember Hannah? This isn't good... he thought worriedly.

"Maybe she'll remember her if she saw her face?" George suggested, speaking up in the silent room.

"We'll see." The nurse walked from the room once more, leaving them alone.

"Would you like me to ask the nurse to take a look at those scratches?" George offered.

"I'm fine," Meagan stated flatly.

"Then, I think I should leave...you want your personal space, and I'll give it to you. Focus on getting better. I'll be waiting for an update." George said.

Meagan remained silent, deep in thought, as George left the room. Hannah appeared around the corner, her eyes dimming when she saw him. "I'm so sorry about last night, what I did. I hope you forgive me. I wanted to apologize to Meagan, too. How's she holding up?"

"I know it was the rum talking. Listen, let's forget what happened in the bathroom. I'm not sure if you want to see her," George informed, passing by her.

His jeans pocket buzzed against his leg, making him jump. George pulled out his phone, checking who had texted him.

I'm waiting outside of our hangout spot when we were younger, the park out by the baseball field next to the willow tree. Do you remember, George? We weren't always into gaming. I have to talk to you about last night. I'll be waiting, so hurry!

"What is there to talk about, James? I'll be back." Paranoia immediately flooded George as he rushed out to his car, the morning light feeling warm against him. An immediate contrast to the frigid hospital. He pictured the faded blue blanket lying on the grass, hiding behind the old willow tree from the sun's rays, watching hilarious videos, dishing the dirt, and venting. So, how come he'd suppressed those memories? Maybe it was because he thought James was only there for the snacks.

Why would he choose to rendezvous there, of all places?

George snickered to himself, "probably to teach me a lesson on my paranoia."

The park was vacant; George scanned the area to see if he could spot James. The only sound came from the leaves blowing over the grass.

His truck isn't even here.

In the distance, George could see a faint figure on the horizon. When George walked closer, he realized it was James with his back to him, watching the clouds out in the field.

After reaching earshot, he pointed to the sky. "Look, George, doesn't that cloud look like a snake?"

George continued narrowing the space between them, following the direction of James' plump finger toward the sky. "That cloud doesn't resemble a snake to me at all. It looks like a long blob."

James shook his head, turning around to face George, "I should've known you don't even have your imagination anymore. So, have you snitched on me yet? I figured I'd give you a night before your paranoia consumed you." His eyes darted sardonically from George's eyes to his cheeks, adding, "When you lie, your face and ears turn a rosy pink."

"I haven't told a soul, but your speculation about my paranoia was spot on. I'm still trying to process exactly what happened last night. Is this the only reason why you called me out here? To reminisce in childhood memories and remind me how I'm faint of heart? Thanks, but you've already expressed your hatred before." George started walking back to his car.

"Turn around, I'm not finished talking. I couldn't sleep at all! My roommates didn't come home last night. They probably passed out at another party. Besides that, did you even watch the news this morning? All that's left of the vehicle are pieces of burnt metal, the blown engine, and shards of glass with blood on them. The car we hit last night must've caught on fire after we left. They haven't released any information on how the fire started, but the mayor released a statement to contain it. No bodies have been identified yet. To contain the fire, they'd have to be in those damn forsaken woods! George, if they launch an investigation and somehow link this back to us, we could go to jail for a millennium!" James' dramatic voice grew fierce.

He was tipsy when he was driving, don't forget that.

George had already spun around, "If you would've listened to me in the first place, none of this would've happened!" Rage began to fill his body, hating his 'friend' who never listened to him. "Stupid decisions and actions result in consequences, sometimes deadly consequences! If you would've let me drive, or not have drank as much, no one would've died!" George puffed in fury.

"We're in this together, remember that," James spat harshly, "If I'm going down, then you're going down with me. We're bros until the end."

"AHAHA!" George screeched, his laugh echoing across the field to the trees. "This is your burden you're carrying on your own. I'm not snitching, but this isn't my fault." He turned around to leave when he heard a metallic click.

"I know you all too well. You're a witness, a second-hand driver. Turn around and face me like a man."

As if in slow motion, George turned to face James, who was pointing a gun at his temple. "That's better. Besides, if you don't confess to the police, you're guilty by association. If you do go to the police, well, you won't live long after that. POW!" James pretended to pull the trigger, smirking.

Cold sweat broke out on George's palms, his hands twitching. "Why did you bring a gun with you? You're going to kill me now? Is that how you're going to resolve this?"

"Shit, I just made you piss your pants, didn't I? Eh, I'm not going to kill my best friend, unless he doesn't cooperate, that is. We're going to take a ride. Now will you do the honors and take the lead for me?" James still had the gun trained on George's temple.

George didn't budge, "You're insane, you know that? What if I'm willing to die here?"

"Quit babbling. We all know you're too pathetic to die. Honestly, I wish you would just do as you're told. I guess we have to do this the hard way." James raised the butt of the gun, then slammed it down on the back of George's head. George fell limp onto the grass. Immense pain spread from the back of his neck to his forehead. The ground below him started to spin. His eyes closed, and darkness surrounded him.

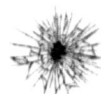

"Rise n' shine!" James splashed water in George's face, making him snort and choke. "Did you sleep like a princess?" He asked sarcastically, taking the gun from the holster pinned to his waist. "We're almost to the rendezvous, and once there, I'll decide your fate. I can make it look like you were the one feeling guilty about killing them in the crash last night." James continued, "I'll be a free man walking, and you'll be the pawn you were always meant to be. If I were you, I'd take a good long look at how you're going to beg and plead for me to spare your life!" He burst into furious laughter, his tongue clicking up and down like a serpent.

Does he want me to piss and shit myself? Is this really how I'm going to die? A staged suicide? He won't get away with it. Meagan will know...won't she?

"Even if I do die," George croaked, interrupting his mirth, "Meagan

134

will know that I wouldn't kill myself. She'll know!"

"Is she your girlfriend or something? You did beat the hell out of that Dom guy for her. Besides, faith in others will only get you killed in the end," James advised, turning on his signal.

George peered out the window, the sun blossomed a tangerine haze on the horizon, "She's not my girlfriend. She was there for me when I was about to do something stupid. She saved me, and I tried to save her! But it didn't turn out the way I wanted," he said, talking more for himself than to James.

He must be taking me to the town's outer limits. The forest is there. I can't run away. Where would I go? I made a promise to Meagan that I wouldn't give up on myself. So, what am I going to do?

Make your decision fast. The clock is ticking.

You again, are you a saint or an angel? Perhaps, an instinct?

I told you I am what you want me to be. Nothing more, nothing less.

George closed his eyes, trying to concentrate.

I'm not a coward, and I don't deserve to die. Take the gun away from him – or, my better option, swerve him off the road. I hope I'm right about this.

George opened his eyes, watching James carefully.

"Ya' know, I think your suicide would serve me the perfect scapegoat plan. Meagan won't have time to think about you. She's been marked by him." A laughter spilled out of him— a chuckle at first, but gradually, it transformed, twisting into something manic.

Here's my chance.

With a fast movement, George grabbed James' wrist, digging his fingernails into his skin. James' laughter turned into a snarl. The truck swerved wildly, tires screeching in protest as George strained against James's hold. George refused to let go, his fingers locked in a desperate bid for survival.

George managed to push the barrel toward the windshield, but James' grip remained firm. Struggling with James to gain control of the gun, George lurched forward and sank his teeth into his wrist. Letting out a howl, James' finger pressed the trigger, and a gunshot discharged with a deafening roar, blowing through the windshield. George pulled his body back from the deafening gunshot, his ears ringing.

James swerved across both lanes, while George grabbed the gun that'd landed in the floorboard after it had gone off. He pointed it at James. "I don't think you plan on dying today, James. I suggest you pull over and tell me about what attacked Meagan last night."

James retracted his hand, wiping blood on his pant leg, not replying, swerving a third time, narrowly missing a car. A loud honk erupted from the passing vehicle, and James managed to regain control of the wheel.

George buckled his seatbelt, one hand resting on the trigger, and the other held the panic handlebar.

"You wouldn't shoot the driver. You'll die too!" James gritted his teeth.

"I'm not going to shoot you. Instead…" George jerked the wheel to the right, feeling the center of gravity shift to the left as the truck flipped onto its side.

Chapter 16

"You still don't remember me? I'm the ginger with all the funny memes!" Hannah's eyes lowered, knowing there was no use in trying.

"I'm sorry, Hannah. I just don't remember. I think you should leave." Meagan replied unremorseful.

"Yeah, you're right. I wanted to apologize for not being there, but now's not a good time," Hannah murmured, standing up.

Meagan dismissed Hannah's apology. Instead, she asked, "Before you leave, will you tell my grandmother to come in so I can talk to her?"

"Mhm," Hannah hid her face, walking out.

"Thanks." Meagan scratched her bandages.

The nurse walked back in a few seconds later. "I'm going to check your fluids first, while you wait for your grandmother."

Meagan shook her head, "My head feels like an endless fog, I can't remember anything about that girl. It's quite scary...but I'm surprisingly calm."

The nurse changed the IV bag, then lifted Meagan's head up,

unwrapping her bandages while talking, "You'll probably have to go to neurotherapy after you get out of the hospital, but I wonder if this memory loss is temporary or if the memories are being blocked by any damage to the neurotransmitters. It could be that a shock wave was sent to your frontal lobe, blocking the memories. Either way, honey, I hope it's only temporary."

The nurse threw the bandages in the trash as she wrapped new ones around her head.

What if I forget everything? What will I do then? Would it be worth it to live?

"Everything else is in good check. Dr. Lawrence should be on his way now. I'll be here to check up on you every couple of hours. If you have any problems before then, hit the nurse's call button on the side of the bed."

Meagan nodded, "I will, thanks."

After a few minutes of solitude, both her grandmother and Doctor Lawrence stepped through the curtain simultaneously.

"What do you mean, some memories are blocked? Did she hit her head that badly?" Her grandmother demanded.

"Honestly, these cases are hard to determine!" Dr. Lawrence coughed and cleared his throat.

"Wh… What!?" Meagan's heart pounded; her forehead began to sweat, and she felt dizzy.

"I want you here until the swelling subsides," Dr. Lawrence began, staring down at his clipboard. "You were lucky enough the damage didn't paralyze you, but it did cause enough damage to block certain memories. The results indicate that your frontal lobe, with the hippocampus, has taken the damage. I doubt you'll regain any of them."

Meagan was silent, not knowing what to think.

"There is no way of getting her memory back? Dr. Lawrence, please tell me there's a chance for my grandbaby to remember?" Her grandmother pleaded.

"Hmm, there's about a ten percent chance she'll regain it, but I'm putting a referral in for a neurologist, and if that doesn't work, one can only hope time will be on our side. She'll stay here for a few more days to make sure nothing else happens." Dr. Lawrence took his patient's chart and left the room.

Meagan remained silent, the fear of not remembering anything growing on her every second.

I don't remember this girl, Hannah. I seemed to remember what happened to me, I remember my childhood and grandmother, and I still remember Becca and George...

Her breath eased a bit.

"Honey, Becca wanted to see you before she left to go back home," her grandmother informed.

Meagan froze in fear, whispering, "Becca..."

Her grandmother stared into Meagan's eyes. "Becca... your friend? You were at her birthday party last night. Anyways, I'll leave you two alone," before Meagan could respond, her grandmother left the room.

I remember the birthday party... but it's all a bit of a blur to me. Who knows what memories I've lost?

"M... Meagan?" Becca emerged in front of the curtain, her eyes watering.

"Why are you crying? Don't give me waterworks, please," Meagan replied, crossing her arms. "It's freaking me out."

"I wanted to apologize to you. I feel like it's my fault! I was the one who invited Dom to the party. I didn't know that he and Amanda were a thing. If I hadn't invited him, you wouldn't be here right now. I'll take full responsibility, and you don't have to forgive me if you don't want to," Becca cried.

"I remember last night, if you want me to be honest. I need to pretend I don't, so the doctors don't question so much. Besides, I was pushed by...well, we're not sure yet, and we can't risk them finding out we were, you know where," Meagan stated flatly.

"You don't even sound like yourself anymore, but I wanted to see if I could help you remember Hannah before I left," Becca informed her, adding, "During the summer, we had a girls' night with Hannah. You told us you were glad to be friends with us because we were supportive of everything you wanted to do. And before this, you stayed at my house for about a week before you told your grandmother about your parents contacting you about how you did with your final exams. I understand now that you stayed somewhere you felt appreciated because you wanted to get out of your parents' house. I told you last night that no matter what, we'll be there for you. Please try to remember Hannah!"

"I'm sorry, but I can't. It's all a blur to me. Is George still here?'" Meagan asked.

Becca hesitated, saying uneasily, "He was here, but now that you mention it, I haven't seen him in a while."

"Do you have my phone? I need to text him," Meagan's eyes searched around the room for her purse, not seeing it.

Becca reached into her back pocket and pulled out her phone, "Here. Have at it."

This is Meagan. I'm using Becca's phone. When you get this message, please come to the hospital as soon as possible! I do have feelings for you. I need you to know that! We also need to figure out what pushed me! We need to regroup.

Meagan pressed send, then handed Becca her phone. "I didn't want to scare George, and I don't want anyone else to know— I'm not sure what it means, but—" Meagan ran her fingers on the marks down her throat. She gritted her teeth, and a stinging sensation flared through her skin.

"When did you notice this?" Becca asked worriedly.

"George pointed it out. Something's not right. Anyways, I know you need to get home," Meagan replied, laying her head gently on her pillow. "If he texts back, tell him to be careful."

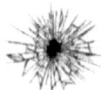

Do you see it, George?

See what?

All of your memories.

Flashes of memories flew through George's head at the speed of light. In just a few seconds, the flashbacks had reached his memories from the age of eight.

Do you remember what I said?

I believed in myself, but either way, was death inevitable?

Not that. I told you that I could be a saint, or I could be Satan.

The memories kept zooming by at a fast pace, reaching age twelve memories.

You were trying to help me, my instincts.

Or was I trying to get rid of you faster for your sins? Now is the time to decide what I am to you. Time waits for no one. So, George, what have you learned?

His memories became more depressing as he got older. By now, he was at age fifteen.

I've learned that I'm stronger than everyone thinks I am. I've learned not to be so gullible all the time. I've learned that I'm not alone: my friends are there for me. I've also learned you're not a saint or Satan. You're a part of me, and you're my subconscious!

Prove to yourself that I am you.

George thought for a moment, stumped. At this point, he was seeing recent memories of Timothy at age eighteen.

Time waits for no one.

That may be true, but you will obey me! I won't die just yet. You will keep me alive.

Meagan had fallen asleep while waiting for George to text her back. While appearing completely knocked out to those around her, inside her head, she was locked into a realistic, dream-like world.

"I hope you're not angry with me, sis." Michelle stood in front of Meagan, frowning.

"Why would I be mad at you?" she asked, feeling confused.

"I'm the one who blocked your memories," she admitted, a soft white glow illuminating around her.

"You're blocking my memory?" Meagan's words carried like thunder across a black and white world that seemed to be her mind.

"You must understand it's for the right reason to…" she bit her lip.

"Why?" Meagan demanded.

"I can't tell you yet. You must understand this for your own good. You must wake up now." Michelle snapped her fingers, and Meagan's eyes popped open in shock.

What the hell is this madness? My dead sister is trying to teach me a lesson. How much more insanity can I take before I have to be locked away in an asylum?

Her eyes wandered around the dark room looking for Becca. "She's gone," she whispered.

She noticed the note lying on the table and snatched it up to read.

I stayed two hours to make sure I gave George enough time to text back. He never did. I have to get some sleep. Honestly, I'm a bit worried; it's not like him. I didn't want to wake you because you were sleeping so soundly.

Love, Becca.

I can still remember the kiss he gave me that day. It was better than—

"Clear a room, stat!" A nurse's shadow ran past her curtain, breaking her thoughts.

"This one is in critical condition! He's losing too much blood. We have to stop the bleeding! Prepare for surgery!" Four nurses scurried past her curtain.

What's going on?

Meagan listened closely to hear what the nurses were saying, "Huh? He said something. Meagan? Who's Meagan? His mom? Hurry! He's losing consciousness!"

I must've heard them wrong. The nurse didn't say my name.

"What happened?" she heard another nurse ask.

"Paramedics said a truck was turned over. Looked like it flipped a few times before landing in a ditch. Get this, the driver seemed to have fled the crash, and a gun was found a few yards from the scene. Devastating."

Truck? Another person? That can't be George...George wouldn't do that...

Meagan pressed the nurse's button repeatedly, wanting to know more information. After a few minutes, her nurse peeked through the curtain.

"Is everything alright? What do you need?" Her nurse glanced at the monitors.

"Who was that? Who are they rolling into the surgery room? Do you know? I have to know who it is!" Meagan's breath grew hot and sharp. Her heart monitor beeping faster as her heart rate began to climb.

"I don't think the boy had any identification on him. The police are trying to figure that out now. Do you possibly know him?" The nurse asked.

"I thought I heard one of the nurses say my name. Is it George? Tell me it isn't George?" Meagan screamed, gripping her hospital gown.

"I don't know, miss. I have to go help them. Please take it easy!" The nurse swung the curtain as tightly closed as she could, returning to assist the others.

Meagan lifted the thin sheet off, then jerked the needles from her arm.

"GAAAAHH!" she screamed in agony, sliding out of the hospital bed. She peeked behind the curtain just in time to see the medical bed roll by. She saw a grimy, bloody face. Bruises, cuts, and open wounds were on his legs and arms. The sight of seeing someone so unrecognizable made her knees tremble.

Oh God, no...

Her head pounded with pain, and her vision began to get dizzy.

"G... George..." she rasped as she collapsed to the hospital floor. The last thing she heard was the curtain coming down around her as she tried to steady herself. The world around her broke, and her heart shattered like tainted glass.

Chapter 17

A sunny haze glimmered through the stray clouds, a subtle change of environment warming George. He stared up, watching the sun play hide and seek with the clouds.

"Wouldn't you like to stay here forever?" a voice from above asked soothingly.

"Yes, I would. It's peaceful," George replied.

"Close your eyes for three seconds, then open them," the deep voice echoed down, and the sunshine grew hot on his skin.

George felt his eyes flutter shut. Blackness shrouded his breathtaking view.

One…two…three…

George's eyes opened. The sun and clouds had returned, but this time he was sitting on a grassy knoll overlooking the sea. The waves rolled up gently, splashing.

"This is beautiful too," George said, rubbing his arms slowly.

"You can stay here, too, if you choose." Seagulls circled around overhead.

"If I do what will happen?" George brought his knees close to his chin.

"You will have to find out." The male voice replied.

"You know what to do," George directed the voice and said no more.

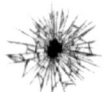

A cold, numbing feeling washed over Meagan as she muttered George's name, the one person she wanted to remember, but there was a stinging feeling in the back of her brain. More memories shattered, and a white light soon faded to black.

"It isn't right, what happened to you," a familiar, angelic voice stated from above.

"What happened? I need to get back to George! He needs me! I... need... him...," Meagan's eyes filled with salty tears as the darkness overtook her mind.

"You want to remember your friend, but what about me? Michelle..." the voice seemed distant.

In her dream-like state, Meagan wiped her tears, her brain searing with jolts of agony as each memory became either unrecognizable or tainted. She wasn't sure if she even remembered her sister.

"Urgh, my head feels like it's about to explode!" Meagan grabbed her head with both hands, applying pressure to reduce the throbbing.

"Does this jog your memory?" the voice said.

Meagan watched a young woman appear in the small white light, just enough for her to make out the figure. Lavish blonde hair, hazel eyes, and a smirk caused Meagan to shudder.

"You're not... it can't be, Michelle?" Meagan replied reluctantly, the pain inside her head became apparent across her face.

"Yes, it's me, your big sis— here in the flesh! I'm glad you're here with me," Michelle informed, stepping beside Meagan— her presence calm and soothing, subsiding the pain.

Meagan focused on her surroundings. A dimly lit asylum hallway, surrounded by peeling paint and smeared blood on the walls. The corridor was deserted, except for the soft flickering white glow of the hallway fluorescents. She started to tremble.

"Don't be afraid," Michelle whispered, her voice bouncing off the cold walls. "I'm here to help you find a way out."

"Where are we?" Meagan murmured, anxiety setting in, thinking someone could hear their conversation. She watched Michelle move down the hallway.

"It's better if I show you," Michelle answered, enticing her to follow.

Distant screams and whispers filled the stale air, making the stillness even more uneasy. Meagan felt a chill run down her spine, but when Michelle placed a steady hand on her shoulder, she somehow felt grounded.

Michelle stopped Meagan in front of a wooden door with a number plate engraved that read "Room 314." Her eyes locked onto Meagan's. "Your memories are in there. Are you ready to face them?"

"Why would I need to face my memories?" Meagan challenged. The whispers of patients growing in volume.

"Don't you want to keep your memories?" Michelle shot back.

Placing her hand on the door handle, Meagan's heart raced with anticipation and fear from not knowing what lay behind the door. She hesitated.

"Open the door, Meagan," Michelle hissed, her voice dripping with malice. "Your memories are waiting... and they're screaming to be freed."

As Meagan turned the handle, the door creaked open, revealing a room made from body parts. Stretched out and sewn together skin formed the four walls, legs and torsos created a couch with a coffee table and lamp made of arms next to it— the soles of each leg planted firmly to the ground. Faces protruded through the walls, some familiar, and some contorted in agony.

Meagan's screams were drowned out by the cacophony of terror within the room. The faces groaning, howling, and screaming her name in torment.

Michelle's sinical laughter echoed through the room, her eyes now black. "Face your fears!" she gave a forceful push, and Meagan stumbled into the grotesque space.

"Help us, Meagan. Free us. Help us. Free us," the voices called out to her.

Meagan spun around to see Michelle grinning with dark hollow eyes, slamming the door shut, hearing a soft click.

"Please, open the door!" Meagan begged in the blackness. "Michelle, please! Sis!" she wailed, pounding on the wood.

"You're the one who killed me." Michelle's voice muffled. "Now I'm going to kill you."   A red glow illuminated from the lamp behind her, and various deathly screams rang in her ears. She whirled around to a figure now rising from the center of the room, facing her. It was a conglomerate of faces— her parents, her grandma, Becca, Hannah, Dom, and George's faces were bunched all around its body, everyone's eyes blackened.

"You're not enough" and "You'll never be loved" phrases appeared on the walls, written in some form of dark, bloody liquid. They dripped down, searing themselves into Meagan's soul. The room was a prison of her own making, revealing her deepest fears.

The figure of faces seemed to come alive, its arms, pale and spindly,

150

reaching out for her. She backed up against the door, her chest tightened. She shook her head in disbelief, the faces daunting her. "Die. Die. Die," they chanted.

Her eyes darted around, seeing a hundred arms outstretched, swiping at her. Fear paralyzed Meagan. She felt herself drop to the floor and hug her knees, rocking back and forth as the figure came towards her.

Is this how I'm going to die? George? Someone has to show up, right?

Meagan couldn't breathe, but she kept fighting the haphephobia, the monster enclosing in on her, hoping anyone would come to her aid.

"Touchy, touchy, miney, miney," it taunted, raising a bony finger.

And that's when Meagan noticed something— a large mirror hanging to her left— its surface cracked and distorted. She crawled to it and noticed her reflection staring back, her face twisted in grimace and self-doubt. As she watched her distorted reflection in the mirror, it shattered, blood pouring down the tiny shards. She screamed.

Chapter 18

James had left George for dead, but more importantly, he didn't need to be there with a gun in the vehicle. He winced in pain as he breathed, clutching his ribs.

"Fuck." Every time he drew in air, it stung. He walked toward the woods, looked back at the vehicle in the ditch, and pointed his gun at the vehicle.

"So, long, George," James muttered, resting his finger on the trigger, but realized another vehicle stopping. "Shit!" Using his strength, he threw the gun into the ditch, yards away from his overturned truck, and hid in the woods.

Gotta make another plan. Gotta save myself another way. I was supposed to only threaten him until we ended up in its nest. And now...

James shook his head, shaking the thought.

Let me get to the rendezvous spot.

James had only been there once.

Celebrating the move into our apartment a few weeks ago. I remember my roommates blacking out, and I became angry and restless. I got out of this town, but only moved to the next town over, and now I'm right back where I started. There's got to be more than just here. I stumbled into the woods, drunk and reckless, being sucked in further and further. Little did I know I'd end up at a shitty cabin. It was like the forest drew me to it. No, something else. It spoke in a voice that still haunts my dreams— to plead for my life, a life for a life. As long as I fed it the perfect vessel. George, it kept snarling. It wanted my best friend. I laughed it off as a drunken hallucination, but now I'm desperate enough to consider it the only solution.

"George had to make everything complicated. He isn't the type to keep anything a secret." James talked to himself, brushing branches away from his head, knowing he was close to the spot.

I know good and well, they'd never step foot in the woods. It's forbidden. All these people are blind. They're too scared to be taken to jail. Not me. I'm going to get out of this shithole.

"Aggh!" James' ribs were on fire. His breathing was becoming faint.

Just a little further to the cabin.

The trees grew closer together. James thought they were enclosing him until he could see the shattered windows of the battered shelter. James looked back at the thick trunks, which seemed to squeeze tighter together, and the branches seemed to push him toward the door.

Maybe I can get the Weaver to go and get George from the vehicle. That's what the journal I found on the altar called it. Yeah, okay. This fucker wouldn't even show itself last time.

James knocked three times. He heard fumbling around and noticed a sour stench.

Death. It smells like death.

"Did you bring him?" it asked in a deep, scratchy voice.

154

"I got him just off the road. He decided to be a nuisance ..."

"Did you forget the deal?" it interrupted James.

"I didn't forget. Your specimen jerked the steering wheel and caused me to crash my truck. I can't go back up there. The police will connect me to the crash. I was hoping we could talk." James forced the aching pain of his ribs away as he spoke.

"We're talking," it grunted in dissatisfaction.

"Face to face. I'm not scared like I was the first time. If you hurry, we could go back and get George together," James compromised.

The weathered door creaked open, and James stood firm.

"Ah, James," it rasped. "You think you can toy with me? You, who are already mine?" The Weaver's red gaze seemed to bore into James' soul, making his skin crawl.

He could feel his back on fire and realized it radiated from the claw marks he received from his first encounter.

"George is beyond help now, but you... you're right here with me. And you'll stay that way." With each word, the demon's presence seemed to grow, its darkness spreading, and James felt himself crumble beneath its unyielding gaze.

James, speechless and afflicted by broken ribs, cradled his left side.

"That wasn't part of the deal! You agreed you'd show me the world beyond this town if I got you a worthy vessel. I brought George nearly here!" James protested.

"The ritual can't be done from a dead or unconscious body. They must be alive! Nearly doesn't cut it. It's the only way, the journal explains this. Don't worry. You'll get to see the outside." The Weaver informed, approaching James when the door slammed shut. "I need a vessel. I need someone, anyone. I'm dying, especially waiting for you to bring me the perfect specimen. But this form is not one I can keep any longer. Are you getting it now?" It glared at James.

"You mean…I'm…" James trailed off.

After moving, I left George behind years ago. After him ratting me out to my parents the day before the move… he deserved it. He deserves this! I deserve to be free, to get out of Arcae by any means!

The truth hit James like a slap, his face contorting in shock and horror. "No, I won't be your vessel! Go and get George, now!"

The Weaver grinned devilishly, "You made a deal with the devil."

James turned white. He could feel his blood run cold.

Back then, I confided in George I'd figure out how we could get out of this twisted town and venture out into what was beyond. Until he blabbed to my parents at the time, and they never trusted me after the move. I snuck out and did what I wanted, but now…

"That smell…" James murmured, the air sour, the shack had a thick scent of burnt flesh. Gagging on the smell lingering in his nostrils, bile burned in the back of his throat.

"You did a number on your truck last night. I was there at the crash. I needed human blood to keep alive, but the bodies were charred. The fire started immediately after their death on impact. You're just as tainted as I am, James. A murderer. You were willing to sacrifice your best friend. For what? Freedom?" it spat.

A black mist surrounded his face first, then his shoulders, all the way down to his feet. He didn't feel scared; in fact, a weight was lifted from his shoulders. His fingertips and toes felt tingly, and his brain relaxed.

"I really thought you could do this. It looks like I must do everything around here," its voice circling around James.

"I can bring you someone else…." James started.

"One chance," it intruded.

James felt the sharpness of his breath ease, and then his oxygen cut off. He was pulled up a few feet in the air toward the rotting beams holding up the roof.

"Let me show you!" the Weaver rasped.

I'm going to die! He's going to use me…

James could feel the black mist become frigid like an invisible hand squeezing his neck, his eyes fluttering shut as he passed out in midair for a moment.

I wanted my revenge. I wanted to see life leave George… I want him to suffer… not me…

"Make a deal with me, and I assure you I can see what your heart most desires. Let it consume you, let it control you, and you will see. Come James. Let's begin the ritual." The demon said, seeming to be able to read his thoughts.

His feet returned to the ground. He had one mission. He remembered where he'd found the journal a few weeks ago— perfectly placed in the middle of an altar in the back room of the cabin.   Black candles cast flickering shadows on the walls, and puddles of dry blood painted the floor of the chamber. The air, thick with the stench of char and smoke from two bodies badly burned and blackened, were slumped in one corner of the room. The smell of death tingled James' nose.

A deer antler skull sat atop the makeshift altar, adding decoration behind the journal; it seemed to watch him with cold, empty sockets. The number 666 and inverted crosses were drawn in blood behind the altar.

"No…this… can't be… I want revenge!" James said, cringing at his surroundings, and attempted to run, but he had no control over his feet as gut-wrenching pain was sent through his body.

"Revenge is served best cold." the Weaver's voice darkened.

James gritted his teeth. "Get out of my head! I'm not participating in your ritual!" His trainer shoes stepped in the red puddles across the floor, tracking footprints as he approached the altar. His hands reached out, and his fingers touched the spine of the worn leather as if he knew exactly which page the ritual started. Scribble filled each page front and back in languages he couldn't understand. His fingers stopped.

An unearthly roar, deep and menacing, came from James' throat, speaking in an unknown language— possibly Latin. He allowed it to take over, reading verse after verse, his eyes rolling in the back of his head until the room turned black.

"SCREAM!" It commanded, its voice scathing.

James heard his bones cracking and popping, and a sharp stabbing pain transmitted throughout his body. He was blinded, suspended in the air, while feeling the presence of the monstrous shadow towering over him. His blood-curdling screams rang throughout the cabin, but only for a moment. His soul felt disconnected from his body, seeing the Weaver's mouth open wide, revealing jagged teeth. James' soul could only watch it bite down on his flesh, eating him from the neck down. James' head lolled to the side, his eyes frozen in a permanent scream while blood dripped from his body, painting the floorboards red.

Chapter 19

Becca crawled into her bed, exhausted from staying up all night and morning. She checked her notifications one last time before slumping into her pillow. Nothing from George. Instantly, her eyelids grew heavy while wishing she could've done more to help Meagan.

What seemed like a few minutes, a soft nudge on her shoulder woke her, and her dad hovered over her bed. "Hey, kiddo, can we talk? I know you've had a long night, but I've been thinking about what happened to your friend, Meagan."

Becca blinked several times. "What's wrong, Dad? Meagan's fine for the most part, just recovering." She sat up and yawned.

"That's just it— I don't think she slipped and fell from a water balloon fight like you said. As a paramedic, I've seen some weird stuff, and something doesn't add up. She wouldn't be running around in a pretty dress, Becca," her father pointed out.

Fuck, James was right, this was a shit excuse. I can't risk it— but I've always told dad everything since mom...

'I want to know what kind of friends my daughter has been hanging with. Can you tell me what happened, angel?" his words were a soft blow. He never used her nickname unless he was serious.

"She was dared to jump from the roof to our pool, but she ended up hitting the bottom." She let out a heavy sigh. "It's all my fault! I could've stopped her, and I didn't." She shook her head; her blue jay painting on her canvas caught her eye.

"Kiddos these days, geez Becca, I wanted to ask because... well... I was on call a bit ago," he rested his hand on her shoulder. "It was a pretty bad truck accident. I helped search around for some ID after we took him to the hospital and finally found a wallet. It's George, Becca. He was found on the outskirts of town. It's pretty bad, and he's losing blood. I know you haven't had much sleep, but you should go back to the hospital for your friend."

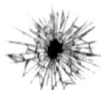

"Um, excuse me," Becca said as the receptionist typed. The clicking from the keyboard echoed throughout the lobby.

"How can I help?" She paused and waited.

"I was here a couple of hours ago for my friend, Meagan, she—" Before finishing her sentence, a familiar, deep voice interrupted cooly, "I need to know where a patient is located, his name is George."

Becca turned toward the voice, her nose scrunched at a stench of decay, but did a double take when James stepped up beside her, his blonde hair glistening with sweat, his muscles tensing in his tank top. His eyes, though. Something was off with his eyes. She couldn't put her finger on it.

"George who?" the receptionist demanded.

"George…" James hesitated.

The receptionist crossed her arms. "Well, I can't help you if you can't provide me with a last name and your relation to the patient under HIPAA."

James stormed from the desk, frustrated. "I'll find him myself. Is it Lovelle?" he asked himself.

Becca's heart skipped a beat.

He didn't even recognize me.

"James?" Becca called to him.

James halted. "Hey, Becca. All of this is tense. I didn't see you there."

"Did George tell you where he was going? Maybe taking a drive to clear his head? You know, we have two friends here. I just don't understand… and James… are you feeling okay? That smell…" Becca's voice turned soft with disbelief and concern.

"That's why I'm here, to find out what happened, but I figured his parents would've been here by now. Why haven't they called them?" he grumbled, balling his fists. "I haven't been sleeping, just need a shower and some rest."

At that moment, a nurse rushed into the hallway. "The patient in room 110 fell and hit her head. The girl isn't responsive. I need help! Is there any family here right now? Maybe a familiar voice will wake her up."

Becca's world constricted; the receptionist's words delivered a devastating physical blow.

The receptionist searched the monitor, then turned toward the nurse. "Room 110, that's Meagan Phin."

"Her grandma should be in there with her," Becca blurted. "That's my friend! I was just here earlier with her."

"Well, she's not. So, you're up. Come on." To her left, the nurse motioned her to come with her, and to her right, James had disappeared. She felt she had to choose a friend and leave the other behind.

Where did James go?

Becca felt time was moving in slow motion, and there was no time to make a decision. A decision that could cost either friend's life.

"Well?" Meagan's nurse asked impatiently.

Becca didn't rely on her heart or brain to make the decision, but her gut to outrun death's grasp on her friends.

Tears streamed down her face, and her ears heard the thumping of her heartbeat as adrenaline kicked in. She stumbled into the hallway, the light dimmed, and she feared losing one of her friends. She burst through the heavy door, accessing patients' rooms, and through the curtain to Meagan's room. A bright light poured over her, barely able to see through tears. She was mentally and physically exhausted.

"I'm here, Meagan! Hun, please wake up! It's going to be okay, don't give up on me!" Becca wiped her tears away, feeling Meagan's icy fingers beneath her own.

"If this is my belated birthday present, that's not happening!" Becca sniffled. "I never got to open my gifts. I wanted to wait until you were feeling better."

Meagan's fingers twitched hesitantly.

Becca massaged them softly. "I don't care if you don't remember me. I just need you to respond." She watched the nurse nod as Becca grabbed Meagan's other hand. Meagan's chest heaved, gasping for air. Becca's gentle massaging seemed to be triggering a reaction. She noticed her body tensing as if defending herself.

"It's me, Becca," she whispered, hoping Meagan would relax.

Meagan's eyes snapped open, and she thrashed her arms and legs wildly in a panic. "Don't touch me! Get away!" her voice hoarse.

Becca quickly pulled back, giving Meagan space as she continued to panic. Filled with concern, she watched Meagan's fearful gaze darting around the room.

"Look, I'm not touching you," Becca threw her hands up, backing away slowly. But Meagan didn't seem to hear her; her confusion and disorientation evident on her face. As she came back into reality, her panic subsided, focusing on Becca.

"I'm sorry," Meagan whispered, her voice shaking. "What happened?"

The nurse fluffed her pillow, answering, "You were trying to run after the nurses and doctors, even ripped your IVs out. You said someone's name and blacked out. You were knocked out for about half an hour while we stabilized you. Your friend here decided to help bring you to. Whose name did you call out? You seemed so concerned."

Meagan's face became perplexed. "I don't remember ever calling out. Where am I?" Her head flopped back into her pillow.

Becca's forehead broke out in a sweat. "Do you remember me? It's me, Becca. You're my best friend."

Meagan turned to her, "Best friend? No, I don't... I don't have any friends."

"...I'll go get your grandma, just rest," her voice becoming shaky.

The nurse watched Meagan intently. "Go, now, thank you. I'll have her taken care of. I need to get Dr. Lawrence to examine her again."

Becca backed away and rushed out to the waiting room, spotting Meagan's grandmother walking down the hall. "Hello, again, dear. I thought you'd gone home? I was eating in the cafeteria."

"Meagan fell again. The nurse is there with her; she could use you," Becca explained quickly.

"What on earth?!" Meagan's grandmother scurried off past Becca.

"Where's the ICU?" a stern voice asked behind Becca.

The same receptionist from before concentrated on her monitor, replying: "You need authorization. Past here to your right through those double doors," the receptionist answered, not peeking around the screen.

"Fuck these hospitals," he grumbled, catching her eyes. He sped off in the opposite direction.

"Wait! James! Please!" Becca called, while nurses and doctors swarmed past her. He ignored her, continuing around the corner. She jogged past the check-in desk, but he was gone. Becca sat down in a waiting chair in defeat, her eyes starting to fill once more.

What happened to George? Did he try to hurt himself? Or did someone try to hurt him? I can't even go back there, and his family isn't even here.

Becca's leg shook anxiously, peering at the ICU entrance, realizing she needed a key card. More surgeons and nurses ran past her.

She knew where they were going.

It's impossible that James vanished into thin air. Did he get through the doors? I need to see if they've even called George's parents.

Becca stood up and turned to face the main desk.

"My key card? Where is it? Cassandra? Did you hide it again? I was gone, not even ten minutes!" Irritated, one of the nurses was rummaging through her drawers.

"Julie, I didn't see it, I didn't take it!" Cassandra she replied defensively.

What if James ... but how? I need to get back there, too!

Filled with determination, Becca marched to Cassandra and Julie and slapped her hands on the receptionist's desk. "I know what happened to that key card. My friend James is worried about our friend George. Because he isn't family and we're the only ones here actually concerned, he stole your keycard from you when you were distracted." Becca's eyes darted to Cassandra.

Julie sighed heavily, and Cassandra crossed her arms, saying, "Oh? Is that so? I'll go take a look, Julie. Stay right here. I'll be back." Becca watched as Cassandra made her way to the key card terminal and swiped her card.

I just have to wait for the perfect moment and sprint inside. I should be faster than her.

The double doors flung open.

Here's my chance!

Before Becca could think again, she sprinted through the hall, passing Cassandra and ignoring the shouts and screams.

"I need to see if my friend is okay! I need to know what's going on!" Becca rounded the corner. About ten rooms down, Becca could hear an authoritative voice yelling something about stopping the bleeding. She darted to the threshold and saw a bloodied face, the body unrecognizable.

"George? GEORGE!!!" Becca fell on her knees, screaming. She couldn't make out what the doctors and nurses were telling her. Arms lifted Becca, her feet like weights dragging on the floor.

Where did James go? I don't see him…

Becca finally managed to murmur, "What…happened…please…he's my friend…"

"Get her out of here! We have to keep him stabilized," the surgeon commanded

Becca raised her head, her eyes swollen, just able to make out Julia and Cassandra, who had hold of her arms, sitting her down in a chair.

"Did any of you see another person, a young guy with dirty blonde hair?" Becca broke down in a sob, feeling guilty she couldn't have been in two places at once.

Meagan is fine now, but George is on his deathbed. He was barely recognizable…

"We can't find the guy, but we did locate Julie's keycard on the floor. I'll have security take extra precautions so no one else unauthorized is back here. They can question him when we find him. Did you need water?" Cassandra kneeled beside Becca, staring aimlessly at the floor, shaking her head.

"Cassandra! Get her out of here!" The surgeon's deep voice shook Becca from her daze. "We need all hands on deck, he's lost too much blood, we only have one unit to give him…Cassandra, have you contacted his parents or relatives?"

Becca shook her head feverishly, "I need to see him! He needs me!" She cupped her face in her hands, not knowing what to do. Her friend was bleeding out, and she might never get to see him again.

Chapter 20

"Hey, is this George's mom? Hey, this is Cassandra. I'm a nurse at Arcae Hospital. I'm so sorry for bothering you, but there's been an accident involving your son. He has lost a lot of blood, but with his rare O- blood type, we only had one unit readily available. I urge you to come in. He's in a stable condition, but at any point this could change. Are any of you compatible?" Cassandra informed. "Hello, are you there?"

Cassandra backed away from Becca, straining to listen. She leaned against the counter.

The other end became still, no reply. "Are you there?" Cassandra repeated. "I know this can be extremely difficult to hear, but I need to know you understand what I'm asking."

"I'm here, and we'll be there," his mom replied flatly, her tone lacking warmth.

Cassandra opened her mouth to speak, but the phone went dead. "Great," she murmured.   "Well?" Becca demanded.

"All I can say is she's coming," she replied, hanging up the receiver.

"WHEN?" Becca's voice stretched across the lobby.

"I find it fucked up, the lack of emergency. I can't say anything, but she's coming." Cassandra explained.

'This is too much, I need some fresh air," she replied, leaving Cassandra at the desk.

Becca paced back and forth on the sidewalk, growing in panic— worried about George's blood transfusion, and desperate for a solution. She stared at her phone and thought about trying to get a hold of James to find out why he was acting the way he was, but remembered she never got his number.

What if...? What if he has the same blood type as George?

"Becca?" a familiar voice called out from behind her.

"Huh?" Becca shoved her cell in her pocket, turning to see Timothy raising an eyebrow at her.

"What are you doing here?" he probed, stepping onto the sidewalk beside her.

"Why do you care?" Becca remembered the turmoil he'd caused George not too long ago.

"Geez, what did I do to you?" Timothy kept his eyebrow poised, waiting for her to answer.

"Why are you here?" Becca demanded.

"I help volunteer with the blood drive. I donate blood, and give out water and snacks. I'm trying to build my college resume. Now, what about you? Are you donating?" Timothy took a step closer.

"I'm here for George and Meagan..." Becca trailed off, her anxiety heightened.

Timothy's eyes bulged. "What? George...?"

Becca stared down at the sidewalk. She sighed heavily and sat down on the brick wall, focusing on the purple tulips planted behind her. Her hair blew in her face as she spoke. "Yes, George. Were you called by one of the nurses? I mean... can't they see how bad he is? His family is just taking their sweet time, and the nurses don't even know what the fuck is going on!" Becca screamed as she broke down. Her nerves couldn't handle any more.

Timothy put a gentle hand on her arm. "What happened?"

Becca shook her head, her voice lowering. "Why do you even care?"

"Look, I get it! I fucked up! But I still care about him." Timothy replied empathetically.

"He was in a car crash. I'm not sure about all the details. He needs another blood transfusion. They've managed to stop the bleeding. I feel like all of this is my fault!" she admitted.

"Why do you think it's your fault?" Timothy pressed.

"Yesterday was my birthday...and I'd never had a party before, so I thought throwing one would make up for all those years of dealing with my mom leaving on my birthday. If I'd been paying attention to my friends, they wouldn't be in this mess. I didn't even think to check in on George because I was so worried about Meagan. First my mom, and now my friends." Becca hung her head down in shame, while Timothy listened intently.

"Don't blame yourself, it's a coincidence," he reassured. "I think I might be able to help. I have a rare blood type."

The words were music to her ears, hope flickering to life. "Do you think that's why they called you? Could you be a match?" she asked.

"I know I can. I have O negative, which means I'm a universal donor." Timothy clenched Becca's shoulder. "I'll do it. Let me speak to the nurses so they can start immediately."

He's willing to do this with no hesitation. Does he regret gaslighting George this summer?

"If you're doing this because you feel bad…" Becca started.

"I'm doing this because I still love him! The longer we debate this, the less time we have." Timothy's voice cracked in a higher pitch.

"I know, I know. I'm sorry," Becca replied gently, realizing she had set aside her bitterness.

Timothy nodded. "Are you coming?"

"Hannah, before we go into Meagan's room, I need to talk to you." Dom grasped Hannah's arm as the sun overhead beaded down on her face. Dom locked the car, giving her an unforgiving glare.

"Were you serious last night?" he asked, his voice low and urgent. "About being interested in me?"

Hannah's heart skipped a beat; her gaze met his. "Y… yes," she stammered, her cheeks flushing.

Dom's eyes locked onto hers, his expression fervent. "Good, because I need you to do as I say. Can you do that?"

Hannah nodded, her mind racing with questions, but she knew she had to trust him for now. "Wait." Her voice trembling. "I don't understand why Meagan doesn't remember me. It's like I'm invisible. Last night at Becca's party, when I stopped you, I felt seen for a moment. But now, with Meagan not remembering me, I'm scared I'll be forgotten, ignored, like I don't matter."

Her words spilled out in a rush, "You giving me your number last night felt like a lifeline. I couldn't believe you wanted to talk to me after I confessed my interest in you. But now, I'm terrified it's all just a fleeting moment, and you'll forget me too." Hannah's eyes searched Dom's, seeking reassurance, "Can you understand what it's like to wonder if anyone would even notice if you were gone?"

Dom leaned over and pinned Hannah's wrist up against the seat. A fresh spicy sandalwood aroma wafted in her nostrils that she hadn't noticed before; his expression was stern. "Focus on following my lead, Hannah, and play your part by staying here."

She could feel the hotness of his breath inches from her face. "I can," she squeaked.

"You're so fucking hot when you're submissive. If this goes well, I'll invite you over so we can work on your fears," he replied seductively, his thumb caressing the bottom of her chin.

Hannah leaned in. "Do you have feelings for me?" She noticed his thick veins bulging from his wrist and up into his forearm, tensing. She clenched her jaw, feeling his grasp grow tighter.

"You'll find out later," he answered and released her, breaking the stare.

Hannah rubbed her wrists.

"Where's Meagan's room?" Dom asked, unlocking the door.

Hannah hesitated before responding, "It's room 110."

"Becca, is there anything I can do? For Meagan?" Dom's helpless voice came from behind her.

Becca opened her mouth to reply to Timothy and stopped in her tracks, watching Dom walk up to them. "What the fuck are you doing here?"

"I felt guilty and wanted to apologize." Dom's voice was steady, looking Becca straight in the eyes. "It was an accident, Becca. She fell."

Becca narrowed her eyes at Dom, her suspicions growing. "Dom, what happened out there... You know... Meagan could've died."

Dom raised his hand. "Did you see what happened?"

"No, but—" Becca started.

"It was a tragic accident. I'm glad she's okay." Dom's expression remained calm— the sound of his voice almost detached from reality.

Becca's skepticism grew. "An accident? You and she were arguing, Dom. You brought another girl to my party, and I didn't even know about her. She ran out of the house because of you!"

"You don't know what you're talking about. I've been trying to help Meagan," he said coolly.

Timothy stepped forward, "Becca, stop. Let's just go," he suggested.

Dom's eyes lock onto Becca, a subtle smile on his lips. "That's right, Becca, go. I'm trying to help Meagan and Hannah."

Becca's face reddened at the mention of Dom and hearing Hannah's name. "You know, Dom, your intentions aren't good for them— or for anyone, for that matter."

Timothy jerked Becca's arm. "Are you coming or not? We don't have time!"

Becca crept quietly down the hallway, her eyes fixated on Dom's retreating figure as he made his way into Meagan's room. She hesitated for a moment, wondering if she should've gone with Timothy to do the blood transfusion, but her curiosity got the better of her. She didn't trust Dom.

Carefully and quietly, she approached Meagan's room as she heard Dom's smooth voice, "Hey, babe. I was thinking we could hang out with your grandma when you get out of here. I'm sorry I wasn't here sooner." Becca's eyes narrowed through the slit in the curtain at Dom. What was he playing at?

"Can I help you?" Meagan's grandma asked, her eyes focusing on Dom.

Dom smiled charmingly. "Hi, I'm Meagan's boyfriend. She's told me so much about you at work. I was worried sick about her."

The crow's feet in the corner of her eyes relaxed. "You can call me Josephine. It seems I don't know much about my granddaughter's life."

Becca watched, amazed, as Dom seamlessly played the role of Meagan's boyfriend. Dom inched closer to Meagan, but not enough to touch.

Becca watched Josephine throw her hands up in excitement. "Oh, Meagan, dear, I'm so glad you've found someone nice. You two make a lovely couple."

Meagan looked confused, her eyes darting between Dom and her grandmother. "Uh, yeah... I guess so," she said with uncertainty.

The twists in Becca's stomach made her uneasy. This wasn't right. She stepped forward, her voice low, but urgent, "Meagan, wait—"

"Wh... who's there?" Meagan asked.

Dom's eyes flickered to Becca's, a warning glint in their depths. He smiled, "Hey, Becca. What's up?" his voice sweet.

Becca's gaze locked onto Dom's, a silent threat passing between them. She knew she had to tread carefully. Dom gripped the sheets until his knuckles grew white, his fingers digging into the thin fabric.

"Nothing," Becca said finally, "Just...nothing," she repeated.

"Dom's smile grew wider. "Good. We were just having a nice conversation about our plans for this upcoming week.

Josephine stood up, her eyes shining with excitement. "Oh, yes! I'm just glad my sweet Meagan is okay. Maybe we can have a family dinner next week?"

Becca felt a surge of rage. This was getting out of hand. She took a step forward, her voice rising, "I don't think that's a good idea—"

Dom's voice cut her off, his tone sharp. "Actually, Becca, I think that's a great idea. We should all get together soon."

Becca's eyes flashed with anger. She knew Dom was trying to manipulate her, to keep her silent. She took a deep breath, trying to calm herself down.

Dom approached her, his voice dropping to a whisper, his words meant only for Becca's ears. "You know, Becca, I think it would be a shame if certain people found out about your little group venturing into the forbidden woods. I'm sure they'd be very interested in hearing about it."

Becca's heart sank. Dom had her right where he wanted her. She couldn't risk exposing their secret, not now. Her hands felt tied, her voice trapped in her throat.

She forced a smile, her eyes locked onto Dom's, playing the part of his scheme. "Have a great time, guys. I'll catch up with you later, Meagan." As Becca turned to leave, she felt Dom's eyes bore into her, his gaze heavy with triumph. She knew she'd have to find another way to stop him, but for now, she was trapped.

Meagan's voice called out after her, "Becca, wait! What's going on?"

Becca shook her head, her eyes warning Meagan to stay quiet. She knew Dom was watching, waiting for her to slip up. She had to get out of there before things escalated further.

Chapter 21

Timothy sat beside George's hospital bed, his eyes fixed on the steady rise and fall of his chest. He couldn't help but feel a pang of desperation, seeing George like this— vulnerable and helpless. Timothy's fingers itched to touch him, to hold his hand or brush the hair out of his face. But he restrained himself, knowing it wasn't the right time.

As the nurses worked around them, Timothy's gaze never left George's face. He memorized every detail— his left eyebrow swollen and stitched closed, bruises and cuts decorated his face, and a faint smudge of dried blood lingered on his cheekbone. His skin was pale and clammy, and his left arm in a cast. Timothy's heart ached. Why did he ruin a good relationship?

He'd do anything to protect George, to make him safe. Anything to be near him, to be the one he turned to. Timothy's thoughts swirled with ideas on ways to fix his relationship with George and to make him whole again.

The hospital room faded into the background, his focus on the blood travelling from his vein to George's. He felt like he'd be waiting forever for George to wake up, to see those piercing eyes open and know he was okay.

Timothy's fingers curled into fists, his nails digging into his palms. He'd wait as long as it took, do whatever it took, to make sure George was safe.

Once her adrenaline died down from Dom's threat, Becca felt exhaustion wash over her entire body. Becca fell into a daze, staring out the window from the waiting room. Her eye caught a cardinal on a branch outside the window. She wished she were one. Where she could fly away, how she desperately wanted to escape. Her 21st birthday hadn't gone the way she'd intended it to.

My birthday always turns into a disaster... just like with mom... if I hadn't messaged Dom to come, we wouldn't be in this mess. Although who knew Dom would upset her this badly? That prick. I feel so overwhelmed. Her grandma said she would keep me updated. I just need to wait and get some rest and hope George's blood transfusion is successful... his parents are some work. But first...

"You look drained. You should get some sleep." Timothy appeared over Becca, realizing she'd dozed off for a quick minute from her thoughts.

"You're right," Becca yawned. "But first, how did the blood transfusion go? Thank you for trying to save George. Can you believe his parents are still not here?"

"Are you serious? He looks pretty banged up, but I'm sure what I gave him helped tremendously. He still hasn't woken up yet, but we can't do anything else now." Timothy informed. "I'm going to try to visit him tomorrow and let him rest. You should, too," he looked down at his bandage before walking out.

"One more thing, before I leave," she said to herself, walking to the receptionist's desk.

"Can I get a pen and paper? I'll get out of your hair afterwards. I promise." Becca smiled, her thoughts settling.

"One sec," Cassandra walked behind the receptionist's desk and handed the materials she'd asked for.

Dear George,

I'm so sorry I left without waiting for your parents to get here. It seems they were in no rush, and it pissed me off. Every minute felt like it was my fault, like my presence was somehow bringing bad karma to those around me. My birthday always seemed to be cursed—the year my mom left, it felt like the universe was conspiring against me. And now, with both of you lying in a hospital bed... I couldn't shake the feeling that I'm somehow to blame.

I have to tell you something. Meagan fell again and... well... she doesn't remember us. Any of her friends, including you and me. Those memories of us just vanished. I'm still trying to process it all, but it's hard to see her like this.

I know I shouldn't have let you leave without talking to you, but I at least tried to make it up by staying here as long as I could. I need to get out of here for a bit. I hope Meagan's memories come back soon. You two have a connection like I've never seen. I promise you I'll be back to check on you tomorrow.

Please forgive me for leaving.

-Love Becca

Becca finished scribbling her apology; tears fell from her cheeks to the letter and splashed on the page. She folded the paper and handed it to Cassandra. "Can you please make sure George gets this? Or give it to the nurse taking care of him?"

Cassandra nodded sympathetically. "Of course, dear. I'll make sure he gets it. If he wakes up."

Worn out, Becca pulled her car door shut and slammed her hands on the steering wheel in frustration. She put the key in the ignition when she heard her passenger door abruptly open.

Becca reached over and slapped James in the face reflexively, being startled. The stench of death soured inside her vehicle. "James! Where did you go earlier? You stole a keycard!" She realized he now wore a hoodie in the summer heat. She breathed through her mouth to avoid the putrid smell.

James rubbed his cheek and huffed angrily, "If you can contain yourself for one second, I'll explain." he leaned back in the seat, his eyes gazing out at the parking lot. "I've still been trying to process what happened."

Becca rubbed her hand, "I've been on edge too. Those woods, and the stories about what goes on in them, but never thought we'd actually go in there."

James turned to her, his expression serious. "Did you feel anything? I know I wasn't exactly... with it, but you seemed to feel something."

Becca hesitated, her eyes darting away from James. "I don't know. It was like a pull or a presence, maybe. It was guiding us further into it."

James raised an eyebrow.

Becca shook her head. "It was guiding us to them, I think. And we are supposed to regroup about this— I mean, something pushed her off the cliff, they said. That's crazy, right?"

James nodded thoughtfully. "Whatever force it was, it seemed to work. We found Meagan, and we got her out of there."

Becca nodded, her eyes still distant. "Yeah, we did."

He cracked a smile. "Now, about the keycard. I've had my experiences. I can blend in if need be. Sorry about not telling you earlier. Here. Maybe you'll have some use for this." James reached underneath his hoodie and pulled out a confidential file.

"What did you find?" Becca's curiosity filled her as James slipped the manila folder into her fingers.

"Consider it your first opened, unexpected gift. Happy birthday. I felt like the bottle of alcohol just wasn't enough last night. I know I can be an asshat, but I genuinely care."

Becca was speechless. Breathless. Her mom's name was written on the tab; her fingers fumbled through the document. "Transferred to Arcae's Mental Institution. Patient... exhibits symptoms of extreme paranoia and hallucinations. She reports seeing and hearing things that are not there and believes that someone or something is watching her."

Becca's face went pale listening to herself read aloud. "Patient's condition deteriorated rapidly, and was transferred for further treatment and observation..."

I don't think I ever told him about my mom... so how did he...

"James... how did you know this was my mom? She... she left a long time ago..." Becca asked her voice shaky.

"You're dad. I spoke with him, after George was admitted. He was a train wreck at first, I had to console him. He thinks he made a mistake letting you have your own party since your mom left. I asked what happened, but all he gave me was an argument. I saw pain behind his eyes and asked what

179

his name was. And here, before I go, I found this, too; it must've been your mom's. It fell on the floor when I pulled the file." James reached into his gray gym shorts pocket and pulled out a dreamcatcher bracelet dangling from his fingers.

Its delicate brown hoop, with a small turquoise stone in the middle, held in place by a web of thin string. A few pieces of the string had been frayed, but the rest of the bracelet had been decorated in black and white beads. Only one feather dangled from the hoop, seeming a few were missing from the thread.

"Mom..." Becca's lip trembled, her tear ducts dried out from all the crying.

"I felt like finding this was fate, and I think George is going to be okay. I overheard them talking about recovery. I'll give you some space, after all, I need a shower, remember?" James chuckled, opening the passenger door and leaving her alone.

Does dad know about this? Other than what happened last night, we always tell each other everything.

She needed to speak to her father. Becca gripped the broken dreamcatcher bracelet, holding onto the only piece of her mother she had.

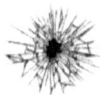

Meagan pulled her legs up to her knees. "I didn't think I had a boyfriend." She looked over to Dom. Her cheeks flushed.

"Of course you do. I'll stay and help as much as I can. Believe it or not, we were working on your phobia." Meagan felt Dom's hand on her forearm before she swiped her arm away. "Our progress has restarted. I came by because I wanted to tell you both how you fell."

"You do?" her grandma said, invested, perking up in her seat.

The room felt tense as Dom's voice rose, his words cutting through the air like a knife. "George and Becca are the two to blame for what happened," he informed, "if they hadn't been caught up in their own problems, they would've noticed something was wrong with Meagan. "

Meagan stared at her hands, puzzled. "I feel like I would remember if people were trying to hurt me, but I don't..."

"Clearly not. Look over your text history with me if you don't believe me." Dom voiced.

"Can I have some alone time with my granddaughter? I don't think accusing people is what she needs right now," Josephine cut in.

"Read the texts," Dom repeated before slowly walking out of the room.

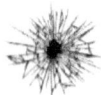

Hannah jerked her hand away, her eyes adjusting to the bright evening sunlight. "So, you're really going to play the concerned boyfriend card, huh?" Hannah's voice was laced with venom. "Calling Meagan your girlfriend like it's going to make everything okay?"

Dom raised an eyebrow, his expression calm. "I'm trying to get our names cleared, Hannah. We need to make sure we're not involved in whatever happened to her. You should be thanking me. Be grateful I got you out of this mess. We planted a seed to rift all three apart." Dom growled.

Hannah's jealousy simmered just below the surface. Now, she saw an opportunity to break him and Amanda apart. "You're really going to pin this all on Becca and George, aren't you?" Hannah asked sweetly, smiling.

"Yeah," Dom replied casually. "I can bend the truth for her to believe. I'm going to create new memories for her." Dom revealed.

"I won't play dumb! Those are my friends! You said you were apologizing. And call it off with Amanda. She's unpleasant to be around with her prissy attitude," she admitted, leaning against his car.

Dom glared at her. "I don't like to be threatened. How about you be a good girl and keep quiet, and I'll think about calling it off with Amanda. You do want me, no?"

Completely caught off guard, having the upper hand turned against her, "Take me home," she grumbled.

"Grandma? I'm so lost. Every time I try to remember something, my head hurts." She winced in pain.

"The nurses and doctors filled me in, sweetie. I promise I'll get to the truth." Meagan's grandmother sat with her at the bedside.

Meagan's eyes began to well up. "I keep having nightmares about my sister, and I need to know if I was the reason Michelle left." Meagan burst into sobs.

"Sweetie, please don't get yourself worked up. I need you to dry those eyes. I need you to listen. Your parents didn't tell you the truth about Michelle." Her grandmother's hands were wrinkled and worn, keeping at a careful distance from Meagan. "I still don't believe it," her grandmother said, her eyes clouding over with memories.

Meagan grabbed her pillow, bringing it to her chest like a shield, listening to her.

"Your sister Michelle was extraordinary. There was nothing she couldn't do. She made straight A's. She was taking college courses in high school. She loved volleyball, was on the debate team, and was the class president at the time. She had so much aspiration, so much energy! When your parents had you, her energy started to shift. Her positivity diminished. I was so blessed to have both of you. She knew your parents had put her on a pedestal so high. They wanted more and more from her. Michelle noticed they were starting to be hard on you.

"Meagan, you have to understand, Michelle tried to reach out to me, but your parents blocked any efforts to see her or remain in contact with her. Michelle snapped. She ran away, but with you. Your parents told you wrong. I wanted to stick with your parents' story to keep it simple, but they blamed you. It wasn't a car crash. I was living far away, and I'm not sure where Michelle was thinking about taking you. You were left, or she left you. I'm not sure. She was delusional."

"But between these delusions, she left you near the road. It was maybe a day, and we were all searching for both of you. We found you first... but by the time we found your sister... all that remained were her clothes. They didn't find her anywhere. A few days later, she showed back up at your parents, naked. She had scars all over, and she didn't seem right. Something sinister happened to Michelle. She blamed her parents and became violently hostile. The police were called and had to arrest her."

Meagan's heart sank to her stomach as she listened, gripping her pillow harder as her grandmother continued:

"They restrained Michelle and took her to the Arcae's Mental Institution. That's where it started. I saw it with my own eyes. Folks going into the woods and coming out deranged. That's why the woods are forbidden. My dear, have you ever heard of a wendigo? Native Americans believed spirits in the mountains would get into a host by means of cannibalism. They claim there's one that lives out in the..."

"Sorry to interrupt, but there's a detective here that would like to speak with Meagan," a nurse said from the curtain.

"I'll be back soon, sweetie. I'm sure they just want to see if you remember anything." Meagan hesitated, but leaned in and allowed her to kiss her forehead, still processing the truth.

After her grandmother left, Meagan nodded at the nurse— her head pounding.

Chapter 22

Becca stormed into the house, her frustration rising, seeing her dad passed out in the chair. "Dad, we need to talk," she said, her voice loud and firm.

Her dad looked up from his chair, a mixture of surprise and wariness on his face. "What's going on, Becca?"

"You know exactly what I'm talking about," Becca replied, her eyes flashing with accusation. "James told me you two talked at the hospital. What were you discussing?"

Her dad rubbed his temple. "Uh, geez, I never talked to James. Between the car crash and getting your friend to the hospital, I didn't have time to talk to anyone. You're the first person I talked to when I came home."

Becca's eyes softened. She wanted to believe him, but it didn't explain how James had a medical file on her mom. "Don't lie. I read Mom's transfer papers. How did he know about Mom?"

Her dad sighed. "Angel... I didn't talk to him. I have no idea what you're getting at. You're the only one—"

"Don't use my nickname against me... especially if you can't tell the truth. Leave me alone." Becca said, backing away toward her room. She slammed the door and locked it. She grabbed her paintbrush.

The paintbrush glided effortlessly, her running mind winding down with each brush stroke—a cardinal forming on the canvas. Painting was therapeutic to her anytime she was stressed out. The night crept in her room, casting long shadows across her face. Her eyes felt droopy as she finished the final touches of her new masterpiece.

Becca's head hit the pillow and slipped into an unconscious state. She was back in the hospital's entrance. The sun peeked its head from under the horizon, and a calm breeze gently blew into her face. A firm grip jerked Becca back: it was James.

"Hey, ow! Stop with the surprise scares! What do you want?" Becca questioned as James jumped at her remark. She jerked her hand away.

"What are you doing out here? The nurses need you!" James answered hastily.

"You're a bad liar," Becca retorted.

James didn't budge.

This doesn't feel like a dream...

"You have to save George and Meagan! It's all on you!" James informed.

Becca rushed back inside, the ICU doors open, but it was too late. George and Meagan lay motionless on their beds next to each other, their faces pale and still.

A voice whispered in her ear, "Why did you allow your friends to die?" She realized it was her mother. "Just like you did to me? Why'd you let them take me?" The words cut deep, and Becca felt a wave of guilt wash over her.

"I must be dreaming... I must be..." Becca murmured to herself.

"What makes you think you're dreaming? Hey, hello?" James asked from behind.

Becca turned around, the dream shifted. She stared in awe, her eyes meeting glass chandeliers and dark purple velvet wallpaper embroidered with gold roses.

"Where are we?" Becca wondered, seeing a dark mahogany podium.

"Our date, silly," James answered, ushering her over to a black glass table with two purple leather chairs and two glasses of wine awaiting them.

She'd never seen this restaurant before.

"You were going to explain your first masterpiece, a painting." James slid one chair out.

Becca took a seat. "My first painting?" she repeated.

"Yes, the one on the wall," James pointed behind her. "Go on, tell me about your painting," James urged, intrigued.

Turning her torso, Becca's eyes glimmered in excitement. Her first masterpiece hung on display. She stared at the icy mountain and the purple haze created with strokes so seamless and carefree. A shadow of a little girl stood in the distance, and a snowman about her height holding her hand. In the distance, an outline of a fortress.

Then the memories flooded back to her. The pain she felt, a memory she repressed. She faced James.

"I'm listening." James' eyes fixated on her.

Becca's mouth went dry. She grabbed a wine glass and sipped the chardonnay. Her taste buds expected it to be bitter, but it tasted sweet like cherry pie. It was thick like blood, but she sipped again.

Barely audible, she whispered. "I painted myself." She closed her eyes, seeing how blinded her younger self was. "The girl in the painting is me, frozen in time, right before... everything changed," she confessed.

James didn't comment; he was quiet and sat listening intently.

"The painting came at a time when I was so alone," Becca continued, her voice crackling. "My parents were always busy, and I just wanted someone to talk to, someone to see me. One snowy day, I escaped into my imagination, into the woods, and made the snowman. It was my friend, and that's where I fell asleep— lying on the ground, watching the snow fall from the trees.

My parents didn't notice I was gone. My dad was the first to figure it out. This was the winter before my mom was taken. They found me almost unresponsive in the snow, hypothermic and alone. It wasn't until that summer when they took her away that things changed. My dad finally was able to notice me." It took every ounce of willpower for her not to break down.

James took her hand. "I know. I wanted to see the real you."

Becca stared at their hands intertwining. "The real me?" She scoffed. "I painted the moment before I lost it all. The moment before my world changed forever."

James studied her, remarking, "I see it represents your pain. Nonetheless, it's a breathtaking painting."

"My pain…" Becca whispered.

"It shows your independence, but also your want for attention. Well, you have my attention." James revealed.

"I wanted to ask you, how'd you know about my mom?" The hair on her arm stood up as she asked.

James didn't reply; instead, his grip tightened around her fingers, squeezing. Her fingers cracked under his strength, his muscles tensing.

"Ow! What the fuck, James!" She tugged her hand, but he had a firm grip. His demeanor changed.

She cried out and stood up. James did the same, then pounced on her. She felt his fingers around her neck. The dream darkened, and Becca felt herself being pulled apart, her consciousness torn from her body. When she woke up, she was standing in the forest— feet bare, bleeding, and her legs trembling. She looked down at her hands, and they were no longer hers. They were pale and gaunt, with long fingers dripping with fresh blood that seemed to be moving of their own accord.

Becca tried to scream, but the sound that emerged wasn't hers. It was low and raspy, and it seemed to come from somewhere deep within her chest. Her mouth moved, but it felt foreign— like someone else was speaking with her face. She stumbled through the forest, her legs carrying her forward with a jerky, unnatural gait.

The trees loomed closer, branches seemed to reach for her, and the sky above became overrun by black clouds. The air thickened, humming with a presence that pressed against her back. Before she could turn, an invisible force yanked her backward. Her arms flung out, suspended. Rough briary vines thick as rope bit into her wrists, anchoring her to a tree.

Becca's body was frozen in fear, but inside she screamed— soundlessly, endlessly. She tugged at the bonds with everything she had, but her muscles didn't respond. It was as if something else had moved in, pushing her soul out. Her thoughts echoed in a hollow mind. She wasn't dreaming. She was occupied.

This has to be another nightmare, right?

The darkness swirled at the edges of her vision, creeping inward like ink in water. A chill slithered over her skin, and she suddenly became aware of her vulnerability. The forest air licked at her bare flesh. She was naked. Exposed. Helpless.

Then— a flicker.

A pulse behind her eyes. A heartbeat not her own. The pressure inside her skull cracked. She gasped, a real breath—hers. Her head lulled forward; she was still tied to the tree. But the feeling lingered— like something had worn her skin, and might return.

"Becca, sweetie, wake up," James whispered, emerging from the darkness, carrying a firelight. Yellow light caught the edges of his face. He loomed over Becca, his thumb grazing her chin, the touch sending a shiver down her spine. "Exhaustion must've consumed you, left you vulnerable... so fragile." His words hung in the air with an unsettling intimacy.

The stench of rot and wet soil reached her nostrils, and she coughed in his face.

James growled and wiped his cheek.

"Where... where am I?" Becca croaked, heart thudding. "What is this place?" she squinted, adjusting to the faint light, making out a dry, rotted cabin door and a soft white glow from its windows.

"Back in the woods, silly. You felt my presence before, no? The eerie feeling? Unnatural." James purred.

"Did you follow me home?" Becca mentally replayed her drive home, realizing she was too damn exhausted to even notice anyone behind her.

James snickered: "We have a winner! I didn't want to ask for a ride, or else your father would've denied our conversation, and I would look like a liar. I stole the keys to that nurse's car. I watched you through your bedroom window until you fell asleep."

James crouched behind the tree. "By the way, I'm through with this." Becca watched him return, clutching a handful of hair. Cassandra's hair. Her eye sockets were black, and a frozen scream was stitched on her face, with blood dripping from her severed head. James rolled the head over to Becca's foot.

Becca swallowed hard and turned her head, squirming at the rope, wincing in pain as the thorns ripped through her skin. but her arms remained tightly bound. "Who the hell are you?"

"Angel!" her mother's voice dispersed from James' lips.

Her blood iced. "Mom!?"

"Some people call me a wendigo. Others mimic. Shapeshifter. I'm forever evolving. I call myself the Weaver. I made one tiny mistake, and it was allowing a human to try to do the dirty work. Now? I wear them like masks. This body is breaking down, but yours? Yours is fresh," the Weaver explained, scratching off flakes of skin.

"You're a demon," Becca murmured to herself, noticing a red glimmer in James' eyes. "Why me?" Becca asked, alarmed.

James grinned maliciously. "Simple. You see, George is the perfect vessel. He's strong, resilient... and I need his body to fulfill my purpose. That's where you come in, Becca. All I had to do was lure you into your dream. You revealed to me your passion, your deepest desires, and your trauma. That's all I needed to get you vulnerable. I used this." He reached into his pocket and threw her mom's broken dreamcatcher bracelet at her other foot.

"Why do you need my body?" Becca asked.

James glared, and her heart thudded against her chest. "Your soul. You'll be an empty shell, and I'll wave you around like a puppet. And once I'm close enough, I'll discard you and take George's body for myself."

Becca's mind reeled in terror as the Weaver's plan unfolded. "And it wouldn't just be George who suffers," James continued, his voice deepened. "Your father will fall too. But not by my hand. No— You'll be the one who kills him."

His fingernails twisted and grew into black talons with a sickening crackle. He dragged them under her breasts, not with lust, but like a butcher tracing where to carve. Becca screamed, feeling vulnerable. Her mind splintered.

"Tell me, Becca, do you know how your mom died?" he hissed. The Weaver's words were a twisted game of psychological torture, and she was trapped, unable to escape the horror that was unfolding.

Becca shook her head, but her body betrayed her—her limbs went limp, her thoughts slowed to sludge as she hung from the trees.

"It's your fault, angel," her mom's voice erupted from the Weaver. "Why did you burn me? You started the fire."

Becca closed her eyes, shaking her head, denying her mother's voice. "I was only eight! I didn't know! I asked for help all the time—and you and dad just ignored me! You went out into the woods one day, and shortly after, you became deranged and started the fire— I was trying to make you happy and cook on my own! Dad told me you left; I repressed what happened for so long!"

Becca burst into a sob.

"It's your fault," her mother's voice pierced her heart.

This isn't real, this is a nightmare! I need to wake up—I have to!

With her eyes clenched shut, she took several deep breaths, then she flung her eyes open. The Weaver had vanished. She was still stripped bare, tied to a tree in the suffocating night. The moonlight flickered through the branches.

The solace of the night soothed her for a moment, but just for a moment.

Then pain. A searing bolt of pain through her neck. Her scream died in her throat. Tears streaked her face, and she bit her lips hard enough to taste blood.

"You're too innocent for this world," the Weaver breathed into Becca's ear.

Becca swallowed hard. His body began to twist and contort, his skin graying, his eyes turning a milky white. His limbs elongated. James' transformation accelerated, his face distending into a grotesque, antlered visage. He was no longer human, but a monstrous creature, driven by an insatiable hunger for human flesh and souls.

The Weaver's maw opened wide, revealing rows of jagged teeth. Shrilling sounds drowned out Becca's screams as the creature's hot, rank breath washed over her. It lunged.

Claws tore through her skin, and Becca felt something intangible— her soul— being yanked out thread by thread. She was trapped, unable to escape. The wendigo's jaw closed around her head, she drifted—falling through darkness, her breath gone, her vision dimming.

Her last thought came in fragments:

George…Meagan… Dad…

I didn't mean to.

I won't get to open my birthday presents.

Happy… birthday… to me…

Her heart gave one last beat.

Then stopped.

Chapter 23

Dom reviewed the plan in his head one more time, opening his closet.

Hannah wants me to break it off with Amanda, which I'm fine with. She's just another waste of space, just like the others. The end goal is to get closer to Meagan. Using Hannah is just the icing on top.

He pushed his clothes aside, uncovering the wall panel in the back of the closet. He brushed his fingertips across the newspaper clippings. The headlines of each girlfriend from this year and last year read "Missing Teen, Have You Seen Her?" Each of the girls' haunted faces lingered in his mind with the dark truth of what happened to them. Their innocent smiles in their photos knew what he'd done to them.

Their fears killed them, not me. I was only trying to help them get over themselves.

The doorbell's sudden chime shattered the silence, jolting Dom back to reality. For a moment, he stood there, mind struggling to shift gears. Then, he composed himself, smoothing out his clothes, and closed the closet door— hiding his secret.

He made his way to the front door and realized Amanda was just a doll. Just a pretty face.

Dom greeted her with a grin, motioning her to come in. "I'm glad you were able to come over on short notice tonight. I prepared a little dinner to get us in the mood."

Amanda's smile faded slightly as if something was on her mind. "You did? I wanted to see and talk to you."

Dom tilted his head slightly, "Oh, about?"

"About what happened last night. I did what you asked. I tagged along with you and was a bitch to the others. After we left, I was hoping I'd get what I wanted, but you only dropped me off at my house. We need to talk about that." Amanda walked past Dom and sat down in the kitchen. Dom turned around, shutting the door and following.

"From what transpired last night, I wasn't much in the mood, but I cooked us a special meal tonight. You know— romance to get us in the mood." Dom explained, standing on the opposite side of the table. He wanted to butter her up before letting her in on what he had in store for her.

"I'm only hungry for what's in your pants, Dom. And since you didn't hold up your end of the bargain, I wanted to raise the stakes. It felt one-sided." Amanda replied.

Dom raised a brow, moving around the table to tower over her. "Cut to the chase."

If we aren't having dinner, and it seems as if she isn't staying long, and she's asking these stupid little questions, why bother coming over?

"Well… I've been doing a lot of thinking, and I know we hadn't been together for very long, but I need to be with someone else. I just feel like you try too hard, telling me I have all these fears. I mean, look, I'm not afraid of anything."

She batted her eyelashes, glancing at the covered pot on the stove. "Okay, I see the candles and wine— are you trying to seduce me?' she said with a nervous laugh. "You're sweet, Dom, but you're really not my type. I go for guys who aren't so, um, intense."

"It's just... you seem kind of sensitive. And honestly? A little dark," she continued as Dom took a seat, "and I think I need to find someone I can have a fling with— nothing serious," Amanda admitted, her voice running through the words smoothly as if rehearsed.

He'd never had any intention of being with her. He needed to know her deepest fear, to exploit it, to use it against her.

"So that's what this is," Dom said, his smile tight. "You want a warm body, not a connection.

Amanda tilted her head unapologetically. "You read me right." She began playing with her nails, avoiding his eyes. "Summer's almost over. I don't plan on leaving for college with regrets."

"You brought someone else?" Dom asked, confused.

"Timothy," Amanda responded.

His face didn't change, but the chill in his eyes deepened. "Didn't know he was into girls."

"Neither did I. But turns out, he's more flexible than I thought." She smirked, teasingly. "We were thinking... maybe a threesome? I have him on speed dial." Amanda waved her phone in her hand.

"So," Dom stood up from the chair, "you want a threesome when you haven't even had sex with me yet?"

Amanda watched him, "Like I said, that's another reason why we wouldn't work out. I said I'd ask for both of us."

Timothy, hmm... tch... both of them try to get in everyone's pants. Wow, gotta hand it to them, they fooled me, but I always have the last laugh.

"That's too bad, because I prepared a kinky night for you," Dom shrugged, her words not bothering him an ounce.

"Oh? What did you plan?" Amanda asked curiously.

"You're going to let Timothy fuck you, remember? I wouldn't want to impose." Dom turned around so she wouldn't see his devilish grin.

"Well, now you've caught my attention. What...did you have planned?" Amanda probed. "I didn't take you as a kinky type of guy," she added, as he saw her simpering from the corner of his eye.

Dom fetched a box from the drawer next to the knives.

"Well, if you're THAT curious, Amanda, open the box." Dom placed the scarlet-colored box with a candy cane bow on the table in front of her.

Amanda didn't reply, but stared at it. She rested her fingertips on the lid and gently lifted it up.

"Oh? Hehehe, pink fuzzy handcuffs and a blindfold? You're into bondage?" Amanda ran her forefinger across the soft handcuffs.

"Why not? Felt like your kind of vibe, or am I wrong? Also, thought you'd like a little choke-play too." Dom winked.

"I do... I mean... It's on my list. I have a little time. Here's a thought —why don't you, Timothy, and I have some fun?" Amanda suggested.

"If you ask me, I suggest you start off with one dick inside you first. You need to get used to that first. I have the tool you need to get there. Sorry, sweetie, but I like being the only dominant one," Dom smirked.

Amanda thought for a moment, staring at the pink cuffs, and finally nodded in agreement, "I have some time."

"Good girl, now close your eyes and wait for me to instruct you further," he demanded.

Dom slid over to Amanda and took off her jacket. "Stand up, but keep your eyes closed," he commanded.

Amanda did as Dom directed. He took the box and her hand, leading her to his bedroom. He led her to the foot of his bed. "Now, take your sweater and pants off."

Again, Amanda did as she was told— stripping down to surprisingly lacey scarlet panties and bra.

"Get on the bed," he said softly.

Amanda followed his voice.

"Left wrist out. Be a good girl and I'll do the rest. You'll moan when I tell you to moan." Dom bit his lip in exhilaration as the handcuff clicked shut.

He felt a throb in his pants and allowed his dominance to take over. Amanda still had her eyes closed while Dom handcuffed her other wrist to the upper post of the bedframe. He began savoring the moment, stripping to his silky, black underwear.

Knowing he couldn't risk her peeking, he removed the black blindfold from the box, then slipped it over Amanda's head.

"Relax for me," Dom ordered, studying the slight tension in her leg muscles.

Amanda took a deep breath in and blew it out, nodding, knowing not to speak.

Dom removed her scarlet panties. He climbed on the bed, throwing her legs apart, inching down to her clit, licking, noticing her biting her lower lip. Trusting his intrusive thoughts, he wiggled his tongue more vigorously.

"Moan," he directed as he slapped his lips together.

"Mmuah," Amanda whimpered. "I'm getting close."

"Don't cum yet... You wanted choke play, right, sweetie?" Dom stood up from the bed.

"Yes, sir," Amanda said with a squeak.

"I have another kink I want to share with you, that will make my dick hard as a brick," he replied, reaching for his nightstand and pulling out an acrylic dagger, it's smooth surface comforting weight in his hand. He held it up, the dim light casting an eerie glow on its surface.

"What is that?" Amanda breathed heavily.

"Knife play," Dom smiled at his blindfolded prey. "Just a little something to spice things up," he said, rubbing his thumb at the tip of the blade.

"Is it one of those safe-edge play knives?" Amanda wondered, gripping the handcuff.

Dom didn't answer as he teased her with the dagger, tracing the blade down her sternum, his touch light and deliberate. Amanda's breathing quickened, her chest rising and falling in rapid succession.

"You're trembling," Dom observed, his voice low and seductive. "Are you scared?" The dagger traced her collarbone.

"No," she lied, her voice barely above a whisper, but Dom could feel the fear lurking beneath. "It feels sharp."

He lowered his head and stared at his throbbing dick, and his smile grew with amusement. "Don't worry, I'll take care of you," he insisted with sarcasm.

The dagger traced the patterns on her skin, while Dom's heart beat faster, his excitement building up as he ran the blade down to her thigh.

"Alright, open wide for daddy," Dom threw his underwear on the floor, before kneeling over her head, and shoved his dick in the back of her throat. "Now swallow."

Amanda choked, because of his unexpected action he presumed, but noticed she pulled away from him.

"What the fuck, Dom?" she coughed again.

He felt a rush of power, a sense of satisfaction he felt from his previous victims. With a swift motion, the dagger bit into her arm, precise and deliberate. Blood welled, spilling onto the sheets like ink on a blank canvas. Amanda screamed, the sound of terror echoing in his ears.

Amanda screaming in agony. "WHY—"

Dom held the dagger to her lips. "Shhh." He licked the blade. "I'm an artist. You're part of something eternal now."

Amanda shrieked, her body thrashing and kicking out toward Dom, who, in turn, jumped off the bed out of her blinded sight, and the cuffs held fast.

He backed away slowly and walked to the closet. The hinges groaned as he threw open the door and back panel, revealing the newspaper clippings and photos, his masterpiece shrine. He walked over to turn the lamp switch on and stepped aside, returning to Amanda to remove the blindfold.

"You see them?" Dom whispered. "All of them? Each one gave me a piece of their fear. Their truth. Their essence."

Her eyes took a moment to adjust— then widened, horror bloomed across her face. Dom could see the realization dawning on her. "You're... you're a serial killer," she stammered, her voice weak.

"Labels," he said with a shrug. "All I want is a harmless picture. A keepsake." He opened the top drawer of his nightstand and pulled out a Polaroid camera. "Smile."

Amanda whimpered, twisting her body violently, the cuffs rattling the bedframe.

Dom climbed on top of her, straddling her hips. Her sobs choked in her throat, blood soaking through the lace of her panties.

"Smile," he repeated, raising the camera. The flash snapped. Then another. And another.

He set the camera aside.

"Now... let's find your heart."

He raised the dagger higher, his face painted in blood, and began to carve into her chest. Amanda's final sounds sputtered from her throat, her hands pushing weakly against him—until they moved no more.

Chapter 24

Timothy drummed his fingers on the car's console; his eyes fixed on the house. Amanda had promised to talk Dom into a threesome, and if that happened? It could help him forget about Michael dumping him, about George. He wanted *out* of his own mind.

Timothy scrolled through his phone aimlessly, watching the time roll by.

Amanda told me to stay until she came out, but this is ridiculous. Am I supposed to let them fuck and have all the fun?

Timothy spun the car keys around his fingers, not sure what to do with himself.

I tore George down. I cheated. Michael dumped me. I helped save George's life—but he'd never take me back. So, we're even now, right? No more guilt. From now on, I look out for myself.

A high-pitched scream shattered the still night. Timothy jerked upright in his seat, staring at the house. There were no other houses nearby, so it had to be Amanda.

Slowly opening and softly shutting the passenger door, Timothy

203

crept to the nearest window, where he heard Amanda's scream. The shades were closed, but the lamp illuminated a bulky, silhouette figure standing with an outline of a long knife.

Fuck... did Dom...

"There, smile, you beautiful bitch." Timothy could make out Dom's muffled, deep voice from the closed window, followed by soft clicks from a camera and flashes of light. As Timothy leaned closer to the window, a twig snapped underneath his shoe. Timothy dropped low, pressing himself against the siding in fear of getting caught.

The clicking stopped, and the curtains snapped open.

"Did you bring that fuck with you?" he heard Dom growl from the window seal. Timothy didn't breathe. He didn't even blink.

"No?" Dom muttered, his voice fading deeper into the house. "Gotta clean this shit up."

Timothy stayed frozen in the shadows as he heard the curtains overhead pull closed. His head was spinning. The back door flew open, and Timothy moved to the corner of the house. Peering around the edge, he watched Dom emerge, shirtless and covered in blood, carrying Amanda's dangling body toward the edge of the woods. Timothy pulled out and raised his phone camera, zooming in to snap a few shots. Then something shifted in the moonlight.

A second figure—Becca. She was following Dom's silhouette into the trees, but something was wrong. Her skin was caked in dirt. Her clothes were torn as if she'd been crawling through the woods for days.

What the fuck is going on? I just saw her at the hospital earlier! What have I gotten myself into?

Timothy hesitated, waited a couple minutes, then crept along a straight path into the trees with only one goal in mind, making sure Becca was alright.

She's been going through a lot, but how the fuck is she here? Is she in on it with Dom? What happened between the hospital and now?

His heart thumped louder than his footsteps, which were focused on not snapping another twig. In the distance, he heard two words: challenge and run. Timothy stopped short of the clearing, seeing Dom charge at Becca.

The limp body pressed against his chest. This made the fifth soul for his collection.

Dom kept trudging through the leaves. He wasn't scared of being apprehended. He didn't care. They'd just let him go. The mayor was under his thumb, and the police wouldn't bat an eyelash.

I bet they've never seen a serial killer get rid of evidence like this …

Dom kept walking through the darkness until he came to the edge. Like he'd done with the other girls, he'd dump her into the void. Dom watched her head roll, her neck showing gashes from the brutal carving it'd taken.

"Can I play with her before you waste her?" Becca's voice came from behind Dom.

Dom craned his neck around to find her standing amongst the trees. "Becca?" his voice was rough with disbelief.

"Can I? Before you throw her into the gorge?" she asked sweetly, stepping out of the trees like she'd been there all along.

Dom stared. *What the fuck is she doing here? I never told her where I lived. What the fuck is this awful stench she's carrying?*

Dom laid Amanda down, asking: "How did you find me?"

Becca snorted. "I've watched you for a while. Dumping these bodies into the gorges below. This isn't your first, but you already know that. The mayor really thought he'd killed me?"

Dom's angry confusion made him ball his fists. "When did you become interested?"

"Oh, I've been interested in this routine for a while, but just stood back to watch. I'd love to play with you, too," Becca grinned.

"I'm not into necrophilia, or anything you're into. Sorry, hun, you're not my type," Dom growled impatiently.

Becca's grin faded. "I want to add both of you to *my* soul collection."

Dom crossed his arms, not amused. "You think you can scare me? I could overpower you in a second. And honestly, I love a challenge. You'd better run, bitch."

She tilted her head like a broken doll. He could feel her staring deep into his soul. Dom lunged. His hands closing around her neck, and something inside Becca *snapped*. Her body cracked. Her arms stretched. Her legs bent backward, animal-like. Her eyes rolled white. And then came the scream—not hers.

Dom was strangling Becca, and behind them, Amanda lay lifeless. Timothy covered his mouth as if he were about to scream. Beyond her were stars and an endless black sky. Panicked and awestruck, he watched the fight ensue.

Timothy switched his camera to night mode. It was worth a shot. No one would believe him if he described what he saw. Zooming in, he waited for it to focus.

Becca threw Dom like a ragdoll. Her bones cracked, shifted—until she towered over him. Ten feet tall. Claws. Hind legs. Not Becca anymore. The creature she'd become thrashed about and let out a high-pitched, inhuman squeal.

That's impossible. I'm outta here.

Timothy stopped the recording, turned, and sprinted. He didn't want to see any more.

Would the police even be able to stop this thing? What is it?

As Dom's gurgling screams ripped through the trees, Timothy slammed the car door shut. Behind him, something screeched— long, shrill, and *hungry*. He covered his ears as the windshield began to splinter.

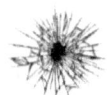

Timothy pulled into the police station, gripping his phone with the evidence. Not the video. No way. He's heard stories about what'd happened to people who wandered into those woods. Arrested if they were lucky. Disappeared if they weren't.

The front desk officer barely looked up when Timothy walked in.

"I need to report a murder," his dry voice said.

That got her attention.

Twenty minutes later, he was sitting across from two detectives in a stuffy conference room, his pictures of Dom—bloodied and carrying Amanda's body— he swiped through all of them.

A sitting detective leaned in. "You said this was taken nearly an hour ago?"

"Yes." Timothy traced his finger and showed them the time stamp.

"Where?" the other asked.

Timothy hesitated. "... last house on Whisperwind Drive."

The detective shifted in his chair; his lips twitched. "And what exactly am I looking at here?"

"What do you mean?" Timothy asked.

"These pictures are dark. Could be a Halloween costume. That blur? Could be anyone." The detective pointed out.

"No, that's Dom. I heard Amanda screaming. He carried her body into the woods!" Timothy protested.

Both detectives exchanged a glance. The one standing nodded and walked out.

The other smiled politely. "We'll look into it."

Timothy's stomach twisted. He knew that look. The same fake sympathy when doctors gave patients bad news. They weren't going to do anything.

Chapter 25

The soft hum of fluorescent lights buzzed above George's head as he lay in the hospital bed, propped slightly upright by a series of carefully placed pillows. His right arm rested in a sling, bandaged from elbow to shoulder. A dull ache pulsed through his ribs— remnants of the hemorrhage that nearly took his life.

Nick, his nurse, stood at the foot of the bed, clipboard in hand. "You'll be discharged later this afternoon," he chirped. "You'll need someone to help with daily activities for the first few days. Family, maybe? Friends?"

George didn't look up from his phone. "Yeah. I'll figure something out."

The silence returned, thick and pressing. It'd been nearly a week since he'd nearly died from internal bleeding. The car crash still replayed and flashed behind his eyes, but it wasn't the trauma that haunted him—it was the absence. Where were his friends? His parents? Was he that easy to forget?

Keep smiling. Don't let anyone see it's affecting you, just like when you found out your dad cheated on your mom. Or when your parents argue and you distract your siblings. Or that you love men. Or when you realized Timothy was cheating on you. Or realizing

James was going to kill you!

You're in physical pain.

It's fine, this can work. I didn't want to die like this. Not from a backstabbing prick like James.

He swallowed hard, turning the phone face down. He'd always figured things out on his own, but now, it just felt empty. His thoughts drifted toward Meagan. She hadn't texted either.

I chose to be alive but—

"George? Can you hear me? Hey, hey!" Nick's sweet voice snapped him back into reality.

"Oh... sorry... I was just..." George trailed off.

Where is he? Where's James? That bastard was going to kill me!

"Don't get yourself worked up. I was just saying I needed to know who was going to pick you up after being discharged. Who should I put down?" Nick asked, clicking his pen.

"Me..." he replied, unsure. He stared past Nick, concentrating on the chair backed against the wall. "My mom left a voicemail on Monday. Said they were leaving me clothes and that Dad wanted me to take responsibility. Handle my own mess, even paying for my medical bill."

Nick didn't write anything. Just waited.

George exhaled sharply. "But they never came. No visit. No clothes." He glanced down at his hospital gown, picking at a loose thread. "Guess I'm walking out in this."

There was a beat of silence before Nick moved forward a little. "What size are you?"

George raised a brow, "Medium? Why?"

"I'm about your size. If you don't mind waiting until my break, I can swing by my place and grab you something more comfortable." His tone was casual, like they were already friends.

George's voice softened. "You don't have to do that."

Nick shrugged. "I know, but I want to."

Nick's pen dropped and clacked on the tiled floor, and without warning, everything seemed to distort. Words caught in George's throat, and the air grew thick. The chair across the room, still harmless, suddenly felt like he was staring at James' empty truck seat. The echo of the gunshot that almost killed him rang out, and his pulse thudded in his ears. He became apprehensive as all the events flooded him, and then the anxiety sank in. He gripped the sheets.

"Did James get away? He was two seconds from shooting me! What if he's out there, right now, waiting?" George cupped his cheeks in his hands, realizing he was taking in giant gulps of air — an anxiety attack. His vision blurred, and his throat closed.

I can't do this. No, no, no, no—

"I can't... I can't..." he whispered, tears springing to his eyes. The beeping steadily increased from the monitor as his heart rate jumped. "He was going to kill me. He was—"

"Hey, George, look at me!" Nick's voice cut through. "We need to get you calm. I know you might be remembering a traumatic event. You're safe. You're not there anymore." His voice firm, but warm.

He shook his head wildly, turning his attention to Nick. "I can't, I can't breathe!"

"You're having a panic attack," Nick said gently. "It's okay. We just need to slow your breathing. Focus on my voice, alright?" He moved closer, kneeling beside the bed so George could see him clearly. "I need you to take a deep breath for me. In. Hold. Out. With me now."

He followed Nick's lead, struggling, pulling in a deep jagged breath, holding it for a few seconds, and both of them let out huffs of air.

"Again," Nick said. "You've got this."

They did it together. Once. Twice. Five times. George still trembled, but the storm in his head began to settle.

He'd taught himself to do this years ago— at ten, crouched under blankets with his arms around a stuffed animal, quietly trying to hush his own world while chaos erupted behind his bedroom door. But this time it was different. Someone else was with him. Someone else was *helping* him breathe.

Nick rubbed George's back. "Good job. You know you've been quiet most of this week, checking your phone. What's on your mind?"

"Sorry, I've never had anyone calm me down before. I'm not used to someone watching me have an anxiety attack either. And... no... I don't have anyone to take me home." George found himself gazing into Nick's honey-colored eyes.

"Oh! Maybe this will help. One of the other nurses handed this to me a few days ago. I should've let you read this sooner." Nick gave a warm, consoling smile, fishing out a crumbled paper jammed in his shirt pocket. "Here."

George unfolded the letter and read it slowly. His heart sank when he finished, but he kept his composure.

George reread it. *Tomorrow. But that was five days ago.*

"My friend... Becca... she never came," he whispered.

Nick glanced up from his clipboard. "No?" He looked genuinely surprised. "I thought she'd at least texted you."

George shook his head slowly. "Nothing. Not since..." he trailed off again. His chest tightened—not just from the stitches. Something felt wrong.

"Well, maybe something came up. I'm sure she meant to," Nick reassured.

George wasn't sure. The silence felt pointed now, heavy.

Nick set the clipboard aside. "Hey, if you're okay with it, I can drive you home after my shift ends. It's better than sitting around here worrying; besides, the doctor isn't going to discharge you walking home with those stitches."

George looked up, grateful. "You sure?'

"Yeah, I don't mind."

But before George could respond, the curtain brushed aside. Timothy strode in with a half-assed smile and tired eyes, holding a small iced coffee.

"Guess who still remembers you exist?" Timothy quipped, eyes flickering between George and Nick.

"I'll just be out in the hallway," Nick informed quickly and stepped out.

"Timothy?...how did you know?" George looked confused.

You said it yourself, clear as day, you weren't going to ever talk to him again.

The soft thumping footsteps came toward him, and Timothy managed to give him a nervous smile. "I brought you a pick me up," he placed the iced coffee on the overbed table, staring at his casted arm.

George took a deep breath, his stomach tying into knots seeing him again.

Timothy took a breath, fingers twitching. "First off—look, I know I messed up— a lot. But... after your surgery, I—" he paused, forcing the words out. "I told them to use my blood. I was your donor."

George's expression went blank. "What?"

"I asked if I could. I wanted to do something right after everything I—" Timothy paused. "I never wanted to see you hurt."

George blinked slowly, absorbing the information dump. "You didn't even visit."

"I wanted to. I didn't think I'd be welcomed," Timothy admitted.

A silence passed between them. George looked away, jaw tight. "How did you know I was here?"

Timothy hesitated. "...Becca."

George's head snapped back. "Becca?"

"I got a call from a nurse, needing my blood type, and I met Becca here. We stuck two and two together. That's how I knew." Timothy looked at the open note on display in George's lap. "You got a note from her?"

George smoothed the page, his voice dropping. "She said she'd come check on me. That was five days ago."

"George..." Timothy's voice changed—lower, more serious now. "I don't think she can."   George's stitches itched. "Why?"

"I saw something. In the woods. Near Dom's place. I followed him out there... into the woods, you know. George, he killed Amanda. Becca was with him. At first, I thought she was in on it—" he broke off, his voice tightening. "She looked like she was changing. Like something... wasn't human anymore."

George's eyes widened. "Shut up."

"I have proof. I took a video—"

"No." George held up his hand, his voice crackling. "Don't. Don't say another word."

"You need to see it, George. You need to understand what's happening—"

"*I said stop!*" George's voice rose, sharp and hoarse. "You're lying. She's fine! She's just busy. I don't want to hear it. I don't want to see anything. I don't want to know."

Timothy froze, mouth half-open.

George shook his head slowly. "Whatever you think you saw... it wasn't her. Don't make this into another game. Not with Becca. I appreciate you saving me, but I never asked you to."

"I just... wanted to make things right," he said quietly. "I didn't come here to hurt you again."

George looked away, eyes glassy, "Then stop trying to force a version of me that forgives you."

Timothy looked like he wanted to say more, but nodded instead, slowly backing off.

Nick's voice broke the tension. "It's time for George to eat." He plopped the lunch tray down beside his iced coffee.

George watched Timothy shift his attention to Nick. "Of course. I've got to get home anyway," he said, scurrying out.

"You're not okay. I can tell." Nick studied George intently.

"I'm fine." He squeaked.

"Stop hiding. I can tell by your voice you're not okay. It's fine if you're not." Nick gently pressed on George's shoulder.

His mask unveiled, and he couldn't hold back the tears. He broke out in a sob. "Nothing is fine. My parents don't care about me, my childhood friend tried to kill me, my best friend is suffering from memory loss, my ex saved my life to hold it over my head, and I'm tired of pretending to be someone I'm not." His face dropped into his hands.

"Oh, boy, you've gone through so much in such little time! I wouldn't even know where to begin on how it feels to be in your shoes right now. I'd cry too," Nick reassured.

George wiped his eyes. "You don't have to be extra nice to me. I'll manage on my own," he said with uncertainty.

I don't want to do this by myself.

Nick gave a small smile. "You *could* manage on your own. But you don't have to. There's a difference."

George looked at him, hesitating. "You still offering a ride home?"

Nick nodded. "Absolutely."

George took a shaky breath. "Would it be crazy if we could... leave a little earlier than planned? Like, right now, early?"

Nick blinked, caught off guard. "You want to discharge right now?"

"Yeah," George said, wiping his nose with the side of his wrist. "I just... I need to get out of here. I don't want to sit around waiting for more people not to show up."

Nick didn't speak right away. He studied George carefully, as if weighing more than just his vitals and charts. Then he gave a thoughtful nod.

"I can talk to the doctor. You've been stable yesterday and today, and if I make a case for it.... yeah. It's possible."

George's shoulders lowered slightly, like some small weight had lifted. "Thank you."

Nick stepped closer, lowering his voice. "Where are we going?"

"I need to check on a few people. It's complicated." George scratched his chin.

Nick smiled faintly. "That seems to be your theme lately."

George almost laughed, but it came out more like a breath. "Yeah. Story of my life."

Nick tapped the lunch tray with two fingers. "Eat something. I'm going on my break in a few minutes, and I'll go talk to the doctor. Afterward, I'll head home and get a pair of clothes for you. If you're serious about this, I'll help get you out of here early this afternoon."

George looked at the untouched food, then back at Nick. "Why are you doing this?"

Nick shrugged. "Because you need someone. And I *want* to help you, George. Not because it's my job. Not because I feel sorry for you. But because I see you matter."

That hit George harder than he expected. He looked down, quietly nodding.

Chapter 26

The soft hum of the car's engine filled the silence as Nick steered the old Honda through the quiet residential street. The afternoon sun filtered through the windows, warming the dashboard. George sat in the passenger seat wearing an olive-green t-shirt and white cargo shorts Nick lent him, with his bandaged arm resting awkwardly in his lap, and a small white envelope clutched in his hand.

"The doctor gave me a note if you need it for work," Nick explained, glancing briefly toward him before returning his eyes to the road. "You're supposed to take it easy for about a month. It includes some recommendations... like having someone help you with basic tasks."

George unfolded the slip and frowned. "A month... great." He sighed. "Guess I'll have a lot of free time."

"Yeah. I figured you might need something to keep you occupied, you know? Just so you're not alone with your thoughts all day," Nick said, rubbing the back of his neck.

George looked up. "Like what? A puzzle?" He tried to joke, but it fell flat.

Nick chuckled softly. "Not exactly. I was thinking more like...a distraction. Someone to hang out with. Like... me... if that'd help."

George turned his head, giving him a cautious glance.

Nick caught it from the corner of his eye and quickly added, "Only if you're cool with it. I mean, just as company. No pressure. I wouldn't overstay my welcome or anything."

George stared at him, unsure how to respond. His chest ached, not only from the injuries but from the realization this was the first time someone had offered to stay, because they wanted to.

Is he flirting? Am I imagining that? Does it matter? He means it.

"You want to keep me company?" he asked, oblivious.

"Maybe I do," Nick said, his voice calm, but his eyes searching George's face before switching back on the road.

There was no pity in them. Just warmth.

George felt a strange flutter in his stomach. He wasn't used to being wanted— for anything, especially not like this.

After a pause, George nodded quietly, "I think I'd like that."

For the first time in what felt like forever, the air didn't feel so suffocating. The drive was quiet after that. George found himself glancing at Nick between streetlights, catching how his jaw tensed when the road narrowed or how he drummed his fingers against the wheel to an imaginary rhythm. He was handsome in a quiet way—nothing loud or obvious, just solid. Grounded.

George didn't say anything. But he didn't look away, either.

Nick slowed as they turned onto Becca's street. "This it?" he asked, nodding toward the trailer by itself.

George swallowed. "Yeah."

Something about the house felt... off. It was still. Too still. No breeze. The tree branches didn't even sway.

George sat frozen, hand on his seatbelt, but not moving.

Nick glanced at him. "You don't have to go up alone."

"I think I do," George said, though he wasn't sure he believed it.

Nick reached over without hesitation and touched his wrist lightly, just enough to anchor him. "I'm right here. Let me help you out. I mean it."

George hesitated, then gave a small nod. "Okay."

Nick slipped out of the car and rounded the front, opening the passenger door with a soft click. "Here," he offered. His thick, warm fingers waved out to him with an invitation. George blushed slightly, taking his hand, his grip instinctive, but the moment he tried to move, pain laced through his abdomen. His breath hitched, and his cast arm moved to his stomach on instinct, trying to cradle it, afraid he'd tear apart.

"Wait," George muttered, wincing. "Shit."

"I've got you," Nick crouched slightly, bracing George as he eased forward inch by inch. Every shift pulled at his stitches, sending a burning ache up through his chest and down his side.

It took both of them to get him upright. George leaned heavily on Nick, his legs trembling with effort. Sweat broke across his brow in the humid air.

"Pain not manageable?" Nick asked under his breath.

"Not even close," George managed a thin, humorless smile.

They took the walk to the porch slowly. Each step felt like it would split him open again. The world narrowed to his feet and the throbbing beneath his ribs. He could barely pay attention to anything else—the peeling paint, the warped boards underfoot; all of it blurred behind the sting in his body.

When they finally reached the top, Nick let him go just enough to let George press the doorbell. His finger trembled against the button, and a soft chime echoed inside.

No answer.

He waited. Rang again.

Still nothing.

Then he saw it— the door. It was open. Just barely. A crack wide enough to let in— or out— a single breath.

"Nick?" George called, voice tight. He felt his neck hair stand on its end.

"I see it," Nick whispered.

George placed a trembling hand on the wooden door and pushed. It creaked open, and a wave of sulfur and rot hit him instantly. George gagged and stumbled back.

"Jesus—" Nick caught him. "George, don't go in—"

But George inched forward, ignoring the burning sensation from the stitches, and covered his nose and mouth. Blood splattered on his face and clothes, and everything felt distant. Behind him, he heard Nick shouting his name—

Then came the wet slap. A curtain of guts dropped from the ceiling with a thick, squelching sound like the house had been waiting for someone to cross the threshold.

George stood frozen. His stomach twisted, and bile burned in the back of his throat. He took a breath in with his mouth, and the stench of decay coated his tongue with sour death.

"I... Is that... Becca?" George barely recognized his own voice, dazed and drifting as if underwater.

"No... It's male." Nick said, his voice felt miles away. "GEORGE!" Nick's voice cracked as he grabbed him from behind, yanking him back. "Don't look." Nick threw his arms around George, pressing him into his chest and blocking his view.

"Becca... where's Becca... who... what happened... BBEEECCCAA!" George's scream tore out of him like an animal in pain.

PLOP.

A dull, meaty sound hits the carpet. They both turned. A man's head lay on the rug.

Becca's dad.

George's eyes widened. His adrenaline surged. He tore free from Nick's grip. "I need to see if Becca's in there... I need to see..."

"Not with those stitches you're not," Nick warned.

"But I have to—" George started.

"You can't track blood in the house, or the police will think you did it," Nick cut in. You can't jump either, or your stitches will pop. We need to think of something else."

George nodded and scanned the yard, eyeing the tarp covering the pool. "What if we laid the tarp over the blood and guts?"

Nick nodded in agreement and sprinted forward into the grass and snatched the tarp with a jerky, upward motion, fleeing back to the house with a long cape fluttering behind. George studied him as he leaned against the wooden railing and, with one smooth movement, flapped the tarp over the gruesome scene; the head watched them tread carefully in.

The trailer was dim and cold. Dust hung in the air. "Becca!" he called.

They passed the living room where they'd played their card game not even a week ago, then the kitchen where he'd dumped the rest of the alcohol. Hallway. Bathroom. All untouched.

Then, the last door at the end of the hall. George hesitated, slowly turning the knob. Inside: a desk, a TV, books knocked off shelves, a lamp tilted precariously on the nightstand. Her bed— the sheets were off, the comforter on the floor. A finished painting of a cardinal and unopened birthday presents in front of her bed, but the window hung open.

No. No, Becca...

George couldn't move. Becca was missing.

Who did this?

His mind spun. Questions collided and overlapped, voices whispered, each one louder than the last, until they no longer sounded like his own thoughts.

Nick grabbed his shoulders and shook him gently. "Hey. Hey, George. Come back to me. You're safe. You're with me."

George blinked, eyes burning, and a sob escaped his lips. His inner child—desperate to be strong— buckled under the weight.

Don't let him in. He'll leave like everyone else.

But Nick said nothing. Just wrapped his arms tighter around George, one hand cupping the back of his head. He rocked him slowly, whispering soft, unintelligible reassurances. And George realized he was careful not to press too hard on his broken arm.

Finally, the sobs settled into sniffles, the only sound echoing in Becca's empty room. Nick leaned back, cupping George's face, wiping the blood and tears from his cheeks.

"Are you okay?" he asked softly. "We need to call the police. Just in case whoever did this comes back. Your friend—maybe she escaped. Maybe she's hiding. Let's get out of here. Why don't I take you back home?"

"No, wait—" George hesitated. "I need to check on Meagan and Hannah. Please, they haven't contacted me either. I need to know if they're okay."

Nick thought for a moment and sighed. "Fine, but then I'm taking you home."

George fumbled for his phone. "I… I'll call," he announced, dialing, peering down at the blood drying on his clothes. "Shit…"

He could feel Nick's eyes evaluate him. "You don't have to say your name. Just report it and hang up."

"No, it's not that… your clothes. They're ruined. I… I'll pay you however much it costs… I'm sorry," George stammered.

"I'm not worried about clothes. You don't owe me anything, it's alright, I'm more worried about you," Nick replied sweetly.

George nodded shakily and pressed the call button.

"911, what's your emergency?" The operator asked.

George gripped his phone, deepening his voice. "There's a body. A man's body. At Lynn Road. 314 Lynn Road."

"Okay, sir, can you tell me your name?" The operator demanded.

"Just... please send someone. There's blood. A head. Guts. I think something really bad happened here," he informed calmly.

"Are you at the residence right now?" The operator probed.

George glanced at Nick before whispering, "No. Not anymore. I just... I found it and left. Please. Someone could still be in danger."

"Understood. Units are on their way." The operator informed them, "Is the front door open? Is anyone inside?"

"The door was unlocked. I didn't see anyone else— but the girl who lives there... she's missing." George replied numbly, keeping it together.

"Do you know her name?"

He paused and closed his eyes, replying softly, "No. I just know something's wrong."

"Alright. Thank you for calling. If you remember anything else, call us back."

George hung up before she could say more. His fingers were still trembling as he exhaled a shaky breath. "Alright, let's go."

As Nick's Honda pulled into Meagan's driveway, George's eyes locked onto a familiar gray Toyota Camry.

Meagan... if this motherfucker is here, I swear I will break him.

"Damn," Nick muttered, shifting the car into park. "You wear your emotions on your face. You look pissed."

George was already unbuckling. "Dom's the reason Meagan lost her memory. He played her, got her thinking it meant something, and the next day... He had a girlfriend. Then he mocked her at Becca's party. And now she has the nerve to ignore me while he's parked in the driveway?" He grumbled, Nick helping him to the front door, fist clenched.

Nick followed cautiously, steadying him. "Still doesn't explain why she would let him in," he pointed out, side-eying the Camry.

"I'm about to find out," George growled, ringing the doorbell hard. "She hasn't even texted me back once."

Inside, footsteps shuffled. Someone stumbled.

"Hold on, Grandma! I'll get it!" Meagan's voice rang out.

Her voice. George's heart clenched.

The door cracked open, and Meagan peeked out. Confusion spread across her face as she studied the blood-soaked clothes. "... Can I help you?"

George blinked. "It's me. George. I... I came to check on you. From the hospital? You—you don't remember me?"

Her brow furrowed, eyes narrowing. "George? I don't... I'm sorry, do we know each other?"

A voice echoed from inside. "Who is it, babe?"

Dom.

George's blood boiled.

Meagan glanced over her shoulder, then stepped outside, pulling the door shut behind her.

Dom's voice got louder. "Is that *him?*"

Nostrils flaring, a wave of rot washed over George. "What the hell... is that smell?"

Meagan looked back at George, ignoring his comment. "Dom said... you might come by. Said you'd probably try to confuse me or say weird things."

George stepped forward, ignoring Nick's quiet warning behind him. "Meagan, we were best friends. You said we were in this together before, just us. I don't know what he's told you, but it's not true. He's the reason you're like this."

Meagan looked overwhelmed, torn between politeness and discomfort. "Dom told me... You pushed me that night. I ran into the woods because of something *you* said. That I fell because I was scared of you."

George's jaw clenched and his stomach twisted, the stitches adding to the gut-wrenching pain. "He *what?* That's not what happened. You were upset. He embarrassed you in the bathroom. I followed you to make sure you were okay."

Her voice grew colder. "He said you'd say that too."

"You can't seriously believe him!" George pulled out his phone, desperate. "Look. Look how many times I've texted you. Checking in. Making sure you were okay. You *meant* something to me. You still do."

Meagan didn't even look at the screen. "I haven't gotten any messages," she said quietly. "I... I don't know what to believe. I don't *know* you."

From behind the closed door, Dom called again. "Everything alright, babe?"

George's voice cracked. "He's manipulating you. He's lying. He probably took your phone and deleted the messages—"

"I think you should leave," Meagan cut in stepping back toward the door. "I'm sorry. But I trust Dom. He's been honest with me. And you're... you're just some guy who showed up all bloody and yelling."

George stared at her. Hollow.

Nick stepped in. "Alright. Let's go."

But George didn't move. He couldn't. He doubled over, Meagan's words hit like a blow, clinching his right arm over his stomach.

"When he hurts you, and he will, I won't be there next time to save you." he warned, gritting his teeth.

Nick had to physically pull him back toward the car.

Doors shut. George didn't say a word.

Nick glanced over. "She doesn't remember you. That's not her fault."

"She's alive," George muttered. "But she's not *her*. Not while he's poisoning her like this."

He stared at the house one last time.

She doesn't remember me. And he made sure of it.

'So, where to now?" Nick asked.

George stared down at his phone.

Hannah. The last one. The only one who might still give a damn.

229

"Hannah! Open up!" George pounded his fist against the screen door. It creaked, and Hannah appeared still wearing her apron from work, eyes sunken, with dark circles. Her ginger hair was in a sloppy bun, and she looked like she hadn't slept in days.

"George...? What time is it..." her eyes droopy, her voice groggy.

George ignored the question, "You didn't answer a single text. Meagan didn't. Becca didn't. You all just dropped off the face of the earth."

Hannah blinked slowly, "I... I've been working doubles. Every day. I took all your shifts— and Meagan's. I needed the money, and they needed the coverage. What happened to you?"

George stepped closer, ignoring her. "Becca's missing, and Dom's messing with Meagan's head. Did you know that?"

Hannah tensed, her eyes narrowing to his reddish-brown stained shirt. "I didn't think it was my place, George. But no... I didn't know he was doing that to her. Not like... that. And Becca... missing?"

"You knew." His voice rose in agitation. "You knew Dom was messing with Meagan. You knew something had happened at Becca's party. You saw how upset Meagan was."

"I didn't want to be involved. I just wanted to keep my head down," Hannah mumbled.

"Well, good job." George snapped. "Becca's missing. Her dad is dead. Someone hung his guts from the fucking ceiling like party streamers. I watched her dad's head roll across the carpet." He grabbed the hem of the shirt and waved it around, proving the gravity of the situation.

"What...? Oh my god, no..." Hannah uttered in horror.

"She said she would come by the hospital to check on me. She didn't. And now she's gone." George's voice trembled with fury. "Timothy told me something's wrong with her. That she's... changing."

"Changing?" Hannah responded.

"He claims she's not herself. Claims he saw something in the woods. I didn't want to see the video. I couldn't. But he said she transformed. Like she wasn't even human anymore," George clarified.

Hannah staggered back from the threshold. "What the hell are you talking about?"

"I don't know," George replied sharply. "But I know you knew something and said nothing. You wanted to stay out of it? Well, guess what, Hannah? You're already in it."

"I didn't know it would go this far..." she choked. "I didn't think—"

"You didn't fucking think. That's the problem." He cut her off, bitter.

"George..." Nick spoke softly from behind.

"If Meagan dies, her blood will be on all of us. But especially you. You could've said something." He turned before she could answer, storming back toward Nick's car. Each step on his own felt like a knife twisting into his stitches until he fell up against the car, almost collapsing.

"You have some explaining to do," Nick replied, holding him up to catch his breath.

Chapter 27

Meagan closed the door softly, pressing her back against the white painted wood. Steam curled around the hallway, the scent of citrus shampoo barely masked a sour, earthy odor wafting through the air like wet leaves rotting under the sun. Dom emerged from the bathroom, towel slung around his neck, water glistening on his shoulders. His skin was flushed from the hot shower, but it did nothing to hide the unpleasant smell clinging to him.

He raised a brow. "That wasn't the pizza guy, was it?"

Meagan wrinkled her nose subtly, "No. It was George."

Dom rolled his eyes. "Oh? What did that weasel want?"

"He was checking in on me." She crossed her arms. "He seemed worried. And... he thinks you have something to do with my memory loss. I want to know why you two have issues. He was also covered in blood."

Dom huffed a humorless laugh. "That weasel's always been jealous. He can't stand the idea of someone else helping you. Covered in blood, eh?"

Before she could respond, her grandmother stepped into the hallway holding a delicate object in her wrinkled hands. It was a dreamcatcher—

intricately woven with pale threads and baby blue beads; a small feather dangling in the center.

"Meagan," she said, ignoring Dom, "I finished the new one. I thought you might like to hang it above your bed tonight."

"Oh," Meagan said with a faint smile, stepping forward to admire it. "It's beautiful, Gram."

The moment Dom saw it, Meagan noticed, his face strained. His eyes darted between the dreamcatcher and her grandmother's face like he was reading something hidden beneath her calm expression. "Cute," he muttered, shifting in place.

Her grandmother's eyes barely narrowed, "I've always believed in protection. Especially these days. A properly made dreamcatcher... can ward off more than bad dreams."

Dom ran a hand through his wet hair, looking restless. "You believe in all that spiritual crap?"

"I believe what I've seen," her grandmother stated without hesitation.

Dom turned his attention to Meagan. "So let me guess. George filled your head with paranoia, and now you're doubting me?"

"I just want answers," Meagan replied, but there was a tremor beneath her words. "I just want the truth. Something happened to me, and everyone keeps acting like it didn't. The doctor, the therapist... none of them understand a part of me is *missing*."

Dom's mouth opened, then closed again. His eyes flicked once more to the dreamcatcher. She followed his gaze, and the feather hanging from the center swayed gently, though the air had gone still.

"I should go," he said abruptly, grabbing his shirt off the banister.

"What? You just got out of the shower," Meagan said. "You said you'd stay for dinner."

"I changed my mind," he muttered.

She stared at him. "Because of that?" She pointed toward the dreamcatcher.

Dom didn't answer; instead, he pulled the shirt over his head and headed for the door without another word.

Once he was gone, silence filled the hallway.

Meagan's grandmother reached out and placed the dreamcatcher into Meagan's hands. Her tone dropped low. "He didn't like being near it. Did you see how he couldn't stop staring at it?"

Meagan nodded slowly.

"There's something off about him," her grandmother whispered. "And the smell on him? That's not just bad soap. That's the smell of rot."

Meagan swallowed hard. Her fingers tightened around the threaded circle.

"As long as this stays unbroken," her grandmother said, "this house will stay protected. But you—" she observed Meagan carefully, "you need to trust what your body's telling you. That boy might still look like Dom, but something's different. Something's *inside.*"

"How do you know it works?" she asked quietly. "The dreamcatcher, you said it keeps things out, but how can you be sure?"

Her grandmother's eyes softened, but the weight of a memory darkened her face. "Because I've used one before."

Meagan stared at her.

"It was Michelle," she admitted.

Meagan blinked several times, stunned. "Michelle? What do you mean?"

"I had a few up in my bedroom for decorations, but only to ward off the bad dreams at the time. I happened to be in my room when that thing showed up here, wanting me too. It would only come to my bedroom door, and I quickly caught on and shoved one into its face. It screamed and clambered away into the woods, and shortly after, the mayor announced and enacted a law to prevent all of us and the other two sistering towns from going into the woods."

A thundering, pounding series of knocks startled them both. They exchanged nervous glances; it didn't seem friendly.

Her grandmother turned sharply. "Stay behind me."

Meagan set the dreamcatcher down and followed her cautiously to the door. Through the front window, a tall woman in a pale gray blouse tucked into dark navy slacks, with sleeves rolled to her elbows, waited with a clipboard tucked beneath her arm.

Her grandmother latched the chain carefully and pulled the door open a few inches. "Can I help you?"

Meagan recognized the female detective as the one who'd interrogated her previously. Her voice was calm, "Have a minute?"

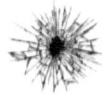

The heat outside hadn't broken by early evening. The cicadas screamed in the trees, and the sun hovered in the woods, casting an orange-spotted haze across the horizon. The Weaver walked barefoot down the gravel drive, shirt damp against its back from the shower that failed to rinse it clean. It still stunk. The human body could only hide rot for so long.

It squinted at the road. A car— plain, silver, government-issued— sat tucked behind the tree line. Engines off. Tinted windows up.

It grinned. The Weaver unlocked Dom's phone and opened the dial pad. There was no hesitation, just calculation. The memories of Dom crawled back into his skull, feeding what the Weaver demanded. Dom had connections.

"Investigator Monroe," the voice answered, a touch of suspicion already in her tone.

The Weaver kept its eyes on the car. "You're looking for answers about Meagan, right?"

Silence on the other end. Then: "Who is this?"

"You already know who I am," it said smoothly. "And you know where I just came from."

The Weaver stepped off the driveway casually, walking along the grass, away from the house. "She wasn't dared to jump off the roof. She was running into the woods and found something... unnatural."

Another silence.

"She'll deny it. But her grandmother's keeping her isolated while she recovers. Ask her why," it quipped, flicking its tongue over its teeth.

Click.

The Weaver didn't need to say more. A good investigator knew the truth lived in the gaps. Phone still in hand, it made the second call, this one more performative.

Hannah picked up on the second ring, breathless. "Dom? Hey, what's up?"

Dom's voice emerged, soft in tone. "I just wanted to say I'm... done with Meagan."

Hannah's breathing seemed to mute. "She's changed. I don't know, it's like being around her makes me sick. I think her grandma's messing with her head." Its voice lowered. "It's not my problem anymore."

"Oh?" Hannah asked curiously.

"I was wondering... Can I come over tonight? Just to talk. I need to be around someone real and who understands," he admitted.

Silence.

"Yeah. Sure." Her voice finally came through, tired and strained.

"Thanks, Hannah," the grin stretched. "You've always been good to me."

It hung up, exhaling slowly as Dom's face shifted slightly. A twitch at the jaw, a flicker in the eyes. Another piece of Michelle rethreaded inside, reshaping its intentions. The Weaver didn't just want to eat. It wanted *isolation*. It wanted to separate the herd. And Meagan needed to be *alone*.

Chapter 28

Nick shifted the car into park and sat quietly for a long time on the curb beside George's driveway, soaking in everything he had told him. The silence wasn't awkward, but heavy, like he was still absorbing everything George had told him.

"So... the thing that pushed Meagan off the cliff in the woods," Nick broke the silence. "It wasn't human, was it?"

George shook his head slowly. "No. It was like... a shadow with weight and intelligence—"

"A demon," Nick finished.

George closed his eyes, watching it leap through the air and pushing Meagan. "I didn't imagine it— I felt it. Something dark is within those woods." Her scream echoed through his mind, and his eyes flew open.

Nick ran a hand through his damp hair, exhaling hard. "That's intense. But listen, I'm not going to say anything to anyone."

"You're not?" George's eyes flickered with surprise and relief.

"Hell no. Those woods are off-limits for a reason," Nick stated without hesitation. "You could get arrested just for being there. I'm not risking that for either of us. However, it doesn't mean we can't figure out the truth. Together."

His eyebrows furrowed. "What do you mean?"

"Maybe Timothy captured this demon. He wanted to show you proof— photos, maybe videos. Let's see what he has. If you're telling the truth, and I believe you are, then maybe his evidence will back it up."

George swallowed hard, emotion tightening his throat. "You'd really do that?"

Nick's eyes softened. "You saved Meagan's life, George. If there's even a chance something evil is messing with you, we're not letting it win. But first..." he cupped his hand dramatically over his nose. "... you need a shower. And I need to make sure you don't tear your stitches, and I need to clean them."

George's attention turned to the two-story house, which stood dark and still. The family car was gone. He tried to sound steady, but his voice snagged. "Spare keys under the rug— I lost mine. I'm basically an afterthought to my parents."

Upstairs, Nick pushed open George's bedroom door and froze as LEDs lit *Stranger Things* posters, Funko Pops, and a glowing gaming PC.

"Here we go," George murmured.

"Nerd," Nick teased.

"I'm a *Stranger Things* fan! I also game," George defended.

"I— did you not get the reference?" Nick chuckled, setting his nurse bag on George's Stranger Things-themed bedding.

Nick combed through his hair, scrunching his nose and squinting, "crusty blood in my hair, ugh, I need a shower too."

George met his gaze, and Nick's expression became stern. "Do you want help wrapping your cast so it stays dry?"

George hesitated; his cheeks reddened. "I... I can do it myself."

Nick rolled his eyes, "Why won't you let anyone help you? It doesn't make sense to me. I'd like to understand."

Nick cares for you. Drop the pretend act and drop your wall. He is willing to listen.

"The truth is..." George's lip quivered, "I hate the way that I look, naked. I didn't have the best childhood. I try to be a perfectionist, a role model to my siblings, to show my parents I can be something for myself. All to make them proud. As you've seen, they're never around, or they don't care, so I've developed an independence—"

"Hyper independence," Nick corrected him.

George nodded, his lips trembling as tears welled in his eyes. His voice cracked when he spoke, barely above a whisper. "My body feels wrong... sometimes I stare in the mirror and hate what I see. I think I'm too fat, or not attractive enough... and then I start spiraling. My thoughts don't stop. I get stuck in them until I'm drowning in my own reflection." A sob pushed its way up before he could swallow it back down. "I have depression. Real, heavy, dark depression. The kind that makes you want to disappear. And I almost did. I almost ended my life."

He rubbed his eyes with the heel of his palm, as if he could scrub the shame away. "Meagan... the girl you met... she's the one who saved me. She talked me down when no one else even knew how close I was. I didn't tell anyone else because I couldn't. I still can't. My parents—"

His voice broke completely, and for a moment, he couldn't speak at all. When he tried again, it came out hollow. "They don't accept me. I feel it every time they look at me like I'm a disappointment, and they're in denial.

But I know. I know if they really knew I was gay, or what I was going through, they'd kick me out without thinking twice."

George's chest rose and fell in shallow, shaking breaths. His fingers curled into the fabric of his shirt, clinging to it as if he might fall apart if he let go.

"And now—" he continued, his voice raw, "James tried to kill me. Both he and Becca are missing, and no one knows why. My ex, the one who gave me blood to survive, betrayed me by cheating on me and is the one I must believe has the answers."

He stared at the floor, unblinking. "I blame myself for Meagan. She almost died, and I watched her fall, and I couldn't reach her in time. And Dom—Dom's feeding lies, twisting her against me, and I can't fix it. I don't know how to fight that kind of evil."

His hand fell into his lap, limp. "Hannah's been distant. She's been avoiding me like I'm contagious, and she knew what Dom was up to. It's like everything around me is crumbling, and I'm the only one still standing in the rubble, screaming for someone to see me."

He looked up finally, eyes red, lashes wet. "I don't know how much more I can take. I feel I'm losing who I am or who I'm supposed to be. Am I going insane?"

Nick shifted closer to him, their knees touching, and he reached for George's trembling hand. He squeezed gently, not demanding. Present. There. Real.

"You're not insane," Nick reassured, voice steady, but there was a tightness in it, like his own heart was breaking. "You're hurting. Anyone would be, after all this."

He leaned forward, meeting George's eyes. "But you're still here. Do you hear me? You're still here. Even after everything you spilled to me, you survived things no one should ever have to. And that doesn't make you weak. It makes you brave."

George choked on another sob, and Nick moved instinctively, wrapping his arms around him, pulling him close. George didn't resist. He collapsed into the warmth, into the soft heartbeat of his solid chest. The way Nick held him felt as if he wasn't a burden, he wasn't broken, he mattered.

Nick rubbed a hand slowly up and down George's back. "You're not alone anymore. And for the record, you're cute and I don't see anything wrong with your body."

Shuddering sobs poured out of George's eyes and soaked into the fabric of Nick's shirt. And still, he held him. No judgment. No rush. Just two arms wrapped around a boy who'd been too strong for too long. He'd lost track of how long he'd been cradled in his chest, but Nick only let go when he pulled back.

Nick jammed his hand into his shorts pocket and pulled out his phone, unlocking it. He tapped the screen and handed it to George. "Here, choose a song while I set things up in the shower."

George nodded submissively, thumbing through the music. He heard Nick rummaging through his bathroom, his voice calling out from behind the door. "Towels, check. Wash cloths, check. Cast protector, check. Gentle, fragrance-free, and moisturizing body wash and shampoo, check ..."

George chose an *After Dark* remix and blushed, hearing the water hissing on. "Sorry—nerd again."

"In *Stranger Things*, right?" Nick hung the towels on the rack and motioned for George to come into the bathroom.

"Mhm," George replied, impressed. He recognized it.

He inched his way toward the bathroom. As he stepped inside, he heard a soft click; the door had shut and locked. That wasn't unusual, but his heart still skipped.

He studied Nick as he stepped over to the tub to adjust the hot and cold nozzles to the shower, asking: "Does this feel okay?"

George reached out, running his fingers underneath the balmy water, steam rising slowly to the ceiling. "It's lukewarm. I usually take my showers scalding."

"It's only temporarily. Luke-warm water won't aggravate the wound. Here." Nick grabbed the phone gently from George and pressed play on the remix from his favorite TV show.

Stream curled up around them as the water rained down. Nick's fingers were gentle as he unbuttoned George's pants, pausing briefly, giving him a chance to say no. George didn't. He held his breath as the zipper slid down, and the fabric slipped past his hips, boxer briefs pooling at his feet. His skin prickled, not from the cold air, but from the closeness—his heart thudding with yearning.

He bit his lower lip, vulnerable and unsure.

With procession and minimal discomfort, Nick slid off his shirt, easing it down past his cast and onto the floor. He slid the cast protector over George's forearm.

"Before you get in," Nick informed. "I need to clean your wound and put this bandage over your dressings. It'll help keep the stitches dry and will help scabbing. That's what we want. I'll put some ointment around the sutures too."

Nick set his supplies on the toilet seat and gave George a half-concerned, half-gentle look.

George hovered awkwardly beside him, naked, while the dull throb in his abdomen made him wince. The skin beneath the taped dressing over his stitches felt tight and sore. It made him feel fragile, which he hated.

Nick snapped on a pair of gloves without comment, kneeling in front of him. "This might sting a little."

George nodded and looked away, jaw clenched. He felt the tug of adhesive as Nick peeled the old bandage off slowly, carefully, as if he knew George was barely holding it together.

Cold air hit the raw, stitched skin. George winced again before he could stop himself.

"Sorry," Nick murmured. "It looks good, though. Healing clean."

"Sure doesn't feel like it," George complained.

Nick didn't respond— he was focused, quiet. George risked a glance and saw the wrinkle of concentration between his eyebrows. There was no disgust in his face, just calm hands and soft eyes.

He watched Nick dab a bit of ointment onto a cotton swab, then gently sweep it across the stitches. The touch sent a cold shock through his nerves, but it wasn't unbearable.

"You okay?" Nick asked, glancing up.

"Yeah. Just... not used to being touched there," he admitted.

Nick gave a faint smile. "Well, I'm being extremely respectful of your abdomen."   George huffed a laugh.

Nick tossed the swab and pulled out a clear shower shield—a square sheet with a medical-grade adhesive border. "This'll keep it sealed up while you clean off."

George watched him peel the backing and line it up. The chilly plastic smoothed against his skin as Nick pressed it down with practiced care. Not too firm, not too gentle, just enough to feel safe.

"There." Nick looked up, locking eyes with him. "Good as waterproof."

George swallowed hard. "Th… Thank you. No one has helped me like this before."   Nick peeled off his gloves, "Well, I give a shit."

The words hit somewhere deeper than George expected. He blinked, looking down at his bandaged torso for a distraction.

"I'll help you get in," he offered.

Without a word and using Nick as an anchor, George carefully stepped in, careful not to strain his abdomen. The lukewarm rainfall hit him full-on. The heat clung to his skin almost like a blanket, washing away the remnants of blood, sweat, and fear.

Nick leaned in, voice low and warm against his ear. "I'll be right there."

He nodded, tilting his head back, letting the water pour over him.

The curtain shifted as Nick stepped in behind him. George turned, eyes meeting his—only for a second— before quickly flicking away, pretending to be very interested in the shampoo bottle.

"You're too cute," Nick teased, reaching past him. He squirted shampoo into his palm, then gently massaged it into George's tangled hair.

His eyes dropped before he could stop them. Tracing the lines of Nick's chest, watching the way the water beaded down the ridges of his stomach. His gaze traveled lower, pulse quickening.

He's perfect. Why do I want to kiss him so badly?

Nick chuckled. "Someone's excited," he murmured softly, still working the shampoo through George's hair. "You like what you see?"

"I do, actually,' George admitted, voice barely above the hum of the water. Then, with a soft smile, he traced two fingers against Nick's chest. "But do you like what you see?"

Nick's eyes softened. "Of course I do, dork." He leaned in, wiping away the streaks of blood on George's cheeks. His touch was careful, adoring. Without warning, he kissed him—slow and tender, not asking for anything, just offering.

George melted into it.

Nick's breathing was calm and steady against him, their lips still touching. Nick pulled him closer, the heat between them bonding and swelling.

He's hard, and so am I. This is really happening.

Nick broke the kiss first, a crooked smile on his lips. "See? I told you I like what I see."

Soapy and breathless, George blurted out a confession. "This is dumb, but... I've always had this fantasy of being pinned against a wall. In the rain. Cold, soaked, and kissing. Something about being helpless, but safe at the same time."

Nick's brow quirked. "That's not dumb at all." His smirk deepened. "Is that really all?"

George laughed nervously, but then shampoo dripped into his eyes. He winced, growling under his breath.

"Hold still," Nick gathered George's hair gently, rinsing out the soap. "Lather, rinse, don't complain."

George blinked against the stream, his vision blurry until he wiped at his eyes with his good hand. When he could see again, Nick was much closer.

Without warning, Nick caught George's wrist and pinned it with gentle force above his head, pressing his hand to the slick tile. George's back met the wall with a soft thud, eyes going wide.

"Y… you don't have to…" he started, voice squeaking.

But Nick leaned forward, letting the waterfall cascade over his head. His white-blonde hair clung to his forehead, water streaming down his chiseled frame. His presence towered, at least six feet to George's five-four, but there was nothing threatening in it.

He stared down into his eyes with a smoldering gaze. "Beg me to kiss you, George," he said, low and commanding.

George flushed; something in him wanted to obey. "Please kiss me, Nick," his lips barely pressed together.

Their noses nuzzled together, and his lips brushed George's. "That's a good boy."

"Mmph…" George closed his eyes, mouth parted, heart thudding violently in his chest.

This time, George broke the kiss, his lips tingling and eyes glossed with desire. He leaned back just enough to meet Nick's gaze. "I've been so stressed out my whole life, and somehow even though I'm injured and hurting, you make this all… lighter. I just… want to feel good for once. Fuck me," his voice shaky and certain, let the last two words drop like a bomb.

Nick paused, brows lifting slightly in surprise. "Tempting," he murmured, his voice dark and low. 'But you've got stitches in your abdomen, sweetheart. If I do what I want to do to you right now, it'd risk tearing them open."

He pressed his body closer, George's cock brushing up against his. Their wet skin heated, intensified.

George groaned, biting his bottom lip. "Mmmmmnh... sorry..."

"I'm starting to love teasing you," Nick whispered against his jaw. 'But we both need to be patient."

He grabbed the washcloth, squirting body wash onto it. He lathered George's shoulders, his chest, and trailed cautiously down to his stomach. Careful and tenderly around the healing wound, he smirked, turning George around, letting the gentle spray rinse the soap from his front side. He felt the cloth tingle, gliding across the curve of his ass, teasing him.

"You give your time, heart, and energy to people. Always giving, never expecting anything back. Maybe I want to give you everything." His breath hot on George's ear. "You do like receiving, don't you?"

His knees nearly buckled.

He loves playing too much... if he keeps teasing me like this, I might not last. Nick's gravelly rasp invaded his thoughts. "Fantasizing about me inside you?"

George let out a low, aching moan. "Mmppphh... yes."

Nick exhaled through his nose, visibly holding himself back. Turning and shutting off the water, he reached for the towels. "Soon," he replied. "But not while you're healing. I want you whole."

They dried off in silence, the steam swirling around them. George peeled the plastic protector off his arm, then slid on a fresh pair of briefs with a hiss of discomfort as the soft fabric settled.

"Wanna know what else I love?" George asked, adjusting himself and grinning through the fog of afterglow.

Nick, standing in front of the mirror, slicked his damp hair back and glanced over. "What's that?"

George shimmied shorts up to his waist. "Cuddling."

Nick laughed. "Should've known."

TACK... TACK!

"You hear that?" Nick alerted.

George groaned. "Yeah. Sounded like a pebble hitting my window." He inched to the headboard and peeked through the blinds—just in time to catch sight of someone outside waving their arms wildly.

A pale, panicked figure stood below the window, eyes wide and desperate. "... Timothy?"

Chapter 29

Meagan dried her tears on her forearm; the handcuffs bound to her wrists were tight, biting into her skin so hard she was sure her circulation was cut off. She felt humiliated, confused, and belittled by the female investigator. The woman had questioned her again, asking the same things she'd asked before. Still, Meagan had no answers to give.

But something had shifted. This time, the investigator didn't seem to believe her. Before she could press further, a call came through. Whatever it was, it stopped the interrogation cold. Now she sat in the back of the cop car, wrists throbbing, her thoughts a frantic swirl.

Why the hell did she detain me?

All the woman said was the mayor wanted to see her. But why? What could he possibly want with her? Tears streamed down her cheeks, this time from frustration. Every question she asked was ignored. The officer treated her like she didn't exist, like a piece of evidence, not a human.

And worst of all? She had tased Grandma. Meagan had screamed, begged her to stop. She'd tried to help, but the voltage hit her too, sending her into convulsions before she blacked out and woke up cuffed in the backseat. For someone so petite, the investigator had been disturbingly strong. Had to have dragged her limp body like a sack of potatoes.

Grandma? Is she okay!?

And then... George. He was frantic and bloody. If what grandma said was true about Dom, then I pushed away someone who might've cared.

What does the mayor want with me? She thought again, her pulse in her ears. *I'm just a brain-injured girl.*

The headlights painted the pavement in soft cream light as they turned down a narrow road flanked by trees. Zilch houses. More woods.

She remembered going into the woods was forbidden.

But does the mayor live here? Is he one of those creatures? Does he know about Michelle? Grandma said Michelle was the cause...

Meagan's eyelids grew heavy with the rhythm of the road and the questions circling like vultures picking at her brain. Her head lolled slightly. She hadn't meant to fall asleep, but everything—her brain, her body was shutting down.

"Wake up. We're here." The cold voice jolted her awake. It was the female investigator, her voice sharp and unapologetic.

Meagan blinked several times, dazed. They were parked in a large gravel driveway. Her eyes adjusted to the dark, settling on a farmhouse looming in front of them. It wasn't a mansion, but it was huge—three stories, with a wraparound porch, and surrounded entirely by forest.

ZZZZAAPPP.

Pain exploded through her body. Her limbs locked, then thrashed violently. She crumpled out of the car onto the ground, gasping.

The investigator yanked her upright with an inhuman grip. "Move!" the woman barked.

Meagan stumbled forward like a puppet, her muscles sluggish and tingling with static. Her legs moved, but she wasn't sure how. Every step felt like walking underwater, heavy.

They reached the front porch, but before the investigator could knock, the door swung open.

A woman stood there, porcelain-pale, wrapped in white, fanning her white laced folding fan in the warm air. "We've been expecting you, Meagan," she smiled reassuringly, her pearly, bright teeth glowed an unnatural white. Her tone was gentle, but Meagan felt a sharp chill rise up her spine. She didn't respond.

The woman in white turned and walked inside without another word, expecting Meagan to follow. The entryway was dimly lit, elegant in a cold and distant sort of way. A long tan rug stretched down a hallway lined with doors— white-painted, solid wood, and strange black shapes hung every few feet along the walls. Art? Symbols? Meagan couldn't tell.

Dim lantern-like sconces illuminated every other section of the hallway, casting an eerie rhythm of light and shadow. They walked all the way to the back of the house. As far as Meagan could see, only one room had its door open.

"This is it," the woman in white said. "The mayor is waiting for you inside. I have other matters to attend to." She turned and disappeared down the hallway without another glance.

Meagan hesitated.

"Go on," the investigator replied sharply. "I'll be right here. Not my business what he says to you." She shoved Meagan forward into the room.

It was massive. Bookshelves lined the walls, overflowing with documents. A sleek glass desk dominated the center, surrounded by four lamps and two crystal chandeliers that bathed the room in pale light. A pristine white oval rug stretched underfoot.

Then, slowly, the black leather chair at the far end of the room rotated. A man faced her. Silver hair, a well-groomed goatee, and a stark white tuxedo made him look like he'd stepped out of another world.

His expression was unreadable, but serious. "I need your help, Meagan."

Hannah kicked her feet on the bed with glee, flipping her phone on, her exhausted face brightening.

He really did it! Dom broke up with Amanda, for me! Now if I can just get him to forget Meagan... or at least let her focus on healing. She always knew I had a crush on him, so why do I still feel bad?

Hannah's eyes lit up, staring at the call log before she rolled out of the bed, stripping bare. She admired herself in the mirror as she changed into her strappy, scarlet lace nightgown.

All those extra hours really paid off this week.

For the first time in her life, she didn't just feel beautiful, she felt sexy. She lost herself in the mirror, spraying perfume around her neck and chest.

You never heard from George. Never even checked in on him. Are you going to feel bad about not keeping up with your friend? Although you have been taking his shifts, maybe it's time to enjoy a little Hannah time, don't you think?

"Am I...truly beautiful?" she whispered to her reflection. Before she could shake her daze, thunder clapped outside as her phone buzzed.

I'm here. Unlock the front door.

Hannah didn't remember locking it, but figured her parents must've done it before they left for their third shift at the motel. The house felt lonelier at night, especially during thunderstorms. It was quite common for them to pop up at night since the humidity had reached its peak in the summer weather. But she didn't want to sleep alone tonight. She crept into the hallway, instinctively quiet as if her parents were still home. At the front door, she glanced through the peephole, heart fluttering.

No one was there.

She slipped on her slippers and flipped the porch light on, cracking the storm door. Crickets filled the night air, but no movement. The neighborhood was still.

Hannah frowned at her phone in confusion.

Down here.

She stepped outside; heavy droplets of rain began pouring from the black sky. Her breath caught. A white flash of lightning and another thunderous clap of thunder— Amanda's severed head lay at her feet, her eyes wide with a frozen expression of terror and betrayal.

Hannah tried to scream, but all that came out was hot air.

No, no, no, no, no. That's not Amanda. It can't be. Dom's just playing a sick joke, trying to scare me. Right? He said he broke up with her. He wouldn't...

"Dom! This isn't funny! Where are you?" Hannah called out.

Only the sound of rain drumming the wooden porch responded.

She crouched near the head, and Amanda's eyes suddenly rolled back. Hannah screamed in terror, flinching so hard she slipped on the forming puddle of rain and fell onto her backside.

Dom murdered her. He SEVERED Amanda's head. Oh my God.

Hannah's palms were sweaty. Somewhere she heard her phone buzz again and realized it wasn't in her hand. She searched frantically and spotted it face down, getting drenched in the rain.

Hannah's legs and feet were soaked. Her fingers quivered, water squished, seeping underneath her fingertips as she turned her phone over.

"You don't like my present?"

Hannah began to tremble.

"What about this one?"

A soft thump echoed from the hallway near the kitchen. Another head, this one freshly severed, rolled across the floor like a bowling ball, stopping against her foot.

Her eyes blurred with tears. She shook her head violently, as if trying to unsee what was in front of her. "B... Becca," she whispered.

Becca's pale cheek brushed her ankle, her soulless white eyes stared upward. Her mouth was frozen in a tight, disappointed frown.

Hannah couldn't look away. *She's disappointed in me. She should be. I didn't check in. Not with her. Not with George. Not even Meagan. I was too caught up in a fantasy with Dom.*

Dom. A serial killer.

"I thought you'd be happy to see Becca again, right? She put up one hell of a fight," Dom stepped out of the shadows, butcher knife in hand. His blonde hair hung messily in his face. "Amanda, though... not so much."

"Wanna taste?" he asked, licking the knife dripping with blood.

"They're...both...dead..." Hannah choked, stumbling back. "I asked you to break up with Amanda, not this...and Becca...I'm—" rotting meat, with a sickeningly sweet undertone washed over her, making her cut her sentence short.

"Confused, are we?" Dom said, stepping closer. "Let me clear things up. You've seen me with girl after girl at work. Did you ever see them again afterward?" Dom pointed the blade at Hannah.

"No... I am confused: my best friend's head is right here, and Amanda's is at my front door. Why?" she pleaded. "Why would you do this?"

"I'm in search of a perfect vessel, my dear," Dom answered with a casual shrug. "And Dom isn't it."

"You're addressing yourself in the third person." Hannah's eyes stayed locked on the knife. And then it hit her, a sour, rotten flesh aroma slapped her nostrils. She curled her lower lip in disgust.

"This vessel has done some harm, but not as much as me," Dom continued, pricking his finger with the knife until droplets of blood emerged. "Dom thought he could be like Bundy. Charming. Charismatic. Manipulative. He'd sleep with them... find their worst fears... then slaughter them. You were just another pawn, like Amanda. Like all the others—nipped in the bud."

I wasn't special. I wanted him for so long. And for what? To be murdered? And I was awful to Meagan. I was a jealous bitch. Did he kill her, too?

"What about Meagan?" Hannah probed. "You said you wanted her to be cleared by the investigators, right? They're still trying to figure out what happened. No one questioned me or you. She didn't remember anything... George and Becca weren't present..." Hannah's face twisted. She was angry, scared, sad, and resentful.

Keep calm. Don't show fear. He's unstable. Dangerous. He's never talked like this before...

Dom tilted his head, amused. "Hannah, the oblivious. Yes, I'm Dom.

I mean... I'm a serial killer. But more than that... I'm 'the Weaver'."

He grinned. "If you knew about the girls I was with—didn't you put two and two together? I was never questioned. Do you know why?"

Hannah shook her head. "I thought they quit. Or you dumped them. I never saw anything in the news."

"Because the stories were only printed in newspapers," he scoffed. "And who the hell reads those anymore?" Dom used the tip of the knife to scrape underneath his fingernail.

"You're asking the wrong questions. Use that one brain cell and think. You should be asking me why I needed an alibi?" He grinned wider. "Let's peel back the layers of the onion, shall we," he sneered, swatting the tense air with the butcher knife.

Hannah inched back, her breath caught.

I really am clueless... think... think. Oh my God! I don't want to die... I need to keep stalling. Stalling for what? No one is coming to save you! You're on your own. No, the car keys. They're hanging on the key rack beside the door. If I can inch my way to it, I can have a fighting chance to run to my car.

"An alibi...you said...but there's no alibi, Dom. You're the one to blame, "Hannah accused. "Whatever you did in the fucking closet to Meagan— said something, put your hands on her, maybe even threatened to kill her? Or rape her? She was too upset, and she ran. She ran blindly into the woods."

Her hands clenched into fists, knuckles bone white, bloody fingernails digging into her palms. "The woods," she whispered through gritted teeth. "They're forbidden."

"Keep going, Hannah. You're onto something," Dom challenged, dragging the blade across the wall, carving. "If you realized it that day, maybe you could've told the investigators. But then again... everyone involved would've been detained. And I wasn't there, remember?"

He grinned wider. "Do you know why it's forbidden?"

"It's to keep us safe. It's dangerous," Hannah responded. "For protection."

"From *what*?" he pressed.

"I don't know," she admitted. "They never told us. Just said it was better not to know."

"There's a much bleaker truth," Dom cackled. "Within those trees? There's a demon. A mimic. A shapeshifter. A wendigo. I like the Weaver personally. I detach their heads, wear their bodies, and consume their soul."

He carved a spiral into the living room wall.

Now!

Hannah edged back until her fingers brushed the key rack.

"What are you saying, Dom? Are you... Are you a demon?" Her voice trembled.

He turned slowly, smiling, "I'm looking for the perfect vessel. Dom wasn't it." He repeated, then added: "These bodies aren't able to sustain my presence; they rot."

"And you think I am?" she squealed.

He chuckled, low and inhuman. "George is, but I just enjoy the slaughter along the way."

Grab the keys. Get out! Now!

Hannah held her breath.

I don't want to die. I never wanted to hurt anyone... But I didn't protect anyone, either. I need to warn George.

She snatched the keys from the hook and bolted, her bare feet slapping through the rain. She didn't care. She bounded down the steps, unlocking her car with the fob.

Behind her, heavy footsteps thudded on the porch.

She yanked the car door open, dove inside, and slammed the lock button.

The Weaver reached the window just as she did. "Hannah... I wanted you to see the third surprise." Its inhuman voice was garbled.

Hannah fumbled to start the car, mashing the ignition button. The engine roared.

The Weaver slammed its fist into the glass. A sharp crack bloomed across the windshield.

Chapter 30

George joined Nick on the porch, the coming rain matching the heaviness in his chest. Watching the footage together, Timothy pointed at the video on his phone. "This is what I was trying to tell you! Amanda is dead! Dom killed her and was fighting Becca, and I saw her turn... she wasn't human... I shouldn't have gone into the woods. They're going to detain me. Please don't say anything, please, please... I know what's out there. I just— I'm trying to process."

George exchanged a glance with Nick.

I chased Meagan into the woods. They could detain me too, if they ever found out how she hit her head. But... Becca turning into... something.

"Why were they fighting?" George demanded, confused. "Why would she, or that thing, be fighting Dom?"

"I don't know! I just—" Timothy blew out a breath. "Let me start from the beginning."

Nick stood close to George, protectively. George could feel the heat radiating from his body, grounding him.

"After you didn't want me back," Timothy shifted his eyes toward Nick, "I was telling the truth about Michael. I'm not with him anymore.

Amanda... well, she had been a friend from school, and I wanted to experiment. Try my hand with girls. Apparently, Amanda and Dom were a thing, and then they weren't— well, according to Amanda. She got a text from him asking to meet. I thought she was crazy, but she seemed nervous and excited. I stayed in the car... but about thirty minutes later, I heard screaming coming from inside and then Dom carrying her out into the woods. I followed, and I found Amanda lying on the ground. Becca showed up, and she and Dom started attacking each other. Then... that's when Becca started to transform."

George felt the blood drain from his face. "Transform how?" he asked, voice thin.

"I don't even have words for it," Timothy whispered. "Like those Native American legends. A wendigo?"

George paled.

Timothy's voice cracked. "When I saw her... what she became... I ran. I heard screaming. I panicked and drove straight to the police station, but they didn't believe me. I told them I left when I saw Dom carrying Amanda and heard the screams. They think I made the whole thing up."

George turned toward Nick. "Becca... what if she, Nick— what if she killed her dad? I reported her missing, but…"

"Why are you even here?" Nick growled to Timothy, folding his arms.

"I didn't know who else to go to!" Timothy cried. "I don't have any friends who would believe me."

George's stomach twisted, and he winced in pain from his abdomen. "Becca... She can't be... What if we expel that thing? Maybe we can save her."

"Don't bother," came a hoarse voice from the curb. He hadn't even noticed the car pulling up, only the voice, sharp and soaked in fatigue.

George spun, startled. A drenched, limping Hannah stumbled toward them; her face scraped, strands of hair plastered to the blood on her face, her voice cracked. "Becca's dead."

She stood in the rain like she didn't care, or maybe like she had nothing left to lose. "Hannah, what the fuck happened to you? Why are you dressed like a slut?" George questioned. A strong wave of vanilla wafted into his nostrils.

"Dom," Hannah sobbed. "He killed Amanda and Becca. He— he threw their heads at me."

Timothy rushed to her side, catching her before she collapsed.

George's eyes darted to Timothy. "The video showed Becca and Dom fighting—"

"I don't think it was Dom," Hannah coughed. "It called itself The Weaver. Dom's just a face it wears now. He's been charming girls and killing them. I wanted to be with him, too. I thought he liked me. I didn't know. I didn't know." She coughed again, then asked, "Where's Meagan, George?"

His heart froze.

Meagan had been with a serial killer? No—something worse. Something inhuman. What if it's on his way to her now? What if it followed Hannah?

George's eyes widened, thinking about the black shadow pushing Meagan off the ledge, the scene haunting his mind.

He tried to piece it all together. "So, Dom has been killing random girls. He allured Amanda, you, and Meagan. He kills Amanda. Then Becca, who has been missing, shows up, but she's... not herself. Something monstrous. Then she fights Dom, and now Dom isn't even human anymore? He's, or its, name is the Weaver that might be going after Meagan?"

Timothy nodded, slowly.

George rubbed his temple. A migraine was coming on. It was all too much to take in.

"George," Hannah whispered, grabbing his wrist. "The monster, the Weaver, or whatever it is... well... it wants a perfect vessel. That's what it said. It's been killing people trying to find one. It said it wants you. That's why I think it's circling Meagan. To get to you."

George froze.

The shadow that pushed Meagan... Becca transforming into something unrecognizable... Was it all the same entity?

"It's using them to get to me," George repeated.

"I barely got away," Hannah's voice shaking. "I ran him over. My window shattered. I don't know if he's still out there, but I can't go back home."

"My house isn't safe either," George murmured.

"I have plenty of room at my house," Nick offered. "But my parents aren't fond of surprises. Only on one condition." Nick glared at Timothy. "You stay the hell away from George."

Timothy rolled his eyes. 'This is how I get treated after saving his life?" He turned to George, who flinched.

"Tell your dog to heel," Timothy spat at Nick.

"We don't need to argue," George said sharply. "Hannah needs a doctor, and Meagan might be in danger."

Nick's jaw clenched, "You think I'd let him into my house? After he stalked you?"

George blinked. "What? He gave me a transfusion, visited me, and tried to kiss me while I was knocked out on painkillers, but he didn't stalk me."

Nick's stare was ice.

Timothy stiffened. "Why would I stalk him if he clearly didn't want me around?"

"Because you couldn't accept that," Nick growled. "I saw you outside his room more than once when I was working my shifts. You still love him. But he doesn't want you. Respect that."

Spacing out, George realized he'd disassociated himself from them. His vision tunneled slightly. A bright light suddenly pierced the chaos—headlights.

My parents are home.

"What the fuck is going on?" his dad snapped, slamming the door.

George turned slowly. "Wouldn't you like to know," he replied with a dead laugh.

Nick and Timothy both quieted.

"This is my house," his dad barked, approaching him on the porch. "So yeah, I'd like to know what the fuck is going on."

"What happened to you, George?" His mom asked behind his dad.

George burst out laughing hysterically. "Oh, wow! Now, look, everyone, my parents finally give a fuck about me!"

"George, what has gotten into you—" his mom started.

"No, no, let him finish. I want to hear what our son has to say," his dad interrupted, arms folded.

George snapped. "I almost died twice, but neither of you gave two shits. I almost hung myself! You know who stopped me? Meagan. Not you. Not either of you! Then James tried to kill me to keep quiet about a crash. I've been trying to be perfect. But nothing I do is good enough for either of you! You didn't even come to the hospital!"

He felt a surge of adrenaline, unstoppable now, finding strength in his voice. "People around me are dying. I'm exhausted. And out of all of this bullshit, you want to know what I'm *most* sure about?"

He looked his parents dead in the eye. "I'm gay."

His mother's face crumbled, tears brimming but unshed. His father's filled with rage, his jaw twitched as if he'd been slapped.

There was a beat of silence before his dad sneered. "Oh, really? And is this your fag boyfriend?"

The word sliced through the air, sharp and venomous. George flinched, not because he hadn't heard it before, but because he had. Too many times, from the man who was supposed to protect him. His chest tightened, and he could feel his younger version of himself: the timid, soft-spoken boy who used to cry in secret—curled up inside, listening and remembering.

Shoulders heavy, George's voice shook but didn't falter. "This is Nick. And he's done more for me in the past week than you've done for me in my whole life."

"Don't get dramatic," his father spat. "We gave you everything."

"You gave me nothing but fear. You've been calling me a fag since I was a toddler. Before I knew what it meant. Just because I was timid. Just because I wasn't like you."

His dad stepped forward. "You think the world's gonna coddle you? You think running off with some guy makes you a man?"

George didn't back down. "I think surviving *you* made me stronger than you'll ever be. I think clawing my way through this life without your help makes me more of a man than you've ever taught me to be."

His father's face flushed with rage. "You're not my son."

A clap of thunder rang in George's ears as if agreeing with his dad.

"Of course," he whispered bitterly. "Out of everything I just said, that's the part you heard. Not the pain. Not the trauma. Just that."

He stepped forward, voice rising. "Not the fact I almost killed myself. Not that I was nearly run off the road. Not me having to save myself from getting shot. Not that I've been hiding how broken I am, just to keep things calm in this goddamn house. Not that people are *dying,* and I'm scared every second."

His mother reached toward him slightly, but he shook his head.

"No. Don't. You don't get to act like you care now." He pointed to his chest, trembling. "You have no idea what it's like to grow up in a house where you feel like a stranger. Where silence hurts more than screaming, walking on eggshells. Do you know who filled out my college applications? Who wrote every damn essay and chased down every deadline? Who applies for scholarships and pays for tuition? Who signed every hospital release form by himself because his parents never bothered to show up?"

His voice choked on tears. "Who is paying for physical therapy out of pocket? Who kept pretending he was fine so you both wouldn't have to deal with him? *Me.*"

George was crying now, but he didn't care. "I begged for years for you to see me. To love me. I kept trying to be good enough, to get straight A's, to work, to babysit, to make you proud. And you never even noticed."

His mother was sobbing softly now, but his father remained frozen, unreadable.

"I stopped hoping you'd be proud. But deep down, I still prayed you'd look at me and see someone worth loving," he revealed, heart burning.

He turned to his mom, eyes hollow. "And you. God, I waited for you to say something. To *do* something. I thought if I could hang on long enough, you'd stand up to him. You never did. Are you going to let him do this?"

She hesitated.

He exhaled hard, wiping his face roughly. "I'm done trying. I'm done breaking myself to be the version of a son you wanted."

He turned to Nick. "Were you serious about your offer to stay with you?"

Nick nodded. "Always."

George stepped toward his father; the sudden movement sent pain through his abdomen, and his eyebrows lowered, his eyelids tightened, and his nose wrinkled. "Well, guess what? Your disappointment with a son isn't your son anymore. I'm done. I'm choosing my happiness. I'm not hiding anymore."

George flung his arms in the air, acting tough. The pain in his abdomen had him biting his lower lip.

"George, you need to sit, your stitches—" Nick stepped forward, holding his hand, leading him down the steps.

The cold rain smacked his body, the silence behind him feeling final. Passing the back window of his parents' car, his younger siblings' faces watching, eyes wide and confused.

Nick aided him to his car, "Careful, please," he reminded in a soft breath and opened the door.

George climbed in with his assistance, the weight of the world behind him and tears streaming down his face. He wiped them away with his forearm resentfully.

From the rearview mirror, a streak of white lightning raced across the night sky, seeing Timothy and Hannah step toward the curb, watching them pull away.

"You sure you want to leave them behind?" Nick asked.

"We need to go to Meagan's. She needs to know the truth. I think Timothy will follow, and Hannah will not want to be alone. Besides, the separation will calm the tension between you and Timothy. You were about to rip his head off."

Nick gave a grim smirk. "Next stop, Meagan."

Chapter 31

George noticed the front door wide open as Nick helped him up the porch stairs, trying to steady him. A dreamcatcher decorated the porch. Sobbing drilled into his eardrums.

"Not Meagan, please... not her..." George whispered. He straightened up, ignoring the pull from the stitches, and knocked lightly on the open door.

"Excuse me, is Meagan here?" he asked gently. The sobbing halted.

"Who's there?" a frail voice asked, wary.

"It's George, Meagan's friend. I stopped by earlier. I'm really worried about her. Is she okay?" He stepped onto the threshold.

"George... she mentioned you, maybe a month ago?" the voice softened. "Please, come in. I'm sorry for the state I'm in. Could you close the door behind you?"

George crossed over into the living room, Nick gently shutting the door. He passed a modest two-seater sofa and a small TV on a wooden stand. The kitchen to the left of the hallway was where her grandmother sat, wiping her face with a tissue. Her eyes were red and rimmed with exhaustion.

"Please sit down," she sniffled. "Meagan told me about you, briefly. She said— and please don't tell her I told you— that she felt like she loved you, well before everything that happened. I'm Martha, her grandmother."

"She said that...?" George's heart clenched. "Where is she? Is she okay?"

Martha shook her head. "An investigator came by... same one who keeps asking the same questions about the night Meagan hit her head. Meagan kept insisting she didn't remember, and the investigator said if the neurologist appointments weren't helping, then..."

"She was taken in?" George asked.

"Yes. The woman said they'd need to detain her for possible entry into the woods." Martha's voice broke slightly. "It's like people around here have forgotten what that place does to people. Do you know what really happened that night?"

George swallowed the lump in his throat. "I do remember. And I hope you won't report me." He hesitated, then added, "It happened at Becca's birthday party. Meagan had a crush on that asshole Dom."

"What did he do? She claimed he was her boyfriend." Martha stood up to rummage through a cabinet and pulled out coffee grounds and a filter.

"I came back because..." George sat straighter. "Dom's dangerous. He's a serial killer. He murdered Amanda, one of our co-workers, and probably others. Maybe even Becca. Or... something else got to her."

"The Weaver, sweetie. You don't have to explain it to me," Martha replied calmly. "If Dom is possessed, or eaten and replaced, he wouldn't have gotten through that door if I hadn't allowed it. My home is now protected. Evil can't step across my porch without being repelled."

Nick stepped forward. "Do you need help? You looked like you were in pain when we got here."

"I was tazed," she admitted. "By the investigator. She was... rough."

Nick moved to help steady her as she sat. "Let me know if you need anything, okay?"

"Thank you, dear," her wrinkles creased, offering him a tired smile. "I'm brewing some coffee if either of you wants any."

"No, thank you," Nick said.

"I'm fine," George added.

Martha poured herself a strong black cup and sipped. "Now, George... you said Dom did something?"

"He played with Meagan's feelings. She ran into the woods crying. She hit her head in the creek. I ran after her, but I couldn't stop the fall— a shadow pushed her. Becca, James, and I helped carry her back, and the paramedics took her from there."

Martha nodded slowly. "Then it's the woods they're blaming. Not her head, not Dom..."

George turned to Martha. "Did they say exactly where they were taking her?"

"They just said she was being detained... but not much else. I figured the police station. I'm too shaken to drive."

"I'll call Hannah," George announced suddenly. He pulled out his phone and stepped away for a moment.

"Hey," he mouthed awkwardly when she answered. "Can you and Timothy go to the police station? Meagan's grandma said she was taken there."

Hannah's voice was muffled but serious. "Yeah, we're on it. Are you—"

"I'm fine," George hung up.

"She's not at the station," Nick spoke up, his voice low but firm.

George turned, confused. "What?"

Nick's eyes darted to him, a shadow growing behind his eyes. "She's not there."

Martha set the coffee down. "Then... where is she?"

"I'll explain," Nick said, "but first... Martha, please, can you explain the Weaver to us?"

Martha hesitated. "I didn't think I'd have to relive this again," she mumbled, staring at her cup.

George glanced sharply at Nick, his stomach twisted.

Why didn't Nick tell me before we came here? If he knew where she was all along...

He tried to stay calm, but his breathing quickened. Something was off. He had no choice but to listen.

Timothy shifted uneasily in the small-town sheriff's office, the stale scent of paper, sweat, and old coffee clinging to the walls like smoke.

"There's no file for anyone by the name of Amanda Bennett. And we have no missing persons report for Becca Lynn. She's a suspect in her father's death, not a victim," the sheriff said, flipping through a thin stack of paperwork, thinking it was proof or something. "Do you have any information?"

Timothy swallowed hard. "What do you mean she's not listed as missing? Amanda is dead. I saw it. And there's weird shit going on, stuff no one can explain."

The sheriff raised an eyebrow. "Is this some kind of joke? A prank? If you have information about the murder of Mr. Lynn or his daughter's whereabouts, we need it on record. She's considered armed and dangerous. Are you willing to go on record?"

Timothy exhaled sharply through his nose. "You've got to be kidding me..."

Before he could finish, Hannah shoved past him, bruised and cut, her limp exaggerated, her eyes wild.

"If we were joking, would I come in here looking like a damn crash dummy?" She snapped.

The sheriff looked her over, jaw tight. "You should get checked out, sweetheart."

"This place is a fucking joke," she muttered, turning her back.

"Agreed," Timothy said, already following her out. "They won't even look into the address we gave them. Let's just wander into the woods ourselves and disappear. Seems to be the local trend."

They stormed out, ignoring the sheriff's half-hearted threats to "not leave town." Timothy yanked open the car door and slammed it shut behind him, gripping the steering wheel like it owed him answers.

"We're on our own," he muttered. "The police aren't going to help us. No surprise there, they weren't helpful last time I went. George left us. He's pissed and for good reason. What the hell are we supposed to do now?"

Hannah didn't answer right away. She pulled out her phone and started dialing.

"What are you doing?"

"Calling George," she replied flatly.

"You okay?" he asked, concerned.

"There's so much going on. How can anyone be okay?" Hannah growled. He noticed her fingers tapping her bruised knee impatiently.

Timothy stared at her for a moment. The scent hit him again— sweet, thick vanilla perfume. He remembered noticing it earlier, too. Too much of it. It was cloying, overpowering, and she seemed to be trying too hard to impress. His nose twitched, and now underneath the sweet aroma, was that... rot? Was she trying to mask something?

His brow furrowed. "Hey, why are you wearing so much perfume? You're practically doused in it."

Hannah barely blinked. "What, are you serious? You're asking me that right now?"

"I just... It's strong. And now I'm..." he sniffed again. Definitely rot. "Did something else happen with you earlier?"

She rolled her eyes. "God, drop it. It's just perfume, Timothy. Don't be weird."

Before he could press her, the call connected.

"George?" Hannah asked, putting it on speaker.

"Hannah?" George's voice was shaky, staticky.

"We're leaving the police station. Meagan isn't here; the police haven't been useful," she said.

"Fuck, her grandmother thought maybe they took her there. Where else would they have taken her?" George asked.

Timothy jumped in. "They're not going to help us. They didn't believe us. I even asked about Amanda, and she doesn't even show up in their system, and Becca's not listed as missing. She's a fugitive. The girls Dom killed? Not even in the media."

"This is fucking nuts," George muttered. There was a long pause before he continued, "Look, I'm sorry for ditching you guys. It was the heat of the moment. Meagan's grandma, Martha, said it's safe there. She can help. She might even be able to take a look at Hannah. I'm going to find Meagan. Nick said—"

The call cut out.

"Did he hang up?" Timothy asked.

"I don't know," Hannah said, staring blankly at the phone. "But I think I know where to go. Let's go there. I remember the way."

Timothy studied her for a few seconds. "Alright... I'll follow your lead."

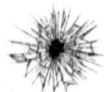

Timothy's mind was racing as they pulled up to the old house. It looked normal enough... but something felt off; he couldn't quite put his finger on it.

"This is it," Hannah lowered her voice. "Her house. But something doesn't feel right. Where's George and Nick?"

"Yeah, I don't see their car," Timothy agreed, sticking his head out the window, noticing only an old pickup and a station wagon sitting in the shadows. Meagan's car looked ancient and untouched. "Maybe they're already gone?"

Hannah didn't move. Timothy watched her hand grip the door handle. "What's wrong?"

"It's a trap," she whispered.

He was about to ask what she meant when the screen door creaked open and a petite elderly woman stepped out. She wore a flannel robe and had a long, graying braid.

"Come on in," she called gently. "It's safe. George and Nick went to get Meagan. I'm Martha. You two must be Timothy and Hannah?"

Timothy nodded, but Hannah stood still like a statue.

"You okay, dear?" Martha asked, hand over her mouth at the sight of Hannah's bruises.

"This is a trap," Hannah hissed to Timothy again.

His heart pounded in his ears. "What? How?"

She didn't respond.

"Hannah, George said it was safe," Timothy replied, swinging the car door. "I know he was mad, but I trust him."

Hannah didn't even look at him; instead, her eyes deadlocked with Martha's. "How is this house safe compared to mine?"

"Dreamcatchers," Martha said simply. "And a protective circle. I'll explain it all."

Timothy stepped toward the porch. "I don't see anything wrong."

"You never do," Hannah responded quickly, her voice colder than before.

He turned slowly. "What the fuck is your problem?"

"You always do what you want. You never care how it affects others," she spat, walking toward him— her limp mysteriously gone.

"What happened to your limp?" he asked cautiously. "Can we just talk inside?"

"Aww, you caught that, huh?" Hannah grinned darkly. "Just kidding. It was an act. I almost had that vessel, but then Nick got in the way. And you— so sweet, always trying to be the good guy." Her fingers stretched and split, bones cracking into talons.

Timothy stumbled back. "What the hell?!"

He barely registered Martha's scream. "It's the Weaver! Get inside!"

He lunged for the porch railing, hand outstretched, but he was yanked back. His breath hitched as he landed on his back; the wind knocked out of him. Hannah— no, this thing— stood before him, transformed.

Her eyes weren't hers anymore. They glowed a deep, bleeding red, and from her skull, jagged antlers twisted toward the sky. Her limbs stretched unnaturally, bones crackling, skin splitting open. Talons glistened from her fingertips.

Timothy's voice caught in his throat. This wasn't happening. Not to him. Not like this. "H… Hannah?" he choked.

The creature grinned with razor-sharp teeth that didn't belong in a human mouth. "Poor, stupid boy. Always tagging along. Always hoping George would love you back."

Its arm whipped forward with a lash, long and unnatural, slashing into his chest. Timothy gasped as pain exploded across his body. He lowered his head and saw red. Deep slashes carved into his skin, forming a symbol he didn't recognize. He trembled. Blood seeped through his torn shirt in diamond shapes and crooked strokes.

"I just wanted... to fix things," he groaned, barely able to speak. His fingers curled into the dirt. "George..."

A sob caught in his throat. He didn't care if this was the end. He deserved it, didn't he?

"I'm sorry..." he murmured to no one. "I was just trying to make it right. I didn't mean to mess things up."

His vision blurred. "I never stopped loving you."

A scream tore from his lungs, but it fell short due to a gurgle of blood. Somewhere above him, the Weaver laughed— a deep guttural rasp of amusement. Timothy's final thought was of George's smile— warm and genuine— and the way he laughed. It used to make him feel like he mattered. Maybe he wasn't a mistake. If only he could've heard his laugh one more time... He let out one last scream, and a final tear slipped from the corner of his eye. His world went still.

Chapter 32

"Nick, please," George pleaded as the tires hummed against the wet road. "Why is Meagan with the mayor? What connection does he have to any of this?"

"I'll explain when we get there," Nick replied, tightening his grip on the wheel.

George frowned. "That's not good enough." He didn't raise his voice, but there was weight in it. "We left Hannah and Timothy again, and I was trying to make sure they got there safely. I still don't understand where you're getting this information."

"They're fine. Just sit back and be patient." Nick pressed harder on the gas.

George leaned back, clutching the seatbelt strap, like it could anchor him.

With his eyes fixed on the rain streaking the window and the black trees blurring past, he asked, "So how do you know where she is?"

"Because I've known for a while."

George turned his head sharply. "But you didn't tell me."

279

"I couldn't," Nick replied quickly, then softer. "Not until I was sure."

"You sound like Timothy," George muttered, more to himself than Nick. "Always 'for your own good,' always withholding something."

Nick's jaw clenched, but he didn't respond right away. The steady rain pounding the windshield filled the silence buzzing between them.

"I want to trust you," George finally said. "But you can't expect blind faith. Not after everything."

"I don't," Nick answered. "You're right to question me. But I had to make sure she was alive first. Then safe. And this place... we're almost there."

George studied him. "Then tell me something real. Not what you think I want to hear. Just something... true. Something you."

"Huh?"

"I only know you're a CNA. But past that? You're still a stranger."

Nick bit his lip, then exhaled, tapping the gear shift. "I like Grey's Anatomy. My birthday's Monday. I'll be twenty-two. I'm a mess when it comes to Italian food and—" he gave a weak, crooked smile, "— green's my favorite color."

George didn't smile back; it didn't warm him. "You could've told me that days ago."

"I didn't think it mattered."

"It does," George peered at him. "When everything else is falling apart, those are the things that matter most."

"We only met this week. I didn't want to give you another reason to feel like you were failing someone," Nick murmured.

George didn't reply, heart empty.

"We're here," Nick added quietly, slowing the car onto a gravel path.

George peered through the windshield, the wipers working feverishly, swashing the rain away. Lightning lit up a colossal white farmhouse, standing shrouded by towering trees, half-swallowed by ivy and shadow. Thunder clapped heavily, and he noticed the porch glowed faintly from old brass lanterns, swaying from rusted chains. It didn't look like the home of a mayor. The mayor. Banning the town from the woods, and he himself lived within them.

"This is where Meagan is?" George asked, throat tightening. "This is where the mayor lives?" His voice faltered.

Nick didn't respond immediately; instead, he carefully helped George out of the car, covering him with a jacket he'd pulled from the backseat.

"Yes."

"And you didn't say anything," George whispered, realizing.

"I was protecting you!" Nick insisted, voice rising. "George, if you just listen—"

George stepped back from him. "You lied."

The porch light clicked on.

"Darling?" A woman's voice sang out. "What are you doing squawking on the porch? You'll catch pneumonia out here in this storm. Get inside!"

A woman in a white, sleeveless sheath dress and a white lace folding fan stepped into view, her golden-silver hair pinned into a twist and earrings that resembled tiny chandeliers. Her eyes fell on George, fanning herself. "Oh, and who's this cutie pie?"

George stiffened.

"This is George," Nick replied, voice suddenly rehearsed. "The boy I've been telling you about."

George's stomach twisted.

He already told them about me? When? How? Who are they to him?

"Oh! You can call me May." She winked at George.

George leaned around May, stepping inside the entryway, taking in his surroundings. The interior was stunning— oak paneling, marble floors so polished they mirrored the antique light fixtures above. They moved into a long hallway, and George noticed a seal was carved into a large wooden door at the end of the hall. A stained-glass dome overhead casts soft, colorful glows on a massive oil painting of the town's founding. But it all felt cold, a place meant to impress, not welcome.

May led them toward the study. "Arthur, our son is home."

Son? He's the fucking Mayor's son? What the hell?

"Send him in," a gravelly voice responded.

Nick leaned into George. "Stay close to me."

He gave a tight nod.

Inside, Arthur swiveled around from behind an ornate desk. He wore a milky-white suit, silver hair cropped neatly, his smile perfect but unreadable.

"Nick, introduce us properly," Arthur said, not bothering to rise.

George stepped forward. "So... you're the mayor."

Arthur finally stood, towering him, extending his hand. "I prefer Arthur when I'm off the clock. And you must be—"

"George," Nick finished.

They shook hands.

Arthur frowned. "Nick told me about your accident. When does the cast come off?"

"Four weeks, minor fracture."

"I was a doctor once, you know," Arthur said, his voice oddly charming. He gently pressed on George's shoulder, manipulating it with practiced fingers.

He heard a crack, and relief washed over him.

"There. Better?"

George nodded, still processing. "I came because... I wanted to know if Meagan was safe. Is she here?"

Arthur's eyes narrowed. "Yes. She's safe. But why don't we discuss that over dinner? We can get to know each other a little first."

"We haven't eaten," May chirped. "Let me tell the cook!"

Arthur watched her leave, then turned back to George. "You're a lucky young man. My son is very... selective."

George didn't know what to say.

Nick wrapped an arm around him from behind, resting his chin on George's good shoulder. "I'll take him to my room while we wait."

The grand staircase creaked as they ascended. He noticed paintings lined the walls— portraits of stern-faced men in white suits, ties, wearing fedoras, and women in pearls. They passed room after room, most of which were closed, until finally reaching the door at the end of the hall.

George stepped in and blinked. It was enormous— modern and sleek, in contrast to the rest of the house's old-fashioned feel. A king-sized bed, oversized TV, rich dark walls with LED mood lighting. But none of it comforted him.

He heard Nick close the door behind him. "We have some time."

George pulled away, his stitches tugged, sharp and unforgiving. "Are you shitting me right now?"

Nick blinked. "I didn't say anything."

"You were about to." George turned to face him, eyes already burning. "This is too much. I'm being pulled in every direction, and you're standing there acting as if nothing is fucking happening, and that makes it worse. Like none of this fucking matters." George could feel his cheeks burning with rage. Nick's expression darkened slightly.

George's voice cracked with fury. "Your parents are the goddamn mayor and his wife, Nick! And Meagan's here? In this house? You *knew*, and you didn't say a word!"

"That's not fair—"

"Isn't it?" George felt his lip quiver, and voice trembling. "You were keeping this from me. This is huge to grasp. "I just ran from my own parents because they treated me like I'm nothing," George continued, voice rising. "I thought I was escaping all of that... and now this? Another betrayal? Another secret?"

Nick stepped forward slowly. "I didn't mean to hurt you. I just... that's..."

George stared at him, searching his face for something real. "Don't!" George's face crumpled. "Don't say it's not fair. You brought me here without telling me where we were going. I thought I could trust you. You knew Meagan was taken here. Your dad is the mayor, Nick! The mayor! And you said nothing."

Nick took another step forward, but George stumbled back, shaking.

"You say we have some time, as if this is a sleepover. Were you planning on cuddling? Watching movies while your parents imprison my best friend?"

"I didn't want to lose you," Nick breathed. "I was scared that if you knew—"

George's eyes filled. "Liar. Fucking liar!" His voice dropped into a whisper, but the venom lingered. "You're just like the rest of them. Timothy. James. Kai. Kat. My homophobic parents. George stepped forward, fists clenched. "I've been lied to my whole life. Used. Pushed aside. But you were supposed to be different."

Before he could stop himself, his fists struck Nick's chest. Once. Twice. Not hard enough to hurt, but enough to make a point. George's broken soul leaked through every hit.

"Liar!" He pounded again, ignoring the searing pain throughout his body. "You're just like them!"

Nick didn't flinch. He didn't raise a hand or step back. He stood there, accepting it.

"Why aren't you fighting back?" George asked, his voice small and shaking, tilting his head upward.

Nick's face darkened in the dim red lighting. Slowly, he reached out and pulled George against him, arms wrapped around his back, silent and unmoving.

George's fists crumpled against Nick's chest. He didn't fight the embrace, but he didn't return it either.

Eventually, his strength gave out. "I don't want to be alone tonight," George murmured, voice barely audible. "But I can't... do more than this."

He turned and carefully lowered himself onto the edge of the bed, facing away, watching the LED shadows ripple across the wall like bleeding wounds.

A beat passed. Then the mattress shifted behind him. Nick settled beside him, cautiously, and wrapped an arm around George's waist, not possessive, not expectant. Just there.

He tried to catch his breath.

"You're trembling," Nick whispered.

"I'm always trembling," George replied, exhausted. "I usually hide it better."

For a moment, they sat in silence, fragile and frayed.

Then, piercing the stillness, came a scream filled with agony, fear, and suffering.

It came from below.

George bolted upright. "Meagan."

Chapter 33

"PLEASE, STOP! I DON'T REMEMBER!!!" Meagan screamed, her throat raw and bloody as she buckled against the leather straps binding her to the iron chair. Her skin was slick with sweat, her eyes puffy from crying, and her eyelids filled with smoke. "Please, I… I'm going to pass out—"

The basement stunk of sulfur and burnt sage. Ancient symbols had been scrawled in crimson blood across the stone walls. The air was dry and sharp, incense smoke curled in hypnotic spirals from an ornate brass censer burner at her feet, seeping into her lungs like poison. The female investigator leaned closer, her spindly fingers toying with the string of obsidian beads she now wore around her neck. Her clothes didn't have a speck of ash on them.

"You don't remember," she snapped coldly, "because something in you is terrified to face the truth. You were there, Meagan. You and your sister. You saw it take her. That thing chose *her*. But you survived, and that means something."

"I was *six!* I don't— I don't remember what happened that night!"

"Wrong," the woman shook her head, the beads clacking together in unison. "You suppressed the memory like a coward. Your mind locked it away for your own comfort. But that comfort comes at a cost, and we are out of time." She turned, lifted a black velvet cloth from a nearby table, and revealed a marble-sized, green glass orb coiled in brass. It glowed faintly, pulsing as if it were breathing.

"What... is that?" Meagan wheezed.

"A memory anchor," the investigator said. "It draws on the energy of the thing that marked your sister. If you've ever been near it, it will force your mind to remember, whether you want to or not."

Meagan thrashed, but the leather straps kept her body restrained. "You're insane!"   "You're the one who watched her get taken," the woman said, placing the orb in Meagan's lap. "Let's see if you scream the way *she* did."

The pulse of the orb grew louder, thudding in Meagan's ears like a second heartbeat. The scratches on her neck seem to react to the orb, burning in agony. Her vision blurred, and the world tilted. Her thoughts were slipping.

A sudden flash— cold night air. Wet leaves. Michelle, screaming.

Meagan gasped and tried to pull away, but her body was already shaking, fingers cramping, and her jaw locking.

"No! Stop!" She cried out.

"That's it... you're right there, aren't you?"

Images flooded in. Michelle twisting, her arms no longer arms. Her eyes gone white. A voice whispering, too deep to be human. "She's mine now."

Meagan's heart pounded in her ears. She could smell Michelle's musty, sour hair. She could hear the snap of her bones. She could feel the Weaver staring at her, then choosing Michelle instead.

Meagan shrieked until she felt blood bubbling in her throat.

Suddenly, a sharp static pop cracked through the room. Meagan's eyes shot open. The door to the basement exploded inward, and the investigator spun, her gun already drawn.

A figure glided down the stairs. Average height, dressed in black shorts and a black V-neck, blood smeared his arms, legs, and face. "Step away from her," the boy replied sternly.

The investigator fired.

The bullet struck his left shoulder. He smiled. The lights flickered; something massive and wrong passed through the room with a rush of wind. The glass orb shattered, and the brass twisted inward on itself.

Meagan watched the investigator try to speak, but her mouth collapsed on itself. Her spine bent backward with a snap.

She fell to the floor. Her eyes whitened. Dead.

The boy knelt in front of Meagan. He had brown eyes, sharp cheekbones, and a little muscle, but not enough to do what he just did.

She tried to keep her composure, but her eyes widened in horror. He looked like someone she almost recognized but couldn't quite place.

"Are you okay?" he asked softly.

"I— who... who are you?" she croaked.

He gave her a crooked smile. "No one important. You're safe now."

He cut her restraints with a flick of his wrist, too sharp, too fast to be human. She slumped forward into his arms. Her head spun with pain and half-formed memories. Something inside her whispered that this wasn't over. Not even close.

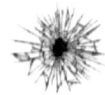

George burst into the dining room, Nick close behind. "You said she was safe! Where is she? That was her screaming!" he cried with rage, rattling his fist at Arthur.

Arthur didn't flinch. He swirled his white wine lazily before taking a sip, his eyes sharp as glass. "It's part of the process. I'm helping your friend Meagan recover her memories."

"You're hurting her, not helping her." George snapped.

"George is right. You never said you'd hurt anyone," Nick chimed in.

Arthur gestured to the empty chair beside him. "Sit. Both of you. Listen."

George's attention flicked to Nick, searching for some kind of ally.

"I don't want to keep you in the dark anymore," Nick murmured, taking George's hands in his. "Let him explain."

George tore his hands free, crossing his arms like armor. "Fine. Explain."

"My family and ancestors are demon hunters," Arthur leaned forward. "Meagan holds the key to ending the demon that's been haunting this town for too damn long. She was there when her sister made a deal with the devil. If we can unlock those memories, she can lead us to the grimoire used to summon it."

George blinked, his breath unsteady. "Demon hunters... Meagan holds the key...?"

"Yes. Stay with me," Arthur pressed. "We need her blood for a sacrificial ritual from that book to trap it for eternity. My colleague is using a technique called memory anchor— a blessed orb to uncloud the subconscious and restore her repressed childhood memories."

George's eyes widened, his lower lip fell, and his pulse roared in his ears.

Sacrifice Meagan... for this town...

"No, you're not going to— I won't let you!" Pain flared in his stitches, making him wince.

"George, I had no—" Nick started, but was cut off by a loud, echoing thud.

May rounded the corner, her heels sharp against the tile. "It's here," she whispered, her eyes darting. "I can sense it."

Arthur shot to his feet. "How the hell did it get through the barrier?"

A sudden draft swept the room, icy fingers grazing George's neck, sending chills down his spine. Then hands, cold and unyielding, gripped his shoulders and spun him around.

Nick's gaze locked on him, urgent. "We have surveillance evidence of your friend James making a deal with the devil. He tried to sell you to a demon, George. I wasn't lying when I said I was protecting you. I still am. It all began with Meagan's sister, Michelle. The car crash... You were no accident to us. My father saw an opportunity and assigned me as your nurse to keep watch. My feelings are real, but the demon wants you."

A hacking cough bled into the silence.

George turned. Meagan emerged from the shadows. Her skin was pale, her eyes glassy, but relief flooded his chest.

"Meagan! Are you okay?" He crushed her into his arms, his casted arm not wrapping completely around her.

"Y… yeah, I'm fine," Meagan answered, wiping her tears. "I remember, George, I remember you. All of it."

"Ow, fuck!" she flinched violently, hissing through her teeth.

George's gaze dropped to the marks, now gashes, raw and bleeding.

Her hand pressed her neck; blood welled between her fingers. Fresh.

"What's going on?" a voice called from the shadows, warm and familiar. "George? Is that you?"

"Timothy?" George breathed.

Nick's voice cracked like a whip. "How the hell did you find us?"

"George, Meagan, the mayor isn't who he says he is. We need to leave. I brought my car," Timothy said, ignoring Nick.

"They aren't going anywhere," Nick countered.

"You don't control either one of them," Timothy rasped.

"Where's Hannah?" George asked.

Timothy's expression darkened. "She didn't make it. One minute she was behind me, the next… Dom tore her apart."

George's breath caught. "Not Hannah. No…" His hand clutched his chest, then gripped Meagan's. "I'm not letting them sacrifice you."

"Come on, George. Let's go." Timothy extended his hand.

"That's not Timothy, George," Nick said flatly.

George and Meagan exchanged a wary look. "How did you get here?" George pressed.

"I... installed a tracker app on your phone when we were dating," Timothy admitted.

George narrowed his eyes, stepping closer. "What did you get me when we started working together this summer?"

Timothy's eyes went hollow. A slow, crooked grin spread across his face. "All you had to do was follow me." He stepped backward into the hallway, swallowed by shadows.

"Meagan, get behind me," George ordered.

Before she could move, the Weaver lunged into view, snatching her arms and yanking her against him.

"I'm done playing games, George," he growled. "James told me you're the perfect vessel. I didn't believe him at first, but after watching you, feeling your strength... you're the one." A low, demonic laugh rolled from his chest.

Arthur's voice rose in shock. "Damn it, how did you get past my barrier? I planted dreamcatchers all around this place!"

"Easy," it sneered, dragging its tongue across Meagan's wounds, making her gag. "I marked her. Every soul I consume rots your little defenses. I'm the reason she can't remember. And I'm the only one who *can* make her remember."

George's skin crawled. "Why me?"

"Your resilience. Your pain. Your potential. Take my offer. Be my vessel, and she lives. I'll make you stronger than you ever dreamed. No more lies. No more weaknesses. No more feeling you're not good enough. Or refuse..." Its voice dropped to a purr. "... and I'll gnaw her pretty little head off while you watch." The Weaver bared jagged teeth like small saws.

"Don't!" Arthur barked. "Come with us, George. We can end this thing. But help this piece of shit..." He raised a pistol; the muzzle aimed at Meagan's temple. "... and I'll kill her myself." Thunder rang through the sky, vibrating the very floorboards beneath them.

George's mind reeled, torn between two monsters. "You're making me choose to kill my best friend?"

Nick's lips parted, but nothing came out.

"I'm creating the timeline one step at a time. You're the fabric to this timeline, George. I'll even prove myself." The Weaver's mouth twisted, and then the voices began.

They layered over each other. Timothy. James. Hannah. Becca. Dom. All of them, pleading in agony, while Meagan squeezed her eyes shut, sobbing.

"George..."

"George..."

"George..."

"Meagan?" he asked softly, shifting his attention to her. "I... I—"

She shook her head, tears streaking down her cheeks. "Either way, I'm dead. What I told you before, about loving you, it never could have worked. Tell my grandmother I love her. I love you, too, George."

She drew a steady breath. "I trust you. You're the only one who can make this decision. I know you'll make the right choice. Remember? We promised to save each other. Looks like we couldn't keep that promise." She forced a trembling smile.

His chest felt like it was splitting open, ribs threatening to give way.

"Don't blame yourself anymore. Remember me, remember only the good memories." She closed her eyes. "I'm ready."

George's heart shattered like tainted glass.

The Weaver's voice cut through the room. "It's time to decide."

George's hands balled into fists. His breath sawed in and out.

"I've made my choice."

He stepped forward into the shadow's embrace.

"I'll be your vessel."

Chapter 34

George wondered who would care if he didn't exist, if he wasn't alive anymore. Meagan, maybe, but all his other friends were dead, and his parents would move on. He figured they already had.

And Nick?

His boundaries were invaded, and he didn't trust him. He couldn't, not after all the information he withheld. Besides, he would move on, having only known him for a week. If he chose himself and Meagan was eaten, then he would have no one.

Meagan...

The glowing red eyes in the shadows grew brighter as he stepped forward. He felt gears turning in his head. Yes, she would lose him, but at least she would still have her grandmother to go to. Martha. She'd have at least one person. Her willingness to sacrifice herself for him proves even more for her to stay, her resilience. He was sick of being afraid.

Behind him, Arthur's voice felt miles away, his words muddled. The Weaver's eyes nodded in approval, and George took another step, shielding them with his back.

"George…" Meagan called, extending her arm out to touch him.

"Dad! Don't!" Nick screamed, and a sharp crack, followed by a high-pitched pop, echoed within the dining room.

George clenched his eyes shut, waiting for the pain to surge or death. Only a loud thud behind him and a shrill gasp and inhumane bellow blared in his eardrums.

He relaxed his eyes and was met with only black. Meagan's arm and the Weaver's glistening red eyes had vanished. He spun, facing the dining room, and watched Nick wrestling Arthur on the floor, battling for the pistol.

"You're not killing him," Nick grunted. "There must be another way!"

"There isn't!" Arthur protested.

May watched in horror, her hand over her mouth in shock.

With Nick on top of his dad's stomach, he forcefully yanked the pistol from his hand and jumped up. "He isn't dying as long as I'm still breathing," he yelled, toggling his aim between his parents.

George didn't have time to contemplate his feelings or hear Nick justify his.

Need to find her… Where did she…?

He followed the black hallway to the front of the house, ignoring Nick calling for him. George bit his lip, jaw clenched against searing pain in his abdomen, and threw the front door open. Light spilled from the porchlight, revealing droplets of fresh blood leading a trail off the steps into the wet night. The storm's silence pressed heavily on the porch.

George drew in a deep breath, "Meeeaaagaaan!"

Crickets answered.

"George!" Nick's voice cracked with desperation, sneakers pounding against the wood. He burst out onto the porch, pistol still in his hand. His shirt clung to his chest with sweat, his eyes wild. "You can't—"

George turned, his body shaking, his face pale. "It has her. I let it take her."

Nick's jaw clenched. He reached out, but hesitated, like he might shatter if he touched him. "We'll get her back. I promise."

His father's voice erupted behind him. "You fool! He was ready to give himself, and you stopped it. Now it has leverage. Now it has her!"

His mother's sob cut him off. "Arthur, enough!"

Nick's hand tightened around George's arm. "Look at me. You're still alive. That means it hasn't finished what it started." His voice trembled, but he forced it steady. "You're the one it wants, not Meagan. That gives us time."

George shook his head, staring at the trees. "Time for what? For it to break her like it broke Michelle?"

Nick's chest burned with guilt, still he pulled him closer, his forehead brushing his. "Time for us to fight back." For a fragile heartbeat, George leaned into him. The storm's aftermath lingered: wet earth, broken branches, and the silence that only comes after chaos.

He knew George's world had been torn apart, but the tension in his muscles grounded him from shaking for a moment.

He felt the pistol rip from his fingers, his father's nose wrinkled and eyes wide. "If you think I'll let this play out again, you're wrong. That demon will bleed, even if I must sacrifice you myself for the town, boy."

Nick snapped, holding George closer, guarding him. "You'll touch him over my dead body."

His father's eyes narrowed, the mayor's mask slipping to reveal something colder, older. "That can be arranged."

George finally spoke, his voice quiet but firm. "Stop. Both of you. This isn't ending tonight. It's just begun." His head returned toward the woods as he continued, "I'll find her. I don't care what it takes. I won't let it kill her. I won't let it win."

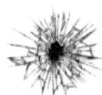

Darkness swelled and ebbed like a tide, dragging Meagan under before spitting her back into flickers of awareness. Her body jolted with each uneven step. Something carried her, its claws hooked beneath her arms, her heels scraping over leaves and stone. The smell of iron clung to her nose, hot and metallic.

She heard it then: the ragged, wheezing breath of the Weaver. Each inhale whistled, wet and broken. It was hurt, bleeding from the gunshot, yet it still dragged her deeper.

"Wake up, Meagan."

Her head lolled.

That voice— Michelle?

She tried to force her eyes open but only saw shadows spilling across the trees. "Michelle?" she rasped.

Her sister's voice threaded through the dark, calm, and hollow: "Don't let it take you where it took me. Remember what happened. Remember the night I died."

"No," Meagan whimpered. The words tangled in her throat. "I can't... I don't want to remember."

She felt the Weaver's grip tighten, talons piercing her flesh. Its voice hissed in her ear, low and venomous. "She belongs to me. Her voice is mine now."

Its blood smeared her arm, hot and slick, dripping from the torn wound in its chest. Meagan's vision blurred again, darkness swallowing Michelle's echo, the trees bending into nothingness.

When her eyes snapped open, she was no longer in the woods. A single candle guttered in the far corner, lighting the decaying wood of a cabin wall. Shadows twisted across the timber, and the air reeked of smoke and rot.

The Weaver hunched before her, its silhouette quivering, its chest torn and leaking black blood onto her chest. Still, its eyes glowed like coals, unblinking.

It leaned close, lips splitting into something that might have been a smile.

"No one is coming," it murmured. "Not even George."

Meagan's body pressed against the floorboard, tears streaking her face as the candle flickered lower.

"... George," she whispered.

The flame sputtered out, and darkness swallowed her.

To be continued...

About The Author

Koda Poindexter is a bold new voice in thriller, horror, and fantasy fiction. Born and raised in Franklin County, Virginia, Koda developed a passion for storytelling under the guidance of his grandmother, who instilled a love for imaginative tales in him at such a young age. With a flair for crafting heart-pounding cliffhangers, Koda's writing keeps readers on the edge of their seats. He has been previously published in Growing Up in the Valley magazine.

Follow the Author

Tiktok: @determined_writer

Facebook: @Tainted Glass

Instagram: @determined_writer

Email: determinedauthorkoda@gmail.com